P9-CJD-044

ALSO BY JOHN DONATICH

Ambivalence, a Love Story: Portrait of a Marriage

THE VARIATIONS

THE VARIATIONS

A NOVEL

JOHN DONATICH

A JOHN MACRAE BOOK Henry Holt and Company New York

Henry Holt and Company, LLC
Publishers since 1866
175 Fifth Avenue
New York, New York 10010
www.henryholt.com

Library of Congress Cataloging-in-Publication Data
Donatich, John.
The variations : a novel / John Donatich.—1st ed.
p. cm.
ISBN 978-0-8050-9438-1
1. Priests—Fiction. 2. Faith—Fiction. 3. Psychological fiction. I. Title.
PS3604.O54V37 2012
813'.6—dc22 2011021809

Henry Holt books are available for special promotions and
premiums. For details contact: Director, Special Markets.

First Edition 2012

Designed by Kelly S. Too

Printed in the United States of America
1 3 5 7 9 10 8 6 4 2

For Mary and Ernesto Donatich

The Lord God called out to the man and said to him, "Where are you?"

—GENESIS

THE VARIATIONS

PART ONE

ONE

It was when driving the parish car that Dominic felt most secular. He was just a guy in a Mercury Sable, driving to and from work, doing errands; he could be anyone else on wheels, someone hard to track. Even though the old Sable was nearly twelve years old, it clocked only 47,253 miles on its odometer and was more likely to die of old age than experience.

He had taken the last two stop signs on a roll. Since he was driving with a suspended license, Father Dominic opened the gate and pulled into the church parking lot with a bad conscience, into the vast emptiness of a weekday morning.

Pulling the keys out of the ignition quieted the dinging in the dashboard. The alarm had rung his anxiety to attention as he sat in the car surveying the church property. The gutters leaked, and the asbestos-lined basement flooded after every rain. The boiler surely would not last the winter. The locks didn't secure, and it was only after they had reported the theft of a gold-plated chalice to the DeSimones, the local organized "family," that the break-ins ceased. Mice or something bigger worried the walls of the rectory. Empty bottles of beer and cheap whiskey littered the corners of the lot; Dominic turned out early every Sunday morning to clear them before Mass. How he hated the clink of glass against glass in the garbage bag, hollow and carnal like a laugh track.

Now in its fifth decade of urban renewal, New Haven was just a bunch of little neighborhoods struggling to assert their integrity. Dom liked the tired maturity of the city's faith—the kind that knew better than to reach a conclusion that believes despite the contrary evidence, despite the improbability of redemption. His church was needed here.

Dominic packed up his portable "death kit"—that little pouch of blessed oils, holy water, a stole and his battered little green book, *Pastoral Care of the Sick*—that he had used in administering Extreme Unction, the last rites, to Father Carl. He leaned over to jam the kit into his glove compartment when in the rearview mirror he saw a flash of movement, a white T-shirt behind a tree. He froze as the girl ran to the next tree—barely a girl, really, a sliver of agitation.

Dolores. Dom had known her since she was a kid in the parochial school—when there still was a school. It was Father Carl who had had the primary relationship with her. They had scheduled spiritual counseling every Thursday night at 6:30 right after the evening Mass, but it was always a gamble whether the girl would show or not.

"One of God's special cases, given us to know Him better," Father Carl had winked, which, again, had confused the younger priest. Dolores was an insistent but erratic presence; she would come to the church every day for a period but then disappear for months only to wind up calling Father Carl at the rectory in a panic in the middle of the night. Then the pattern would repeat. Dom tried to be patient with the girl, but he worried about the toll she took on the ailing older priest. She showed up rarely when expected and often when inconvenient. If her timing was unpredictable, she was even harder to place physically. During his weekly visits to Dolores's housebound mother he barely saw any sign of the daughter in the apartment. Dominic even wondered whether she lived half the time out on the street. The truant officer, social worker and welfare agent had filed their final reports and were done with her. The high school and the state had virtually given up on her. She had turned to the Church in the end.

Father Carl had really been her last lifeline, and when he got sick Dom began to see more of her. She ran errands for the elder priest, made round-trips to the post office and drugstore, brought him books from the library and, then, audiotapes when he grew too weak to read. He began to show up at morning mass in polished shoes. She was desperate to be of use to him, although Dom had always found her to be in the way.

"She must be wearing you out; you need your rest," Dom warned Father Carl.

"What I need is a life I can still help," he replied.

Dominic felt Dolores competing for the priest's affection. A few months ago, in what would turn out to be Father Carl's final public sermon, she had scooped Dom by arriving at the church early, shoving him aside in order to seize control of the wheelchair. She would be the one who wheeled Father Carl down the aisle to the altar, glowering at the congregants in the pews, daring them to look directly at their frail pastor with anything but reverence. But now that the old priest had died, would she be turning to him for counsel? The thought exhausted him.

Wincing at the grunting door (he half expected it to fall off completely any day now), Dominic made hard work of gathering himself out of the car. Glancing at the bumper, he confirmed that he had swiped the mailbox backing into that tight spot. He bent down pretending to examine the scratch while getting a peripheral glimpse of the tree she hid behind. She was so skinny a birch could manage it. He stood up, put his hands on his hips, stared directly at where he thought she would be and walked toward the line of trees at the edge of the lot.

"Hello?" he cried out.

There was no answer. Dom heard the steady roar of the Interstate beyond the concrete barrier at the edge of the shallow woods. His next call was lost in the rumble of a passing truck.

"Is that you, Dolores?" he asked and stepped over the curb onto the soft pile of pine needles. The damp of the earth seeped through the hole in his left shoe he hadn't gotten around to mending.

"What, no coat? Aren't you cold? Come into the rectory and warm up."

"You can hear me, but you can't see me."

"Why is that? Are you invisible?"

"Might as well be."

"Come in; it's cold out. Or I can drive you home."

"Oh no, none of that."

"None of what?"

"Whatever. Sooo, how is he?"

Dom sighed. Would this girl be the first he told? "He's with God now."

Dolores stepped out from behind the tree. He barely recognized her. Long stringy hair, not so much unwashed as unclean. Untreated acne on her forehead. Teenage skinny, probably too skinny. Her very posture was angular and aggressive, vaguely contentious. She was the age at which physiology was temperament. Or was it something more? She seemed somehow hurt.

Dominic cleared his throat. "I'm very sorry. I know how you loved him."

"How do you know that?"

"Well, because I know how he loved you."

He watched the bones of her face fold into an ache; then she turned and ran across the parking lot. He called after her.

As he watched her race down the street, he felt that familiar discomfort he hated in himself: the capacity for pity. He had been prone to it his whole life but had grown to mistrust it utterly; it was feminine and sentimental. It turned on him like heartburn. He had hidden within it, and he had mistaken it for kindness.

Climbing the narrow stairs off the kitchen, Dominic balanced a hot cup of tea on his briefcase; he had forfeited his usual dash of brandy. The hot water steamed in the cool hallway. Much of the rectory had been shut down to save on heating; now it would be kept just warm enough for him.

Upstairs in the library, Dom logged on to his blog. With naive goodwill, he had recently written an essay arguing for the preservation of Our Lady of Fatima Church, which the archdiocese had recently named among the several dozen churches likely to close. There had been a sudden if modest outcry within the parish. The friends of the church were supportive, holding midnight candlelight vigils and prayer sessions. A petition was drawn and signed by the very people who never bothered coming to Mass.

Parishioners came to him with visions. A widow claimed she could suddenly see a teardrop form in the corner of the eye of the marble statue of the Virgin, only it's a blemish in the stone that Dom knows has always been there. He did not disabuse the woman, though, and stayed off the record while she talked to the newspapers. None followed up on her claim in print, thank God. He was glad they didn't take her seriously; the world was right to be suspicious about these sightings: Guadalupe, Lourdes, Fatima, Medjugorje, Queens, and hundreds of others. He mistrusted any literalizing of the mysteries.

It was on the Internet, though, that Dom got his first real idea of how people outside the parish felt about the church and its future. There would be nothing of the Bing Crosby sort of priest for Dom, drawing strength from the supportive folk of the parish. Daily doses of anonymous venom spat through the Web and landed on his blog. Over the last dozen months or so, he had posted his sermons, editorials, daily meditations, personal essays to a small but growing and appreciative audience. His blog had even been linked to several national sites; he had become a kind of go-to guy for reporters watching contemporary Catholicism. His Facebook account collected hundreds of friends, while his social life added none. Most of his readers were either orthodox Catholics looking for blessings or those curious few who came to find out what the fuss was—those agnostics who didn't necessarily believe in the Deity but held on to "their own personal idea of God." As if the purpose of being a god was to be conjured up in the imaginations of those who needed Him.

But it wasn't until the rumors about the closings went public that he got the full blast of those who did not come with sympathy.

29. Comment #1022 by jimmyfox on November 25 at 7:14 p.m.
    Nobody wants you. Just shut it down. Why would you ask us to hold out against all that gives us a little pleasure in this crappy world? No sex, no drugs. Puh-leeeeze!

30. Comment #1023 by indiparent on November 25 at 7:39 p.m.
    I agree. Go to hell! You churches are just recruitment centers for innocent children to be sodomized by the priests anyway. What are you but safe havens for pedophiles. Read a newspaper, people. Get out of town and be in a hurry, Our Lady of Flatulence. God riddance (pun intended).

31. Comment #1024 by holyjizz on November 26 at 12:12 a.m.
    Me again, Father. Let me ask you about that little girl who got shot in Columbine, the one the book got written about, *She Said Yes*. That's what the newspapers reported the girl said when asked if

> she believed in Jesus—with a gun to her head. Turns out the whole thing was a sham. It's more like *She Shit Herself*. That's the humanity of the situation. Am I right, Father?
>
> Let's talk turkey, Padre. When it comes to religion, we're supposed to respect and honor your right to preach superstition and ancient taboos that we wouldn't allow anyone else to get away with. So—we've gotten rid of slavery, cannibalism, the fucking stoning of whores—you name it, the list goes on and on. But in the case of religion, we have to simply annihilate the entire rational evolution of our minds and bow our heads at the effort?
>
> Face it, Father. The fight's over. The world is better off for moving on. The New Atheism: Bring it on.

Dominic typed in a response:

> I recognize a definite zealotry to your atheism. Your attack on religion is not only ideological, it's downright evangelical! It's almost as if your ambition doesn't just want to destroy religion; you want to replace it.
>
> Your certitude astonishes me. I've heard all of it before: that our vision of God is a defense system against the fear of the unknown, a fantasy of anthropomorphic grandiosity, a cognitive response to some ancient offending or frightening mental stimuli. I've heard this all before from social psychology, social-exchange theory, evolutionary psychology, behavioral economics, cognitive science, members of whom inform us that human instinct and intuition are evidence of adaptive behavior, learned fitness, market motives, encoded survival techniques. To give no credence to the wild and unknowable side of consciousness—how small that must feel.

> Faith is that willful belief in what is not possible, or, as Wallace Stevens put it:
>
> —the nicer knowledge of belief
> That what it believes in is not true.
>
> Your legitimate gripe is actually with the Church, which really in the end is nothing more than the social management of the wildness of spirit institutionalized within religion. More than that, it's also the acceptable mechanism for people to safely explore that wildness. They won't like that I write this, but they should realize it's their greatest asset.
>
> Why would anyone not want a greater, more ambitious idea of the human soul—one that can believe in something beyond what it can conceive of? Why wouldn't you cultivate the kind of soul that is able to willfully experience beyond the rational mind and material world, even if illusory? Isn't that in itself a kind of joy?

Rather than press the "send" key, Dominic highlighted and then deleted the response. He knew that he would never win or lose that argument; it would just devolve into name-calling. He would be just another priest arguing with another atheist: "But you're guilty of the same thing you accuse me of; you are trapped within the structural dynamics of your own prejudices." They would get into that "I know that you know that I know that you know" game, like a bad high. Better to resist the easy grooves of careless thinking online: all these people who just wanted to come lift a leg and pee in his yard. Instead, he simply wrote and sent through the line:

> I quote: "To believe in God means to see that the facts of the world are not the end of the matter."—Ludwig Wittgenstein

Funny point in our history, isn't it, for a priest to be attacked like a heretic.

"Whatever you say, say nothing."

Father Carl's last words haunted him. It was as if the old priest had passed invisibly inside the younger, but instead of being burdened Dom felt curiously lighter, happier and excited even—as if they were road buddies off together on some caper.

Whatever you say, say nothing. In the sacrament of Extreme Unction, Dominic had touched with the consecrated oil the eyes, the ears, the nostrils, the lips of the old priest but then lingered, rubbing the oil into the hands. How soft, still, cool and so white: between flesh and marble, man and monument. *Through this holy unction and His own most tender mercy may the Lord pardon thee whatever sins or faults thou has committed by walking*, Dominic said, touching the feet of Father Carl. A douse of holy water, a dose of morphine. Father Carl was nothing but a man and barely that. What was it that Dominic listened for in the sound of that breath held in that grim line of the lips, life or death? And then nothing. Withheld. He had counted slowly and at the twenty-third beat, he listened to the rattle in the man's chest. How many deaths had he witnessed? At what point had they become—no, never routine—but the opposite of something happening?

Whatever you say, say nothing.

The phrase would stick. Even with his cheeks sunken, his bulk weightless on the bed, humming to stay just a little alive, that motherless child, that childless man made the effort to be priestly, significant in his last words, as if they might become famous last words. But who remembers a dead priest?

Holding the hand a bit longer, he had listened for the warmth to cool; he smelled the rank from under the sheets as the old man's bowels loosened. He turned his head away. Is this how a soul at death, at the pearly gates themselves, must look back and first see itself? Soiled and still. How big and true little words pretended to be. Dead. God.

Dom laid the hands across the chest. Old tools in a junkshop. He closed the priest's lids over his eyes. Why did people in the movies always die with their eyes closed? Dom said a final prayer, struggling to let the words settle into meaning; he leaned into their rhythm and fought the hunch that it might just be his own last sincere prayer. He kissed the waxy forehead. He thumbed the jaw to shut the gape of the mouth. Agape. Say nothing. Little Lamb. Lamb of God. Who made thee?

There was much to do. Arrange for the transport of the body from the hospital to the funeral home. But, in fact, many of the details—the choice of coffin, the parish cemetery lot, even the list of eulogists—had been prearranged by Father Carl, who was proud of the fact that he had exacted an "ecumenical discount" from the undertaker. After all the referrals he had given? Father Carl's two brothers were on call, and Dom knew that the answering machine blinking red in the vestibule signaled a neglected call from the elder checking up on things. None of it should wait, really. Nevertheless, he wanted to drift quietly for a while in the depressurized air of the emptying rectory. Weightless and suggestible as a ghost, he wondered the places he might go, the things he might see, might hear. From his earliest awareness, Dominic knew he was given to a mystifying tendency, prone to imagining things around him deeper and more beautiful than perhaps they really were—or had a right to be.

Roaming the halls, he passed Father Henry's room, sealed shut since the priest died fourteen months ago. The door to Father Carl's suite was open, as he had left it. Dominic stood in the doorway as his loneliness warmed its way into the room; his solitude was thermostatic, portable. Sitting on the twin bed made up tight as a military cot, Dominic handled the rosary beads Father Carl had left on his bed table, and resisted the temptation to see human wear in the bevel of the beads.

There was very little the old priest left behind. Not a clue to a single secret. Even if the parish had wanted to honor him as an elder or the chief of a small tribe, there was no personal treasure to bury him with. Where were the things he loved and held on to—the list of which might serve as a kind of biography?

When Father Carl had asked why he wanted to be a priest, Dominic joked, "Why, to have what you have: the girls, the money, the cars, the houses." Looking around, Dom realized he had learned to crave as little as Father Carl. The bureau drawers contained only graying and neatly folded underwear, socks in a limp roll, his personal Bible fraying with Post-it notes, his liturgical calendar, his notes for sermons in copy books, his library copies of Trollope and Nouwen. A beach pebble—the one unpractical item, ostentatious in its useless sentiment. A photograph of Father Carl with his twin brother, at least thirty years old by the look of the Pontiac and their sideburns. In the bathroom, his shaving mug, brush and razor. Under the bed his pair of slippers, his pair of sneakers. He was simple, like a bird, maybe, who loved his few colorful threads but left them behind within the nest. He hoarded nothing.

The absence of belongings, in fact, testified to how little Father Carl regarded his mortal life. The old priest had believed so fervently in the afterlife (almost till the end) that Dominic's own faith had been excited by it. In the old man extravagance of soul was in equal parts to the modesty of the body.

"Of course you can argue that it is improbable—heaven, the afterlife, the Great Merger with Being, whatever you want to call it—but you can't argue with me that it is impossible because I can believe it. To me if it's conceivable, it's possible."

That was what the old man had argued. If irrational or illogical, there was also a beautiful justice to his faith: what ought to be true has to be true. "There's no dishonor in it, you know," he had argued to Dominic, "in believing in something merely because you cannot disprove it."

Dom opened the little white paper bag and took out the sandwich the orderly had given him as he left the hospital. The tuna fish glued the two stale slices of bread together like a gray paste. He wasn't hungry but ate the whole thing anyway, tasting it like medicine. Father Carl had loved tuna and ordered it in a club sandwich with a whiskey sour—"the real stuff, not the mix"—at the Graduate Club every Friday lunch.

Dominic looked in the old man's closet. Sweats on a hanger. Three clerical suits. One double-breasted pinstripe which Dominic took out. He pulled off his sweater and tried on the jacket; the satin lining was cool against his bare back as he buttoned the front. The sleeves hung below his wrists, and as he turned to the mirror and lifted his arms in a mock benediction to his congregation, he braced himself against the unexpected smell of Father Carl that crept up. The old priest had been like a father to Dominic; how difficult it is for a son to love up to a father.

"Call no one your father on Earth," exhorted the Bible; Dominic's childhood had nicely accommodated that.

Dominic took the suit off and looked at himself in the mirror. "You're too sexy to be a priest," one of his bloggers had commented not so long ago. "Even if you were meant to be one," she wrote, "my God, what a waste!"

The mirror didn't exactly corroborate. Fifty loomed just a few years away like a drop-deadline. His workouts had gone by the wayside, and his belly rolled over his underpants. The hair on his chest was graying faster than the hair on his head and grew like a jungle, creeping over his shoulder. Wasn't there supposed to be the equivalent of a tree line to one's torso? Walking closer to the mirror, he saw that he seemed to have the face he deserved: his lips dipped sourly at the corners over the empty space left by the molars that had been removed a decade ago. Worry marks creased his brow. Still, he believed he could whip himself into shape, pass for handsome again, make it on the outside should things come to that. Should the parish close for a fact. Should he be set loose from the Church. Should he become answerable to the charge of being "sexy."

Those hostile comments on his blog—he should find them instructive, be proud of them even. He was too old to have no enemies.

As he hung Father Carl's suit back in the closet, Dominic hummed a song that the dead priest had used to whistle frequently, "Do Nothing Till You Hear From Me." He smiled and understood what he was looking for: Father Carl would "write" his own eulogy by limiting or censoring what might be said. He owed the dead man that much at least: whatever he said, he would say nothing.

"Kneel when you pray," Father Carl had instructed him.

"Kneel even if you aren't able to pray."

Dominic dreaded his evening prayers. The Liturgy of the Hours, November 26, was the Day of the Moon.

> Let us pray.
> Most merciful God, we humbly pray thee: that, like as when thy blessed Abbot Sylvester was devoutly meditating over an open tomb on the vanity of this life, thou didst vouchsafe to call him thence unto the desert, and to adorn him with a life of wondrous merit; so thou wouldest enable us after his example, to despise all earthly things and hereafter to rejoice in his eternal fellowship.

Dominic sat before the still-black window, tracing the filigree of the treetops against the starless but bright night sky, a bemooned sky. He waited for the comforts that reliably came with prayer: for the uphill pull of the eyelids to set at half-mast, for the lips to part and the tongue to go soft, for the tingle at the bridge of the nose, for the lightness at the top of his head. He listened for what he loved about the language of prayer: how it reminded him sometimes of the grit of gravel being stepped on, sometimes of rain running in a gutter, but always of the pinch of recrimination. He tried to pray as young seminarians do, clueless yet stimulated, groups of men sent off like toddlers into a playground. He meditated upon the lesson of Abbot Sylvester, who had looked into an open grave and saw there the disfigured body of a handsome kinsman who had lived nearby, saying, "I am what he was and what he is I shall be."

Sweat broke across his forehead; fatigue pressed at the back of his eyes. The pain in his knees insisted that his body was just matter: what Simone Weil called simple, disobedient matter. He was unable to pray. This wasn't just the usual quieting of doubt, like calling a room to order. This was different.

He worked hard at it, but it was like learning to draw by tracing. Better a copy than a fake. Faith should be authentic, not original.

His prayers reached for the moment when the words lost meaning and began, simply, to act. But not this evening. The failure startled him, like a child who looks up to discover that the legs he clings to do not belong to his father.

"Pray every day, Dominic," Father Carl had said. "It's like money in the bank."

But his body disobeyed. He was starving; his stomach rumbled, and his head ached. Sluggish, constipated, swollen with false starts. Not subservient to his will, but selfish. He craved; he was hungrier than he had ever been. How unlikely this physical rebellion, as if the rocks on the beach were to rise up and colonize elsewhere. He felt the corrosion of conviction deep in his bowels. He dropped to his knees and invoked the antique panic of Psalm 70.

Be pleased, O God, to deliver me!
O Lord, make haste to help me!

His knees, experienced as a yoga master's, ached under his weight and gave in. He fell to his side, hugged his legs to his chest and let the pressure radiate between the shoulder blades on his back. He turned over onto his belly. He closed his eyes to block the rush of images coming at him. He laid his head in his hands, pressed the warm curve of his fingers against his face. The weight of his head in his hands moved him, as if he were another gazing upon this picture of anguish. He had lain in this pose the day of his ordination—prostrate: a young man so eager to be saved and to save. That day seemed so long ago; the image itself an anachronism.

Dom rubbed his eyes until they ached, and the very blindness made its own images. He watched the nervous movie unfold: psychedelic constellations, arid deserts of cracked skin and creeks of blood; even this self-abuse had the colors of cosmic illusions.

Save me, O God!
For the waters have come up to my neck.
I sink in deep mire, where there is no foothold. Psalm 69

His prayers had been stripped of belief, authoritative and petrified like a dead language. They were impotent even as he ground his hips against the hardwood planks of the floor, unforgiving of the unwelcome bulge in his pajama pants. "A common affliction," he told himself with consolation and condescension. He was like an adolescent again. Now in his middle ages, he couldn't even bear himself in pants. His flesh rushed and engorged while his spirit withered and shrunk. The mind was willing, but the flesh was materialist, insistent. Prayer, in fact, had become an irritant like his morning erection: objectless, unfocused, unloved, unloving.

"Listen, Dominic, the big challenge is not to keep believing but to believe again and again, to start all over," Father Carl had exhorted. "Day by day. Day after day. From scratch. Every day."

He tried to pray as he had been able to as a young man, tireless and ardent, with that once-in-a-lifetime sense of attainment young men have. It had come to him so naturally and so blessed. He even used to think he had a gift for it. Now he felt plain foolish. His entire inner life—so credulous, so accredited, so historically buttressed by centuries of theology—now seemed merely ridiculous. What could he do, given the failure of his praying, but simply talk.

Failed Prayer Number One
In prayer I am never alone, both the dreamer and the dreamed.
Even our nightmares deliberate. He who could save us is almost always
too late, almost never on time.
You and I, though, we're right on schedule: Here I am, prostrate before You, in
this ancient pose this late in the story. You recede as the day emerges, impressing
upon me You're going missing.
I'll go out for You again tomorrow.

"Pray like you still believe," Father Carl had said. "Let it sneak up on you."

Failed Prayer Number Two
"Lord, open my lips. And my mouth will proclaim your praise."
Psalm 51.
I will listen for you all night long. I am beside myself listening
for You.
Here, in the aftermath of You.
I am comfortable with Your absence so long as I know You are
there.

He worried that using the second person in his prayers was presuming too much—as if he was admitting his own person by implying a listener.

He slept for a while without dreams. When he woke several hours later, stiff and wary, trying to remember why he felt afraid, he wiped his mouth on his sleeve, rose to his knees and continued where he had left off.

Failed Prayer Number Three
All is still—"Dead quiet," Father Carl used to call this kind of
outside,
as if telling the future.
I awoke hoping that I had changed in some essential way; that
I would
know exactly what to do; that I would recognize Your guidance
though it had not been given.

All summer long, trying to ward off this crisis, Dominic had read outside the liturgy for his morning prayers, looking for inspiration from Chinese poets of the eighth century; Californians from the last—but he found the simplicity of their spirit overly burdened. Their openness crowded him. He had stood in the predawn and tried to feel virtuous before the beauty of a single leaf that fell at his feet. He tried to free himself of promise and be in the moment. His breathing would grow heavy at the proud pressure of being "present," the bias that so much depended on one's attention. In any event, his prayers had stopped asking for anything long ago. He wanted to return to his own enraged universe before which he lay watchful, helpless and expectant.

> Failed Prayer Number Four
>
> With prayer, practice does not make perfect.
>
> Tragic as I feel, this must look pretty funny: me, here on my knees, smelling the failure of will on my hands.
>
> I am the eroding beach that makes the ocean picturesque.
>
> My spirit is suspicious of epiphany: all that blissful filling.
>
> I have never felt so much filled up with You as infiltrated and occupied.

At five, Dom dressed and went to the chapel to walk the Stations of the Cross before the parishioners filed in for the 6 a.m. Mass. At Communion, he dropped the host onto the furtive tongues of the daily dozen that still bothered to attend. He knew their habits: Tony, the tall old man who took it too high on the tongue; Maria, his wife, who winced as if about to be shocked; Ronnie, ever the enthusiast, stuck his out too long, curling the tip; and then there was Erin, the depressed mother whose baby whimpered in the car seat left behind in the pew, running up to the altar at the last moment, as if deliberating whether or not to. Offering her palms to receive the host, she would nonetheless dart her tongue out like a lizard snagging a bug.

Back in the rectory at seven, he ate his oatmeal and fried his egg (he still took the host on an empty stomach) before starting his day. Rounds at the two local hospitals before lunch with the bishop about his and his church's future. In the afternoon, service at the assisted living home, house visits to the elderly disabled in the projects, a chance to answer letters and e-mails before the 5:30 Mass. Maybe another blog post. Dinner at the YWCA annual fund-raiser. In between: trying to organize Father Carl's funeral. Then: facing himself again in prayer.

But first, the happy clarity of his morning walk, which he hoped would soon evolve into a run. He would work his way up the park's wooded trails, switchback up the rock to the top from which he could look at the city's episodic skyline, the doomed dome of his own church, the storied campus, the Long Island Sound, the thickening curve of the sky down to New York City. A fresh powdering of snow had fallen overnight, and the white winter light made him squint. The trails would be precarious; sometimes the world promised to be just too beautiful.

As he crossed the parking lot, he saw something move in the Sable. The windows were fogged; the top of a head peaked up above the dashboard. He leaned in to look.

Dolores rolled down the window.

"What are you doing in there?"

"The doors were open."

"There's no point in locking them; they'll just smash in the windows again. This way they know there's nothing worthwhile inside."

"You should just junk this old thing."

"Have you been here all night?"

"Well, I've just been waiting for you."

"For me? What for?"

"To help you properly bury Father Carl," she said, puffing her chest out. Dominic saw her thin neck as a brave thing, a turtle sunning. The girl darkened just as quickly, sinking into herself. Her face reddened. She looked down at her feet, then raised her eyes to meet his. "I'm sorry. I didn't mean to . . ."

"It's OK," Dom said. "Why don't you go home and rest?"

"No, I came to see you. I want to say confession," she said.

"You want me to hear your confession? Now? There are times posted in the bulletin."

"I can't wait till then."

"Aren't we ahead of ourselves here? I thought you said you had never been baptized."

She curled a strand of hair around her finger. "Of course I've been baptized. I grew up here. I just don't go into that church anymore."

"But now, you want to?"

"I need to."

She stared at Dom until he knew he had no choice. Was this the kind of power she had over Father Carl? This girl—lost—without options, would somehow always get her way.

In the darkened chapel, Dom watched Dolores take off her coat, impressed by the continuing transformation of a little girl into this almost woman. Years ago, he sat next to her on a school bus coming back from the Botanical Gardens in the Bronx; she had fallen asleep with her head against the window, the sunlight illuminating the little spittle that bubbled up in her nostril with each breath. She smelled a little like baked beans.

Now, she wore a tight top that did not quite reach the waist of her low-cut jeans, revealing both the crack of her butt and the pout of her navel. Dom noted the lovely swelling of her flesh—"the hinge of salvation" (Tertullian De res. 8,2)—at the hips, the soft down on her calves. Even in a girl so thin the white extravagance of skin: so clean and helpless and ubiquitous. So much flesh in the world, all forbidden to him. How could something so plentiful feel so rare? Random, uncounted as weeds: that's what we are here on earth—flowering, unappreciated too. And he so lonely amidst it all. She padded heavily down the aisle in her big furry boots that parodied some kind of Eskimo mammoth hunter, scuffing the tiles with the lazy presumption that she had all the time in the world to accomplish precisely nothing.

As a sixteen-year-old she had perplexing looks. She was beautiful at certain angles; today she wore a macabre red lipstick, rounded out like a hot cherry pepper smack in the middle of her pale face. Her skin was usually erupting, flaking; she carried an undernourished cast about her, as if dieting for martyrdom. That was her paradox: her tolerance for her own weakness had become a kind of strength. She carried herself with that difference: she was not made for this world. Father Carl thought that she took herself too seriously; Dom knew he thought the same about him.

Father Dominic settled into the confessional and waited for Dolores. He heard her part the heavy red curtains of the confessional and call out, "Oh-Kaa'ay, here we co'ome," as if she were a frightened child walking into a dark room, trying to fool the monsters into thinking she was not alone. She could still make herself sound like a little girl. She knelt down like a kid too, lithe and tentative in the near darkness, cringing at the creak of the knee stand as she shifted her weight. Why had she had been so afraid to come in here? It turned out to be less like a coffin and more like a phone booth. The curtains smelled of mothballs, and she felt sleepy behind their dimness like an old sweater in a trunk.

A minute passed. She ran her finger along the high trim as if looking for a key. She wiped the dust on the inside of her boot. She grew bored. How would her voice sound in here? She sniffled and cleared her throat, decided to test it further.

"Boop," she ventured in falsetto.

"Beep-boop," she dared a bit louder.

"Boop-de-boop."

The screen slid and let in a soft yellow light and the shadowed profile of the priest behind the grate.

Confession, for Dominic, felt almost clinical; he faced the mysteries of the soul the way a doctor might a network of physical symptoms. What hadn't he heard here: the lovelessness of wives, the remorse of two-bit gangsters in a sentimental mood. The husband who admitted he could no longer bear the thought of making love to his wife of twenty-three years, tormenting himself with fantasies of her death. How could Dominic reassure him that his villainy was one of the most common complaints he heard? How many wives had he smuggled off to shelters? How many confessors came to him seeking advice on negotiating wills, fights with their boyfriends, even investment questions? None of it ever surprised him; all of it made him envious of lives free to transgress. For these people, sin ended up more disappointing than trying to be good.

He was bored with the generic sinners; most people believed they were basically good. Hope depended on their naïveté. Dom was tired of them; they reminded him of himself. It was those with buried sins, secret fears that had ossified into trouble who fascinated Dominic. He was compelled by those transgressions that attracted not just his compassion but his curiosity: the prepubescent boy who, after a severe bout of diarrhea, was terrified that he was turning into a girl getting her period. Or the middle-aged woman who went to Rome to apply for an exorcism but got married instead. Or the man who became impotent in bed with his wife and was afraid that, unable to ejaculate, he would begin urinating inside her. Or the businesswoman in a panic attack on her morning commuter train, convinced that her fellow passengers intended to eat her alive.

Secrets rarely keep their original shape. Once buried, they begin to rot from within or compress into a crystalline hardness, the way fear and desire collude to produce an elusive individual soul. While the shrink might ask a patient what he feels, a priest is more likely to be interested in what a penitent fears. With the sacrament of confession, the Catholic Church had figured this out early: the creation of a dark and different silence to which one repaired to invite the soul, a ritual in which one might be dug up, buffed, reevaluated. Dom had persuaded Father Carl to shut down the sterile reconciliation room with its face-to-face frankness and reopen the traditional confessional. What happened inside the darkness confirmed for Dom the aspiration of Catholics to live their lives inwardly, to schedule regular self-reflection. He wondered too about the eventual loss of this ritual in the future: Would it be one more roadblock to the unconscious? Would we find redemption in the pillbox?

He knew Dolores would not disappoint. He nodded at her and waited. She had been briefed how to begin, but there was only silence. She appeared in a violet outline, shadowy and penitent. The wire grate pixilated her image. Dominic took a disciplinary breath: impure thoughts tormented him most reliably here in the dim light of this big box. He had spent years welcoming lines of women to kneel before him in submission, heavy and open like peonies in a garden after a rain. He regretted every missed opportunity, every lack of transaction between them in this dark, intimate space. The only thing he would ever leave inside a woman was by proxy. A blessing. He would stare as a woman spoke, watching her mouth deepen into a hole of dark against which a tooth might flash like a silverfish. Sometimes he wished the mouth would just talk dirt.

"Yes, my child," he started, surprising himself with his sepulchral mumbling. Who was he now? He sounded just like Father Carl, as if he had been possessed by the elder's manner. Still, he could feel that insipid smile on his face, benign and hopeful like a virgin at a dancehall. Wipe it off!

He pinched a thumbful of his cheek, twisted it and winced. He waited.

"I forget how to start," she whispered.

"Bless me, Father, for I have sinned," he prompted her.

He heard his words back in her voice, timid yet formal. She sounded so much younger than her years in here. Words that began with a hard *c* or *g* would catch in her throat; listening to her, he always had the urged to blow his nose.

"It has been 'x' since my last confession," he prompted her again."

"I forget."

"OK, never mind. Tell me what you want to confess," he said.

Dom waited. He heard her sigh.

"I'm not sure I've done anything wrong."

"Well, you came here for a reason, right?"

"Why I came here? In the first place? I guess I just wanted to talk. I find it kind a wild that big hairy grown-up men—like you—get up there at the altar and talk about, you know, Love, like with a capital *L*. And didn't even seem embarrassed by it, you know? It just seems impossible. . . . And nice."

Dominic waited through her pause.

"Also, I just wanted, or thought I ought to tell you something that I feel which is so bad."

"What is that?"

"I don't know. I think I just need to talk to you about my feelings."

"OK. I'm listening."

"It's just that I get so upset. I get really confused about everything."

"How so?"

"Well, I know that I want to be really, really good, deep

down—a better person than I really even know how to be? Like being good isn't good enough? I want to be good so badly."

He kept quiet.

"But it's like only after being bad that I know how hard it is to be good. Or even that I'm the kind of person who can be good or holy."

"What makes you think you've been so bad?"

"I really don't know if I should tell."

"I can help you. Listen, our failures are important too; they teach us to know ourselves, to see ourselves as God sees us. In some ways, our troubles may lead us to our true selves."

"I don't know. I just, like, *feel* everything so much. All the awful things in the world. And not only the awful things but just people, like, walking around, doing things, thinking they know how to run their lives."

"Do you feel like you don't know how to run your own life?"

"Well, but even the big things like that giant earthquake where so many people—SO MANY PEOPLE—got killed. I can't even understand that number. All this starvation, people starving. AIDS. Just so much suffering—but I see the pictures and they are so real, and are we supposed to just pretend? Just walk on by and pretend everything's, like, normal? I feel nobody is doing anything. Maybe I need to do something."

"Yes, but how are these your . . . ?"

"I don't know I don't know I don't know."

She started to sob.

"OK, easy now, Dolores. Let's slow things down."

"And global warming and the poor, poor polar bears. And I stand here, you know, like everybody, helpless to help. We just go on, like, I don't know, watching television and eating, eating, eating—just stuffing our faces. I can't even keep up with the horrible stories. I can't, I can't even count how much this happens. How can you even believe in a future this way? How can you expect me to believe in God? Why is He so freakin' complacent?"

"Dolores, shhhh. You're shouting now. Let's start again."

He heard her go quiet; the silence exhaled with a punch in the gut. The girl fell with a bang against the back wall of the confessional.

He scrambled out and picked her up from the floor. She clung to him tightly while her body shook thinly. Her collarbone pressed so hard into his Adam's apple he had to disengage her before she hurt them both. This is what it must feel like to be a father—that which she called him. How much she needed him might hurt him. It was over quickly. She quieted; her body went limp. He stroked her hair, greasy and uncombed; she was a little, feral animal in his arms, but one comforted by being captured, wanting to be saved from her wildness. This was what he was for, he told himself: to see one individual's pain so clearly, to acknowledge that misery is everywhere and to reassure that the power that will save is also everywhere.

They sat down, and he laid her head in his lap until the cold of the marble floor numbed his butt. Dolores had stopped crying, but her little sniffs sounded substantial in the still dark of the church. The impropriety of their embrace burrowed between them. Dominic cleared his throat, shifted beneath the girl. She turned and leaned against the end of the pew.

Dominic straightened the curtain of the confessional.

"Are you OK? You fainted."

"I know; I've been feeling sick in the mornings."

"What's the matter? Are you ill?"

"I don't know. I feel like I'm going to throw up."

He held her as she dry-wretched. The suggestion of vomit lingered in the air.

"When was the last time you ate something?"

"Not since yesterday."

"You'll need to eat something."

"No, no. I couldn't."

"Let's get you to a doctor."

"No. I won't go. I know what's wrong, anyway."

"Tell me."

She looked at him dead on and said, "OK. What the fuck."

Taking a deep breath in, she exhaled. "Whooo. OK. Truth or Dare?" She let out a big sigh and looked to the side. "I'm pregnant."

Dominic fixed on the dainty gold cross hanging around her neck and was calmed by the sight. No matter what, they had this in common. He knew this girl.

"I'm sorry. I guess I was scared to tell you."

"Why?"

"For all the obvious reasons."

"Dolores, stop being coy with me."

"I'm not. I'm just . . . ashamed."

"Do you know who the father is?"

"I'm not sure."

"There was more than one?"

Dominic could not tell whether the look she shot at him betrayed contempt for his lack of experience or shame for her own.

"Why don't you go to a doctor?"

"I won't go. I hate them, that whole world. They're worse than priests." She smiled at him. "You can have that for your blog."

"Dolores, you have to see someone."

"I will. I will. I'll go for a midwife. That's how my baby will be born."

"Who's going to take care of you?"

"Who ever does?"

"Do you want the baby? Can you take care of it?"

"What choice do I have?"

He looked at her solemnly. A moment passed.

"You're kidding." She stared at him with wide eyes. "What are you telling me?"

Dominic stared at her silently.

"I can't believe you."

"I'm just pointing out that you are very young and that you have . . . choices."

"You're a real piece of shit."

Dolores sat up to all fours, like a cat.

"Wait. Just listen to me for a minute."

"So this is the great advice of a Catholic priest."

"I haven't said anything. I just want to help you think through . . ."

"No, you didn't say anything. You never say anything."

They sat in a tense silence until Dolores picked herself up.

"I feel sorry for you, Father Dominic. I mean, what if I told on you?"

Dominic felt a door slam inside his gut.

"Don't worry. . . . Anyway, nobody believes me about anything anymore."

She walked down the aisle.

"You believe me, right?" she asked before leaving the chapel.

Dominic sat in a center pew allowing the chilled shadows to settle around him. Looking up at the rose window, he could see that the leading was eroding even further; it was going to fold in on itself if attention wasn't soon paid. The whole circle buckled toward its concave center, and its purposeful light now fell fragile, as if the tension point of its buttressing would be the cause of its own collapse.

• • •

Dominic crossed over the green river via the condemned but not yet demolished bridge. He felt righteous walking instead of driving: the green thing. He really should just garage the car, wait out his probation, do the right thing. Father Carl used to remind him that being a priest didn't earn him special rules. He'd have to get the bus schedule to Hartford for his meeting with the bishop the next day.

At the far side of the bridge, a homeless man held out his hand; Dominic put his head down and patted his pockets to signal they were empty as he walked quickly past.

"Have a good day," the man called out after him. "Hey; the least thing you can do is to wish me a pleasant afternoon."

Dominic picked up his pace.

"I'm not invisible, you know," the man called after him.

"No, but I might as well be," Dominic thought. "I deserve a good kick in the ass for that," he said and made a mental note to address the theme in a future sermon or Web essay: a homeless man complains that he is made to feel invisible by people who turn their head and hurry past him without acknowledgment. But the real trouble belongs with those passing by: it is they who are made invisible. It is they who hide and decide not to exist. That is the challenge the homeless present: to deny them is to deny ourselves. It would make a great homily with just enough regret to delude a Sunday morning.

Dominic grunted. Must every encounter, every image he stopped to apprehend—must all of it warm the heart, charge the soul, make the point, mean something? He was sick of it.

At the other side of the bridge, he saw Ronnie digging for clams in a tide pool of brackish water. His dog was sleeping beside him; an AM transistor radio lay between his paws spitting out conspiracy theories. The old bitch barely looked up when Dom called out, "Hey, Ronnie, you sure you want to be eating that stuff?"

"Eat it? Hell no. I'm gonna sell it."

"Ronnie, come on, that isn't kosher."

"What do you know about kosher, Father?" Ronnie laughed. "Our shellfish used to be famous, you know. I just wanna return to the glory days. You know, like Sheepshead Bay or up in Wellfleet."

"You're gonna kill somebody someday with that, Ronnie." Dom shook his head. Ronnie was a regular at the AA workshop Dominic led on Saturdays at 6:30 just after the evening Mass and before the temptation of the pub crawl. Ronnie had joined them seven years ago after he was in a bad car accident that had injured his back and forced him to leave his construction job and live on disability. But Dom knew it was all a scam as he watched Ronnie rake the sand and collect his polluted haul. Every time he saw the man at a bowling alley or softball game, he wanted to rat him out, but it was just another injustice he had to wink at. Father Carl had talked him out of it, saying it wasn't his job to be God's cop.

"It's very simple, Dominic," the old priest had advised. "The bottom line for most people, the golden rule for everybody, is to treat others as you would be treated yourself. The difference for priests is that we have to learn to treat other people better than we can expect them to treat us."

It sounded good at the time—even comforting in its challenge—but Dom knew there was something off: the selfless benevolence of the comment covered up its superiority. That's how martyrs get made; torture them as one might, no one can touch them.

Dominic had the key to Building 4 of the row of projects behind the train station where he saw several families on a weekly basis, making sure they had not been forgotten and had been given food, checking that social services were keeping the place habitable and, most important, serving them the Eucharist. He unlocked the heavy fire door with its quick return. Despite the cold, he could smell the urine snap in the frigid air, sharp as smelling salts. Climbing the concave steps to the third floor, he rapped his knuckles against the apartment door.

"Mrs. Alfano?" he called. There was no answer and he paused, his head bowed in attention. He always expected the worst on these visits, knew it would happen one day. Somewhere inside he even knows he looks forward to it. But he heard her call out, "Father, is that you?" His key stuck in the door, but he sighed and scraped himself into the front room.

She sat in her red vinyl armchair; the plastic, glow-in-the-dark rosary beads wrapped around her monstrous fingers, soaking up the daylight for their nocturnal life. Many times on entering this apartment, he wished he were as good a priest as Father Carl, and not feel the tremor of repulsion that crept up his spine. He would look at this woman and see her "incandescence," as Father Carl would have called it: "That is truly what I see, Dominic, I see the Lord in their eyes, the way the heart shines. I see a brightness around them. You'll reject the word, Dominic, I know, but I see them as *luminous*." Dominic did reject the word—not just for its pretension but because he was genuinely blind to it. In the endless lines of people who came to be in the presence of the elder priest he saw nothing but dark need and drab loneliness—as well as a lack of realism by those who expected him to be if not omniscient certainly ubiquitous, tending to each one individually all at once. "Be here, now," he reminded himself.

"How are you today, Mrs. Alfano?" Dominic asked. Although she was widowed over fifteen years ago, she went by nothing other than her married name. After her husband died, she rapidly gained the 170 pounds that tipped her over the 300 mark and shrouded herself in the black mourning dresses she wore too many days in a row. The smell of body odor pervaded the place like the gloom of her grief, stained into the lurid varnish on the walls and the tattered weave of the upholstery.

It was hard to believe Mrs. Alfano had ended up this way. She had always been a proud beauty. As a younger woman, she used to volunteer in the parish: soup kitchens, CYA benefits, Girl Scout meetings. However modest the occasion, her hair was always up in a complex beehive, high and contrived. She wore good dresses and high heels; there was something about her belted waist and high-heeled ankles that was "worth watching," as Father Carl put it. He had always imagined a kind of orthodoxy to her physical life at home: meatless Fridays and unprotected sex were just two of the rules Dominic knew so many in the community used to obey—those who didn't "keep two sets of books."

She used to flirt with Father Carl in that chaste way a young fiancée would a future father-in-law. But widowhood had determined her now; she wore nothing but black and had "let herself go," as people say, a step before wanting to be taken away.

Dominic leaned over as the old woman kissed his hands. When she moved in her seat he could smell the vinegar in her clothes, unfolding like a wet and crumpled washcloth left to dry. "This is what I am for," he told himself: "to love the unloved, to refute their unlovableness."

"Has the social worker been here this week?" he asked delicately.

"Yes, but I told her I don't need her. I don't need anybody but you, Father. Bless you, Father."

"And your children."

She grunted. "One uses me, and the other hates me."

"I wanted to talk to you about Dolores, Mrs. Alfano."

"I have nothing to say. I have no power over that girl."

"Is Dolores in some kind of trouble?"

"I don't even know where she is half the time. It's up to God what happens to her. After all I've done for them. Say what you will about Marco; he has some respect for his mother. He comes to visit. But that girl, ahhh."

"She doesn't look well to me. Are you sure everything's all right?"

"Who sees her? You see her. Father Carl sees her, maybe too much. Anyways, I have a hard enough time looking after myself. She wants to look like Saint Theresa, that's her business."

"I called the school. They tell me now she has stopped going altogether."

"They called. They talked to her. They sent two shrinks, social workers—what? Three. Nothing helps, and they gave up. Who can blame them? I've given up. Why do you bother me with this now? You're upsetting me. I'm getting upset. Look what you've done."

She rocked in her chair; her arms rubbed against the plastic covers with a dry snort. Dominic looked away. The TV was tuned to the Catholic station with the sound turned down: Channel 99, the last before the infinite static. After he left, she would pilgrimage through the channels, walking through the stations backward, stopping to chat with the nice ladies on the Home Shopping Network, charging hard against her credit card limits.

"OK, OK." Dom tried to calm her.

Week after week, he tried to get her to look at her life, her daughter's life, try to persuade her to go into assisted living quarters, whose van could get her to church, help her do errands. But she was stubborn. What would her husband have said? Instead, Dom traveled to her every Friday afternoon to hear her confession and celebrate the Eucharist.

What really offended Dom was the woman's outdated brand of Catholicism, the mystical heaviness that understood the stories in the Bible as literal truth. Vatican II, postmodern theology, the easing of restrictions, the backing away from the saints—none of it might have happened by the looks of this place. Dominic felt irritated by the heavy symbolism everywhere: the lurid crucifix on the wall with its little plastic Jesus, that carnage of conviction, curling up like a stale Cheez Doodle; the ceramic Madonna banal as a Barbie on the bureau; the saint cards lined up by the days of the week on the table beside her chair. She had a jewelry box filled with rosary beads, little blue bottles filled with holy water on the window sash, a charm bracelet of bleeding hearts. Seeing all this enraged Dominic like some local Inquisitor. He wanted to smash the idols, strip the altars; this was the immigrant's Catholicism, which modern America felt entitled to condescend to. Class, religion, race, weight, ethnicity—these are the things that replace what people might know about other people.

The apartment, her infirmary, had become a little museum of rejected pieties, almost un-American in its fetishization of relics stripped of value but invested with presence. If only he could free himself of the associations, Dom might approach the place with the wit of kitsch. The whole place reminded him of how being Catholic had gone from feeling like the ultimate insider—chosen, blessed, charged—to being marginalized and patronized. He tried to focus on what she was saying, to hear the human soul through the metastasis of her pain.

"Father, you don't know what it's like, really. All alone here. Always alone here. I need you so bad; why can't you come more often? What's once a week? What keeps you too busy for me?"

"I do my best. Come now, let me hear your confession."

"Confession. What do I have to confess? A simple woman, who suffers alone here. I have grief everywhere. My knees hurt, my eyes are bad. All I want now is to be with Jesus Christ. Why won't he take me, Father? It's all I ask."

Dominic looked away. There was a perverse pride in her suffering; she wore her pain so fervently, with a passion lacking dignity. She was the antidote to sophistication, she wanted him to know. She was all spirit: simple, needy, closer than he to the ultimate misery.

"We all know pain, Mrs. Alfano. And what is pain for other than to bring us closer to the Lord's ultimate suffering?"

"Madonna mia," the woman cried out, and Dominic followed her gaze to the bust of the immaculate mother. Its prettiness got it all wrong. This was the mother of all grief who knew the hardness of life, the meanness of birth, the overhanging pressure of what life is for, the need not only to flee but to ascend. For a moment Dominic felt an old, familiar flush come over him. He cast his eyes down; the bare fact of his shoes, scuffed and dirty, grounded him again. This holy woman understood him better than that narcissistic martyr on the cross.

Mrs. Alfano's confessions were ceremonious at best; she had blocked too much of the world out by this point to offend it. Taking in the body of Christ—craving and ingesting it—was the only meaningful sacrament to her. Dominic led her in prayer: *Our Father who art in heaven. Hallowed be thy name. Thy kingdom come; thy will be done. On earth as it is . . .*

She seemed to get smaller as she bowed her head. She made room for it. The room thrummed with their whispered prayers; the old woman worried over her beads, engaging the old story, the teller of the sacred life.

He delivered the host. "The body of Christ."

"Father, slow down, you're rushing."

Dominic repeated, "The body of Christ."

The old woman grabbed his wrist. "Make him take me, Father. Soon, Father. I can't anymore. Doesn't he love me?"

Dominic shrugged her off. "Mrs. Alfano. The body of Christ."

The old woman nodded, said "Amen" and took the host on her white tongue.

He would leave her like this: with the host pasted against the roof of her mouth, contemplating the Fifteen Mysteries. The Joyful ones. The Five Sorrowful Mysteries and the Five Glorious Mysteries.

Dominic heard the heavy footfall of steps and the turn of a key in the lock. Marc Alfano, the erstwhile son, stormed into the room. On break from the restaurant where he worked across town, he always looked tired, like most waiters. He was a big man with a big mouth, and Dominic instinctively squared himself. The two had never gotten along. Marc took his coat off and wiped his brow with his shirt sleeve, stained at the button. He was already sweating from the walk up the stairs.

"Oh," he said, nodding at Dominic, "you're here." He turned to his mother. "Ma, look, I brought you a little skirt steak to fry me up."

Dominic watched the old woman gather herself up from the chair into her walker and make her way into the kitchen.

"Ma. Peppers. Onions. Thanks," Marc called after her.

When she was out of range, Dominic said, "Maybe, Marc, this is a little too much for her."

"What? And take away the one thing she has left to live for?" Marc whispered loudly. He leaned forward. "And what do you know about it anyway? Get something straight. I'm not looking for some kind of guidance from the likes of you. So, just relax, huh?"

He threw himself on to the couch. The air wheezed through the seams of the plastic upholstery covers; everything in the apartment exasperated. Taking his shoes off with a heavy groan, Marc propped his feet on the coffee table. The glass fogged beneath his heels. Belching loudly, he picked up his newspaper and began to read. Dominic stood there awhile anyway, trying not to look ignored, nor to look at the hole in the man's damp socks, their odor mingling with the onions his mother had begun frying in the kitchen.

Dominic looked at his watch, 3:30 p.m., the restaurant worker's lunch hour, and stood to button his coat.

"Let me tell you something," Marc said, looking up at him. "That woman in there is a saint, you know. A freakin' saint." He stood up and paced the room till he stood directly in front of Dominic.

"Let me tell you something else," Marc said; he was the kind of man who needed to silence a room before it could hear him. He pointed at Dominic's chest with his index finger. "Her whole life, she did nothing but sacrifice herself for her children, for me and that miserable tramp of a sister of mine." Marc was getting red in the face, sputtering, "No one understands the depth of her devotion to her family. No one! Not even you, especially not you. No matter how much you come around here."

He was shouting now, as if angry with Dominic for arguing otherwise, for pretending to know her heart better.

Dominic nodded, stepped around him, walked to the kitchen and put his hand on the old woman's shoulder. She turned to receive his blessing and whispered, "I'd ask you to stay and eat something but . . ."

"Not to worry."

As he walked to the door, he heard Marc call after him, "You know, Father, you should pay attention to what people are saying about you priests."

Dominic froze at the door. His head cleared like a vacuum. Paranoia drew on him like a leech. It was so easy to suspect the worst about himself in the eyes of others. He glanced at Mrs. Alfano, who did not look up from her pan, and let himself out quickly.

In the dark hallway, Dominic clutched the railing as a rat moved along the wall not quite as quickly as it ought.

The door opened and Marc called after him, "Yo, Father. Wait up."

He put a beefy arm around the priest's shoulders. "Almost forgot something."

"What is it?" Dominic asked him.

Marc cleared his throat. "Because I like you, Father, I'm gonna help you out."

He handed the priest a wrinkled paper bag. Dominic looked inside and saw a ratty collection of porn magazines.

"You know, Father, I'm sorry sometimes I get a little rough with you. Truth is I feel a little sorry for you; that's why I want to make this gift to you."

"I've got to run," Dominic said.

"Never mind. Go home. Take a look." He spread his fingers and patted the priest's chest. "Let off a little steam."

"Listen, Marc. Thanks for thinking of me, but no thanks. I've got to go," Dominic said, laying the bag on the landing and starting down the stairs.

"Father," Marc yelled after him, "what do you think, you're something special?"

Many priests who want to leave the Church find it easier to do so after their mothers have died.

Dominic was different; he was marked to join the priesthood upon the death of his mother when he was just seven years old. Remembering little of his childhood, he imagined it happy enough in the way most unaware things must be. A dreamy kid, picked up and shuttled about by his mother, barely disturbing her solitude. Watched over by her somewhere in the next room. She without a husband; he without a father. That seemed just fine as far as he was concerned; you don't have to believe in a mother.

Pajama feet: that was the predominant image of his boyhood, a onesie that wrapped him from neck to toe, its flannel softly pilling and consoling, except that he was always too hot in the groin and damp between the toes. Irritated and chafing, rubbing himself red. The baths his mother gave him, leaving him in the tub while she ran around doing laundry and making supper until the water cooled and the soap scum grayed against the sides, until he screamed for her with bluing lips, and she would come and kiss his eyes, her soft breath on the wet darkness, the towel shrouding him, the roughness against the crew cut, and if it were possible he might never again have opened his eyes to find everything different—suddenly it seemed—his mother gone.

That the world could make such a tragedy could mean only one thing: it was there to astonish him. If these things outside him—the late afternoon light on the chapel, the predawn chants he sang—were mysteries able to move him, they must then be solved. They had to have meaning.

"My little secret," his mother would call him. "I want to know everything about you. Just me. You can tell me everything."

With her gone, he would have no one to tell secrets to. There would *be* no secrets then, only an inner life that would always be apparent before God.

He feared that his mother had secrets. He had never seriously tried to find out exactly how she died except to know that she had been in a car accident. A man was driving. One of the priests said to him, unkindly, "She liked that, you know, taking drives with a man friend."

Having no appropriate next of kin, Dominic was shuttled among Catholic foster homes until he was taken to a community shelter in the northeast Bronx run by an old Jesuit, Father Francis, whom he and the other boys called "Ma." Father Francis never objected; he liked being both mother and father to the boys and fulfilled both roles without gender. He looked between sexes as well with his big hips and soft man breasts, his nasal, sitcom voice, his waddle walk, his nervous clucking around the pots of soup on the stove. He looked no one directly in the eye. His constant chatter worried every detail of maintaining the home; he talked to every task that lay before him: "OK. Now you're done. I've taken care of you. And now I have to . . ." His existence filtered between states, somehow membranous, as if a gelatinous film formed between him and the world, protecting him under its insular damp cover.

Toward the end of a hot and humid July, the ten-year-old Dominic wandered the parish grounds, pretending it was a country estate to which he had been exiled. He had always been good at creating magical worlds, in his own image, little make-believe worlds suitable for living and scalable to his imagination. He climbed up to a second floor terrace and balanced himself on the railing. He extended his arms and closed his eyes pretending to be Superman. Preparing himself for flight, his knees buckled, and he crumpled down to the small patch of grass below. Father Francis screamed for the other boys, who carried Dom to the hospital several blocks away. All he had suffered was a broken elbow. But Father Francis's hysteria had set the tone for how the boy would be cared for: he was a fragile gift, vulnerable to their neglect.

From that point on, Dom was excited by the very strangeness of dimension. Troubled by the vastness of some things (the night sky, oceans), he was puzzled by the smallness of his body, an inadequacy of his senses to match the largeness of his thought. How would he ever fit into the great and undifferentiated world outside himself? Who would see him there; who else but God?

The other boys in the house began to treat him differently too, as if he actually deserved better. He was their special case: a good boy with a mother who had loved him; a boy who would have led a proper life except now he couldn't. That he would fall into their lot through no fault of his own, through rotten luck, ought to mean some sort of special fate. He was sent. They watched over him, got his back at school, saved him from the rougher chores, encouraging him, instead, to "hit the books." They talked themselves into his essential "goodness," to which they attributed his lack of aggression. And Dominic, in turn, was pleased at how he pleased others; he became almost addicted to their approval.

The house didn't know what else to do except to groom him for the priesthood. He was good for almost nothing else. Lacking his own family, he would belong to the family of man. He was an excellent student, and Ma appealed to the archdiocese and raised money to send him to a seminary prep school. It seemed absolutely the right thing to do.

At Dom's going-away party, one of the older boys was allowed to bring his girlfriend. It was the first time a member of the fairer sex had entered the inner sanctum. She arrived with a red mop of hair, big-heeled shoes, a tiny miniskirt and a tube top. Dominic had to bite his lip to keep from laughing but was caught short to find the older boys staring hard at her with a serious and intent silence that he couldn't begin to understand yet.

Dom approached his devotion at the seminary prep with all the conviction of a young cadet in a military academy. Faith to him was precisely this: a set of buildings with defined purpose that he would make his way among, fulfilling duties along the way. As he had no real sense of home, he wanted the places he inhabited to define his life. This is where you pray; this is where you study; this is where you promise. And Dominic was nothing if not promise (even if he was nothing in actuality). He learned the charms of the good boy; he inspired benevolence in others. How he was thought about was in fact who he would become.

As with most boys his age, his confession was big and shapeless; he didn't exaggerate so much as cast a wide net that might catch something. His prayer didn't really concern itself with authenticity or lack of it, but with expectation. The future loomed before him with the prospect of the calling; he waited for it through most of his adolescence until he pretended to hear it. He didn't grow up so much as he was called up. Until this moment in his life, there had always been more space in front of him than behind. He pretended to be called forward to cover the fact that he was being pushed from behind.

When asked if he thought about becoming a priest, he didn't know what else to say but that he had thought of little else. "Explore it," Father Francis said. "You're not like the other boys here. They are ultimately good boys, but you—you have a gentleness. Your smile. People want to listen to you."

"How are you called by God?" went the Jesuit mantra, asked first by Saint Ignatius. Dominic heard it as oddly evasive. While the Jesuit course of study was so rigorously prescribed, the essential question of discernment felt individualistic, with lots of wiggle room. The vast spectrum of possible and acceptable answers confused him. No two novices would be called in the same way, leaving plenty of room to doubt the way in which one was specifically called. He wanted discernment to tighten around him, squeeze out the notice of choice. He already had a passion for faith, but he lacked mechanical competence for it; like a music lover with a tin ear. What came first: the calling or your readiness to hear it?

Perhaps this is why he never felt particularly "chosen"; he had decided to choose, instead. He worked hard at discerning the call.

He didn't have a natural genius for it. Like a young groom in an arranged marriage, he figured love would come.

And so he listened and listened and listened until he was convinced he heard voices. Father Francis asked him if he was ready.

"I don't know, Father. I don't know if I'm right."

"Of course you don't, my boy. That's the point."

He complained again to Ma. "I'm making believe."

"That's OK. It is supposed to feel like play. Serious play."

He tried one last time. "I'm not worthy to be a priest," he said to Father Francis, nearly in tears.

"And that is why you'll be a good one."

And so, after these three denials, the story of his life would be told in the progress of the sacraments he took. The mechanics of becoming a priest would mark the chapters of his spiritual autobiography. His faith would be the great thing, his special fate. On the day of his ordination Dominic lay prostrate for the Litany of the Saints, his face pressed into the cool marble floor of the cathedral. It was hard to think against the cold. He tightened his abdomen to keep from shivering. He was being transformed at the naked core of himself even as he took on layer after layer of beautiful embroidered garments. As the bishop made his way toward the young novice, Dom felt both inert and expectant, like a coveted object up for bid at an auction. Did the bishop feel the tremble in Dominic's hands as he lay his own around them in a double layer of prayer? The monsignor passed the holy chrism from which the bishop removed the crystal flask and dabbed the sweet oil of kings into Dominic's palms, rubbing it in vigorously, seeing if it would take. Dominic's hands were then wrapped in fine linen bands; were his mother here, she would have received these after the service, like a military widow receiving the tight triangle of a flag. With his bound hands he touched the chalice and the golden paten of the sacred host. With the archbishop's blessing, a blessing that had its power in its ancestry, through the generations of priests laying their hands on Dominic's head, a gesture that reached all the way back to the twelve apostles, he received the power to change bread and wine into body and blood; to serve the mystery of transubstantiation. The shunt of Grace.

Deus qui incepit, ipse perficiet. God, who began this, will also bring it to perfection.

"A priest forever," the bishop said, never diverting his rheumy eye on Dominic. Dominic nodded and swallowed. What was that, a promise or a threat? Neither. At last, something definitively. Did the bishop sense the doubt in his heart? It troubled Dominic so deeply that he took pains to doubt his very heart itself. Instead. He accepted more vestments being slipped over his head, grateful for the accumulating weight of the garments, as his body needed to be held down against its dissolution.

He closed his eyes and thanked his mother, tried to imagine her happy at his growing into such a good man, of being so purposed. She was his home, and he had lost her; he had only wanted his whole life to honor her, to find her by stepping into the life she might have wanted for him. He was not, like many of his generation, born into a world he would eventually repudiate but into one that he needed to recreate. He wanted not so much to shed his skins but to grow them back, one by one. Girded like this, he would appear before his mother in his mind's eye and ask, *Is this right? Do you find me here?*

Dominic remembers one of the men she went out with in particular. The man had taken Dominic and his mother out to the circus one weekend. Dom was impressed with the way the man licked his thumb to peel off the bills from the wad to pay for the tickets and peanuts. The man had a big mustache and serious eyes. One ear was bigger than the other. He smelled of aftershave and wore two-toned shoes. He accepted Dom's mother's shoulder rub and kiss on the cheek—but not with any great show, as if he understood how closely children observe every detail.

He called Dominic "little man," and the boy loved that. His mother liked it too.

On the drive home, Dom had decided to show how good and clever he was by saying how much he enjoyed the circus except for the trainers whipping the tigers.

"I don't think the tigers liked doing those tricks. Why did those men have to make the tigers so afraid of them?"

The man breathed sharply through his nose. "Maybe they have to," he said.

"Why?"

"Maybe the men know it's important to show the tigers they are stronger. That they must be listened to."

The man kept on visiting for a while. Dom loved learning things from him. He taught him how to tie knots, swim, ride a bike. He remembers playing catch for the first time and the lightness in his stomach in that moment of suspension when the ball lobbed slowly toward him. How he laughed at his own clumsiness as he missed, chasing the ball across the field over and over. In his heart, Dom knew that eventually he would know how to do this. He would get good at it. And what fun that would be. But then he saw the disappointment in the man's eyes.

"What?" Dominic asked.

"Nothing."

"Am I bad?"

"If you were my boy," he said and stopped.

"What?" Dominic asked and held his breath as if he were afraid of heights but had to look down anyway.

"If you were my boy, you would . . . you would know how to do this already."

Failed Prayer Number Five
Remember those ironic gods and superheroes—the ones who
scared us because we understood they were driven by urges
recognized only by their victims?
You would reveal us if we'd just let You.
But it is not we, the beloved, nor your enemies who bother You.
You are terrified by the indifferent, aren't You?
So You must torment those that love You.
Like an abused child, I know what the truth is: it's all my fault.

Dominic was late for his appointment with the bishop and had failed to arrange for other transport; nonetheless, he pushed the Sable to eighty mph on the highway up to Hartford, expecting to see troopers waiting for him behind every curve in the road. Rubbernecking an accident being cleared on the right shoulder, he shuddered at the buckle of the hood and the crack in the windshield, at the impact its victims must have felt. Father Carl filed gruesome pictures of accidents at the rectory in order to show them to the sixteen-year-olds who were so anxious to get their driving permits. Now he would be the keeper of these images.

The old seminary building hadn't changed much since Dom had studied there. With its dark brick facade, formidable and impenetrable, it had never meant to appear hospitable. What was different was that the greater metropolitan area had sprawled right up against the edge of its campus: the mall with its multiplex cinema just to the north and a housing development to the south. It no longer felt like a world apart, but one holding on to its place in the sand. Still, Dominic knew it as one of the few places in the state where his collar signified as clearly as a lieutenant's badges in the barracks, accomplishing two things: he would be both honored and put in his place.

In public, Dominic was used to drawing one of two reactions: condescension or curiosity. There were times the collar kept him as private and hidden as a Muslim wife in a burka. His self-consciousness had become vigilant, as if he had developed a third eye on how he was regarded. It was a kind of power to enter a subway car and have everyone in it fall silent, sit a little straighter. Gentlemen cleared paths for him; old ladies often crossed themselves as he passed. Teenage boys would sometimes smirk and poke each other's ribs. He was more than and less than a man in his black clerical suit: a shadow, a scold, an omen, a guilty memory.

"Good morning, Father Dominic," Carol, the executive assistant, greeted him. "The bishop is expecting you. Let me tell him you're here."

Carol poked her head into the bishop's office.

"He'll see you in a minute. And don't forget to take these home," she said to Dominic, stuffing a little bag of cookies into a pocket of the coat she took.

Dominic knew why he had been called. The bishop was going to "put it straight," give him the "lay of the land," "talk turkey" as if he were a change agent consulting some corporate reengineering project. The last contact he had with the bishop was about nine months ago when he had asked Dominic to prepare a performance for the Northeast Regional Conference of Bishops. When Dominic proudly offered a contemporary, minimalist setting of the Psalms, the bishop said that he would prefer something more "musical next time."

"Father Dominic." The bishop appeared at the door and extended his hand.

"Bishop."

"Can I get you something?" The bishop settled down behind the broad expanse of the partner's desk that took up nearly half the office. Dom marveled at the man: how old could he be? He was like an artifact: salt-and-pepper hair cropped close to his narrow skull. The smallest ears Dominic had ever seen. Black round pupils set in enormous whites, like pebbles in a Zen garden. A pressured smile which he flashed with discrimination, as a strike of lightning. He lacked canine incisors, as if he could sever with just one bite. The man lit like tinsel on a Christmas tree. Beneath the perfect complexion, he must have a skull of sterling silver.

He poured himself a vitaminwater.

"So, Dominic. How is it going? Tell me what people are saying about Father Carl," the bishop asked, rifling through a folder of letters requiring his signature. Dominic appreciated the elegant and genderless Catholic school cursive the bishop wrote across each of the pages.

"No one really knows yet. We haven't announced it."

"Surely the Sisters know."

"Well, Sister. We're down to Sister Agnes, you'll remember, and she is away, visiting her family for the Thanksgiving holiday."

"Right."

Dominic hated the efficiency of this man. After the special citation had been given to Father Carl several months ago, the bishop actually seemed impatient for the old man to die, as if the old priest's tenacity was merely awkward.

"Actually one parishioner came to me, a girl who seemed to know all about it already."

"Oh, who was that?"

"Dolores Alfano."

In the room, the air pressure deflated; Dom felt half afloat, a day-old balloon. The bishop's chin dropped.

"What did she want?"

"She took confession."

"This morning?"

"She seemed upset."

The light from the window dimmed as the sun moved slowly behind a cloud. The bishop simply did not like him; the blunt force of his judgment came down with the finality of a gavel. Anyone brought before him was not presumed innocent. The bishop was a man who knew what he needed to know and nothing more than that. He would prefer not to deal with Dominic, which inspired in the priest a perverse respect.

"There are rules and schedules, Dominic. You'll have to abide by them."

"Yes, Bishop."

"What did she say? No, don't even tell me; I've heard it all before. You know that she's something of an infamous problem for the diocese. I could show you her file." He cracked the knuckle of each middle finger, then folded his hands on the desk and said, "You know, Dominic, as I'm sure Father Carl has told you, the girl . . . overstates things."

The bishop fingered the part in his hair.

"You mustn't make too much of what she says because she will say almost anything. Anything to get you to listen to her."

Dominic said nothing, taking the power of restraint.

"You mustn't speak with her. You'll only encourage her, Dominic."

Another censure. *Say nothing*. The bishop was looking at Dom as if waiting for him to grow up on the spot. These were adult things meant for men more experienced than Dominic to handle.

"Look, Dominic," the bishop continued. "You are a wonderful priest, but you know as well as I that you are sometimes guilty of misguided sympathy. Listen, I am in touch with the mother."

"Oh, but, so am I. We—"

"Let me finish. Anyway, it's not a pretty situation. We are trying to help them both out. It may be that the girl will be sent away."

"Sent away? Where?"

"Somewhere she can be helped."

"Let me try first."

"Dominic, you don't know what you're up against."

"Bishop, with all due respect."

"It's all been decided. It should have happened long ago. Father Carl should never have let things get so far with her."

"What's been decided?"

"I can't divulge the details. We—you and I—that is, have a trust issue."

"What do you mean?" Dominic asked.

"That 'blog' of yours?"

"You actually read my blog?" Dom beamed.

The bishop smiled thinly.

"It's just meant to engage—"

"I'm sure I'm not interested. But you need to think it through. Who do you think you are, some public intellectual? Some Deepak Chopra? What's next, a book? *The Colbert Report?* You are a priest in the Roman Catholic Church. And, anyway, it's not what I called you here to discuss. Just stay out of it for now."

"I'm not sure what you mean."

The bishop shut his eyes and rolled his head back. Then, looking directly at Dominic, he sighed and said, "Our Lady of Fatima."

Dominic took a deep breath. "I want you to know, Bishop, I stand ready to serve. I don't know how much contact you have with the parishioners in our community—sounds like there is some—but I feel there would be considerable support for me to step in as pastor."

The bishop studied him.

"I could even say that I've lived my entire life for such a moment, and, truth be told, I've been functioning as pastor for at least two years anyway while Father Carl was ill."

"Dominic, you know the problems we face as an archdiocese."

"Of course, Bishop, but . . ."

The bishop glared at Dom. "But. But what? Dominic, you can't sit there and tell me that the prospect of closing the parish hasn't occurred to you. It was listed in the newspaper as a candidate, for God's sake."

Dominic felt the blush rise on his face. "Actually, no. I hadn't. I mean, I didn't believe . . ."

"Well, you're more naive than I thought."

"It's a wonderful parish."

"No doubt. But one with crumbling buildings, a diminishing congregation that is changing constantly and seems to need the church less and less."

"I am sorry to disagree with you there. Our Lady has a vital congregation; the community needs a center."

"We're hemorrhaging money."

"We can raise it. People will volunteer to fix the place."

"Dominic . . ."

"We're a small parish, but a vital one. The place is changing. We're catching up to what the community needs. In fact, until just two years ago, we raised enough money to pay for the vouchers to keep the minimum two hundred kids in the school. We could get there again. I'm sure of it. Let's see. We've got the soccer team—our league will be five years old next year; and the kids, they're a beautiful mix. I think there are eight countries represented. The undergrads volunteering ESL, the community breakfasts, the HIV support group, the cancer support group, the AA workshop. We sent close to a dozen high schoolers down to New Orleans after Katrina. Closing a church is not just shutting a building down; it's like turning out a family."

"Dominic, be realistic. The Mass?"

"Certainly not what it used to be; we both know that already. But we still get one hundred, one hundred and fifty . . ."

"Dominic."

"OK, thirty, forty, sometimes even fifty people sometimes at the eleven o'clock most Sundays. We're down to one morning Mass weekdays. I plan to continue Father Carl's excellent annual Mass for all the community families, regardless of faith, who lost children to violent crime. I'll even cook the same dinner—the baked ham and potato salad. You know, he cooked like a Baptist." Dominic chuckled, but the bishop had turned to stone. "But the real work is with the people throughout the day. The counseling. My people really count on my one-on-one consultations."

Dom looked at the bishop, who was penciling a document on his desk; how bored and unimpressed he was.

"It's not nothing," Dominic said.

The bishop's attention picked up at the defeated beat. "And you, Father. How are you?"

"Me? I'm fine; I'll be even better if you give us another chance."

"You'll be taken care of, you know. We'll find another home for you, nearby.

"But as a pastor?"

The bishop looked at him steadily. "I asked how you were doing for a reason, Father. I worry about you a little."

Dominic felt the heavy rumble in his gut. Of course. He must have done something terrible; no one ever had a serious talk with anyone because he had done something well. He spread his legs and hung his hands loosely from the arms of the chair, trying desperately to pose like a grown man who wasn't worried about standing his ground.

"I've heard that you keep to yourself a lot these days."

"I'm allowed some private time, aren't I, Bishop?"

"Of course; it's even essential. If there was any fault in Father Carl, bless him, it was that. He never took time for himself, always gave, gave, gave. Unlike you, I think he almost hated being alone. His outreach, his availability—well, it almost became a kind of neediness. But, anyway, that's not what I'm talking about."

"Have people complained, Bishop?"

"No, no, it's not that. You command a great deal of respect; you even inspire your community. But people do want to get closer to you, Father."

"I'm stunned, Bishop. I don't know what to say. I don't know that I can actually give any more."

"Probably you can't. But that's not what I'm talking about. I'm talking about something simpler, deeper. They want to be given the chance to love you, Father. To reach you as well as being reached by you."

Dominic was silent.

"Don't isolate; accept invitations. Don't spend so much time alone in your room. Don't drink so much, Father."

Dominic looked down; he sat up in his seat.

"Listen, Father, I'm sorry to spring this all on you today. You'll have a little time to reconcile all this."

"Bishop, listen. It's not too late; let's not make this decision right now. We can figure out ways: sell the parking lot."

"We already have, Dominic."

"Oh. No one thought to ask me?"

"It's not just Our Lady, Dominic; it's the whole diocese, the whole Church itself. It's an international crisis. A historical adjustment is needed."

"Oh, Bishop."

"Listen, Dominic, don't preach to me. We are in the real world here. We have to adapt to all the things that are changing."

Dominic stared at his lap. He had come here to be "promoted," to take up Father Carl's congregation; to shepherd his own church. Now it would be going under. On his watch. The whole flock left to wander the borders of the woods in which the wolves howled. Or did he take himself too seriously? Did anyone really need him that much?

"Father Carl should have prepared you better for this. I can't believe he left this whole thing up to me; I'm actually a bit angry with him about this. What did he think, that his dying would change everything?"

"Well, some can't help but believe that."

"You know what I'm talking about, Dominic."

"Is there nothing to be done?"

"I'm afraid not."

"What is your time frame, Bishop?"

"We're working on that. Within the year."

"When will the press know?"

"Tuesday."

"The day of Father Carl's funeral."

"Yes, of course, a coincidence."

"Or not? At any rate, it won't be seen that way."

"Don't be so self-important, Dominic. These are historical times. We are adjusting institutionally."

"What will I say to them?"

"Carol has a packet for you before you go. Read it and take guidance."

"I don't think we can just apply some template to my people. We're not the same as everyone else."

"You're not that different."

Dominic would not know where to go next. All he wanted was to circle around and around the old refectory table at which Father Carl—the old Father Carl, the one he thought he knew—would be sitting, nodding his head and fuming as Dom told him of the stupidity or injustice he had just suffered. Father Carl always dismissed the bishop as pedantic and two-dimensional, a natural-born religious administrator. He possessed the kind of certitude and authority that made the Church appear downright delusional. In fact, this was where he could begin the elder priest's eulogy: "There were certain kinds of behavior that irritated Father Carl most: flash, polemicism, righteousness, a favoring of orthodoxy over subtlety," he would preach, casting an eye on the bishop in the congregation. "While he was strong and principled—even unbending, some might say—he was never unforgiving."

Whom would he talk to now? Dom couldn't simply be expected to go on. He had lost his chief coconspirator, his better collaborationist half. Gone was the other person who believed in the things that held his story together.

Father Carl himself had tried so hard to come to a proper finish. But he ended not with revelation but with resignation, resentment, regret. His life did not resolve itself so much as come sliding to a halt. And with his passing, everything was coming loose. The stick of prayer was losing its tack. Receptivity was giving way to gullibility. The wine was turning to vinegar. The church itself would go to ruins. The spiritual fog that lay over their life in the rectory was lifting; Father Carl's death cleared the air, revealing nothing but the hard line of the self in doubt.

Never had he realized with such profundity that the Church cared less about the saving of a particular soul than the survival of its bureaucracy on a grand scale. The ambassador of the devil, Mephistopheles himself, always took one person at a time—that was his genius and limitation. Evil specialized. Seduction over induction. Christians, on the other hand, fell by the legions. Mass conversions. Like natural disasters, the Church found efficiencies in numbers.

> Failed Prayer Number Six
> I read and I read with the prejudice (on Your behalf) that while study without faith may be heresy, faith without study is surely banality.
> I will study You.
> Read and reread You.
> Stalk You.
> I pretend to wonder at You so as not to worry You. Anger You.
> Frighten myself.
> I will study You.

Dom stopped in at Burger 'N Brew in the strip mall. He ordered a burger and a first martini. And then another. He stewed in the morbid imagery of what would be happening to Father Carl's body. He couldn't keep himself from looking into the open tomb like the Abbot Sylvester meditating on the "vanity of this life", tracking the steps of decomposition. Despite the embalming and the expensive copper coffin, bacteria would gather on the body, creating gases that would break the seal of the casket and attract the insects who would feed and lay their eggs on his corpse. His face, Father Carl's actual beloved face, would swell beyond recognition. His skin, slippery and fragile, would marbleize green and red. Then it would begin to brown. His chest cavity would rupture, allowing greater access to his innards. His bones, fresh and greasy—"green" it was called—would show within a couple weeks. So go the organs. For a brief period, before disappearing, the body would mummify.

Dominic couldn't escape imagining Father Carl bloating and hollowing and disappearing. "It's the beginning of winter," he thought hopefully. "Maybe the body will freeze and keep until spring." Not that it mattered. The priest's body no longer belonged on the earth but to the earth. *I am what he was and what he is I shall be.*

He finished his burger with a brandy and high-tailed it back to the rectory. There was so much to do. He could do it. With renewed confidence, he gunned into the far left lane, pressing the old Sable to a nice eighty mph. This earned him his rightful place in the fast lane. A black sedan rode up behind, nosed him aggressively and flashed its brights.

"What?" Dom said aloud. "Relax." Switching to the right lane, he'd be stuck behind the laggards. That wouldn't do. The sedan would just have to settle in behind him, at an appropriate speed, some fifteen-plus miles over the limit. That was fast enough. Live with it.

As Dom paralleled the next caravan of sixty-five mph-ers in the right lane, he took his foot off the gas, slowing down by seven or so mph. Not braking, not doing anything unsafe, but forcing the black sedan to brake behind him. There was nowhere to go; the driver would have to accept Dom's lead. He could see the eyes of the driver in his rear window. Set tight. Both hands on the top of the steering wheel.

Passing the group of cars on his right, Dom accelerated back up to eighty. The sedan behind him charged into the right lane, and gunned it. If he thought he was going to pass Dom on the right, he had another thing coming. Dom took it to eighty-five, hovered past ninety. The sedan was edging up to his side. Dom scrupulously ignored the driver; he would not make eye contact. Before long, they came upon another caravan of cars in the right lane. He watched the black sedan sidle up to him and give the little surge that calculated whether he could swing in front. Dom gunned the gas and closed the gap; the sedan bucked in its brake.

"Hah!" Dom cried out. He backed down to a strong seventy mph, keeping pace with the last car in the right lane. The black sedan settled in behind him again.

In his rearview mirror Dominic watched the driver roll his window down and place a red light on his roof and then set it flashing. The state trooper, gestured with his left index finger for Dom to pull over into the right lane. Looking into his rearview mirror, he saw the man mouth, "Pull over."

"Fuck."

He hated that the cop had played him this way, that the trooper had the ironic advantage of knowing how the game would end, a preordained entrapment. Dom blessed himself in a hopeless effort to cushion the fall of his self-esteem. (It used to be his anxiety that escalated.) How would he get out of this one?

Now he knew enough to go blank. His sense of moral immunity—that he was mostly good in the big picture, so it was OK to take small transgressions—was his greatest liability.

The trooper got out of his car, adjusted his pants, put on his hat and walked over to Dom's passenger window. He didn't know this cop personally but had come to expect a positive response to his Roman collar. He did a quick survey of the passenger seat: a back issue of *Books and Culture*, his "death kit" still not put back into the glove compartment, the packet from the bishop with the archdiocese seal blazoned on its envelope, a CD set on "The Age of Bach" from Great Courses. Pretty good, respectable signals.

Dom rolled down the window and watched the trooper size him up, scan a flashlight over the worthy clutter in the car and say, “Good afternoon, Father. I just wanted to see how long you’d keep that up.”

“Oh yes, Officer. I must be in my own little world here. All I can really say is”—Dom added a chuckle—“is that I am more than a little embarrassed and very, very sorry.”

“Driver’s license and registration, please.”

“What?”

“Driver’s license and registration, please.”

“Oh, OK. Let me see here.” Dom pulled out his license but made hard work at finding the registration within the chaos of his glove compartment.

The trooper walked back into his car and picked up the radio. Dom shrunk a bit into the seat and imagined the surprise in the faces of the passing drivers at seeing a priest being pulled over. He closed his eyes.

His driving habits were something that Father Carl had always been on him about: parking in yellow zones, turning left on reds. In a traffic jam, he would idle onto the shoulder to prevent other cars from speeding past the traffic. “I don’t understand this attitude of exceptionalism,” he had said. “There’s an arrogance about this I don’t like, like you think you’re special and don’t have to play by the rules or something.”

The trooper appeared at his window again.

“Well, Father, looks like someone up there likes you. Driving like that, you’re not dead yet or in jail.”

“Yes.” Dom frowned affably. “So sorry about that. Emergency. Official church business.”

“Step out of the car, please.”

“You don’t understand; let me talk to Sergeant O’Malley downtown.”

"State matter. Step out of the car, Sir."

"Goddammit, you just don't get it, do you?"

The trooper radioed for assistance. Dom took a deep breath and failed the straight line he was asked to walk. Alcohol registered on the breathalizer test. Presumed guilty. Seven days to request a hearing. Facing a fine of five hundred dollars. A possible six to twelve months of jail time; forty-eight hours mandatory. License revoked for one additional year. The old Sable was impounded, and Dom was escorted to the station.

When they hit construction traffic on I-91, the trooper set his light atop the car and cruised down the shoulder at an easy twenty-five mph. It was in that slow, silent flashing glow that Dominic resolved that he would go through the pregnancy with Dolores: the doctor visits, the sonograms, the birthing lessons, the baby superstores. He would figure out a way to pay for all of that; he would figure out a way for her to go forward.

TWO

"Stop."

James pulls his fingers away from the keys, defensively, as if she were about to slam the cover down onto them.

"Play the rests," Signora Rosa commands. "Why do I need to tell you this over and over? Know not just when but how to pause."

His teacher places her little hand on his big shoulder and presses her index finger into the shallow pocket of flesh above his collarbone.

"The next note begins from within that silence. Fish it out of the ocean. Suspect that it might not come out a fish. Surprise us with what does come up."

Her finger relaxes. Or at least James thinks so. He draws the next note.

"Oof. There are too many blooms in your garden."

He is not sure what she means. He waits.

Clearing her throat makes a small noise; its rattle reminds him just how frail she really is. The lesson is over; he has disappointed her again. He rises from the bench, slides to his left to avoid bumping into her. His sleeves are rolled up to his elbow, and he offers his arm.

She sees the arm before her; it penetrates the lovely nimbus of light she sees surrounding all young people these days. Her fingernails find purchase in his forearm with a force that surprises a shiver up his back. At the point of his give, she rests finally on her perch, the falconer and the falcon.

She is so small; he tries to be lighter on his feet.

"He is strong, possibly too strong," she thinks. "Look at his long arms. Giant fingers. Massive torso. How will I get him to hear his own heart?"

The bagatelle he had just finished playing comes back to distract or, rather, focus her. She sings it for him, stressing the rests, reinforcing her instruction. He listens while the tingling in his skin, the tenderness he feels, narrows. He listens.

They shuffle together to the sofa; she steps forward with the right foot and drags the left behind to meet it. In this she hears the opening of Mozart's Requiem. Call and response.

He came to her to learn how to play. How long has he been coming? How many days a week? She couldn't be sure anymore. She was never surprised when he showed up. She lets him in; he is one of the few who still comes. Surely there are others still; she just can't remember them now. Nevertheless, he was her only student at the School of Music. He was her last connection to the university, and she would make sure he stuck. He would show them on her behalf. Whatever it took, she would breathe the gift into him.

After every visit, James delivers her away from the piano. Like a disinterment, they walk away from the black box, a carriage in a cortege.

He eases her onto the old sofa; her tiny frame barely impresses the lumpy seat. The apartment is a time warp: old and dusty Mitteleuropa, antique rugs, heavy drapes, ornate lamps and gilded clocks, tarnished candlesticks—everything burdened with too much story, with secret and regret. Signora herself lives like a curio in a cabinet.

She deftly hides her left hand, the lame one, in her lap, covering it with her good hand. He steals a glance at it; he thinks about it too much. He is too polite to ask what happened to it, whether it was an accident or some injury incurred during the war. No one at the conservatory ever talked about it, though some said it was an act of domestic violence. He had even googled her, only to find an obscure reference to a promising career cut short by a disabling injury. The more he tried to convince himself it didn't matter, the more he thought about it. It filled him with a restless morbidity, a dead thing that might still spring to life.

Leaning over her, he breathes in her smell of pickled fennel, dares to linger. How dry her face is, an old peach. How white her hair, its young girl wisps tucked behind the ears. Her neck is strong and smooth, as if the sculptor had neglected to age it. He would like to stroke it, fit it into the grasp of just one of his hands. The image scares him as if he wouldn't know how hard to squeeze or when to stop. He is wary, cautious, a bit awed. He observes her the way a naturalist might a rare bird in a salt marsh—watchful but not directly so, with an awareness of how wrong it would be to pretend a relationship and how easy it would be to destroy the moment.

Practicing at home, James hears Signora's voice and the instructive beats between her comments. As he works his way through the Hanon exercises, his fingers move up and down the keyboard: competent as a spider, deliberate like water. He hallucinates the sound of her singing along with the piano, inside the piano; her reedy soprano plays a half-beat ahead of him. He struggles to keep up. The fatigue creeps up his arm, and he has to remind himself to breathe in through his nose and out through his mouth like an athlete.

His fingers feel flat and unsexy this morning; she claimed that each tip had its own libido. But he would march them through the morning drill, settling into a comfortable rigor, getting through it rather than getting it down. His feet grounded on the floor. "Hard shoes," he would have called them as a boy, and he never practiced in anything but. She demanded it.

He corrects his posture in the way that Father Dominic advised their parish choir—"Imagine that a string from the top of the sky was attached to your spine and was lifting you up higher and higher"—as if the discipline of good posture didn't deliberately push itself up from the abdomen but was an involuntary response to a pulling from above. To live life less as a burden and more like a submission to the force that would lift you: this was the trick, the secret of music. A strange bit of advice coming from someone who was so earthbound with conflict.

When James first met Signora Rosa at the conservatory, he sat down at the piano to play the Brahms Mazurkas he had been asked to prepare. She stood behind him, remaining silent for several minutes after he played.

He hesitated, then finally asked, "Shall I go on? Do you want to hear them again?"

More silence. Finally, he heard her shuffle over to him. She ran her good hand through his hair. She uncoiled a single curl between her thumb and index fingers, resting at the top of the pull, then let it spring back into place. She patted his head twice. For good measure.

"I always wanted to know what that feels like," she said.

He wasn't offended, though he might have been. She was curious. He even gave her the benefit of the doubt that she liked what she felt. He was curious about her too. In the end, he decided not to tell anyone about the incident, couldn't bear the indignation his classmates would exercise on his behalf. The process of formal complaint; the calls for resignation; the bureaucracy of resentment. Her connection to the conservatory was already tenuous—as was his. He hated to admit it, but they kind of needed each other. She might in the end even need him more. She needed a hit, a star pupil, an unlikely success story to retire on. She had not been one to quit while ahead; he would be her redemption. He could even prove her right.

"An athletic build is admirable, could be useful," she had said to him in particular, he presumed, but was she also speaking of his type? Was she speaking precisely of his long neck, broad shoulders, thick chest, narrow hips, high butt? His wide nose, full lips, long fingers, big feet, other clichés supposedly common to his race? She had never mentioned the degree of his black skin: "*Roots* black. Your mix is all wrong—more African than American," his sisters teased him. The sheer fact of it had no relevance for Signora Rosa.

"Relevancy?" she said, "what is this relevancy?" when he asked whether his being black would have an effect on his career either way.

But her regard for the "relevancy" of his race was the one thing that could make him rethink her. What she made of him, in the end, would allow him to make something of himself.

Would an audience want to invest in the mythology of a young inner-city black youth forging his way to Bach? A shortcut to redemption. Could he live up to that mythology, behind it even? Could he learn from a seventy-eight-year-old lame woman whose own ability to listen was a last grasp at empathy? He could try to play the way she wanted to hear him; he could reinvent himself at the piano, a new calibration of the musical canon.

She had warned him off some of his mannerisms:

"Throwing your head back like that—what is that? You have found some sudden angel calling to you?"

"Remember, transport is not meant to be your journey. Take your audience with you."

"Who are you trying to convince—the audience listening or yourself? Do you not have the confidence in the strength of your interpretation to speak for yourself? Are you a musician or a shaman? Do you want to make music or fake magic?"

He tried to recall the gist of their last lesson.

He had played the opening phrase prettily, holding the echo.

"You are like the blind gardener," she said. "He was so stunned by the smell of his garden he couldn't work all the colors and textures."

He let go the pedal and struck the chord tentatively.

"Little Bo Peep."

He forced it.

"Who was that—Cain or Abel?"

The next note peeled out like a car shoved into gear; it curled angrily against itself. It hurt like a pinched nerve.

"Foreboding, yes, but keep it mortal. Less Mephisto. More Iago."

He hammed it up.

"Oh thank you, Sir Elton John."

He banged his fists down on the keys.

She smacked the back of his head.

Together they froze. He had never shown his temper to her; he is sure it scared him more than it has her. The roar in the harp dimmed. Waiting for more, he considered the sting spreading against the scalp: how maternal it felt to him. She regretted the thick ache in her good hand.

• • •

At home, James sat at the piano waiting for the music to bring him into focus. He played the phrase over and over again, breathed into its rests. He now knows how to pull it off but is still surprised how the pause starts deep in his abdomen, the drop and lift of desire. His lips open, his eyes soften. He feels his forehead expand across the absence in his skull.

"Find the phrase by letting it come to you," she had told him. "Have you ever tried to catch a leaf from a falling tree? It looks easy, but it's nearly impossible to anticipate how it will go. Make each note fall that way. Don't try to catch it."

This was the way she would want it. He had it now; but why could he never play as well in her presence? Was it for her he performed? She was always there at the keyboard with him, even then, destroying his privacy—the very thing he loved most about playing piano.

Just last night he had even dreamed of her. They were sitting at a restaurant eating dinner at a place he could never afford. He was hungry, anxious before the emptiness of the plates on the table. She was silent. Deliberately dropping his napkin, he bent to retrieve it so he could sneak a peek beneath the tablecloth and examine the lame hand she kept fastidiously in her lap. A fox curled elegantly there like the collar of a coat. He couldn't be sure whether the creature was alive, menacing or timid; its eyes looked straight into his, luring him with the hold of its breath. Would it spring at him in attack? Did it actually wink at him?

Practicing that morning, he heard her voice vocalizing a problematic phrase, encouraging him but not in the usual way. It didn't come so much from behind, pushing or urging him forward but from somewhere in the future, pulling him out of himself, calling from some point ahead of him. He practiced with negation, deciding what instincts, sounds, impressions he would decline, hoping that in the end he would affirm by default. He could work hard; that was in his corner. All those who didn't believe in him, those who told him to stop: it was for them he practiced so hard. He would show them.

She warned him against his predilection for a *dark* sound. "We all want to suggest our playing comes from some dark place buried deep within us, not reachable by others. It's tempting to phrase off-tempo to bring attention to our precious inner lives, our special, individual souls. Don't do that."

"Dark sound." A reflexive wince couldn't be helped. But he was also ashamed of the reflex itself. He needed to choose what to be: a black classical musician or a classical musician who was black.

He knew what she meant, though. He searched for that dull ache in his lower stomach that came with the exertion of sound, as if lifting a heavy weight—when his impotent fingers just could not complete a phrase—a tickle in the groin, that feeling he could access like an abscess, an ache in a hole. The way the pedal reached deep inside the piano's box, as if a prostate shifted the entire soundboard. He almost preferred the sound unstated, unsatisfied, innocent, left in the dark.

Could one sustain a career in music conjuring the inexpressible?

He could put off thinking about a career for a while anyway. He knew very well it might never happen. All he had to concentrate on now was a postgraduate fellowship, a buying of time: that is what he and Signora Rosa would work toward, even though the conservatory had hinted there might not be much of a future for him there. Nonetheless, he believed he could prove them wrong. James had confidence and a capacity for hard work. Signora Rosa believed in that more than in his talent. Helping him prepare for this recital would be her last project. His career would be launched or not. It would all be decided for him that night of the recital, just months away.

He had chosen Bach's Goldberg Variations: important, difficult, previously owned. Formidable powers had occupied, dominated, exploited and disfigured that land; each had left their monuments. What new would he have to say? The piece already had its terrorist performers; their interpretations meant to be definitive and were in the end hostile, murderous. They wanted to kill the piece, didn't they?—make it submit, bury it under the weight of their reading, spoil it for anyone daring to come to it after they had claimed it as their own.

The Goldberg Variations: he could spend a life reckoning with it, pitching himself against it with all the limitations of his technique, with a frustration that can only be described as a kind of philosophical horniness.

Wasn't it the same music that had stopped him in his tracks when he was a little boy, dragged by his mother to the house she cleaned every Friday? Standing at the study door, unseen, invisible, James watched a man work his way through the entire piece, transfixed. It was the first white person he had ever seen. The man winked at him when he finished playing and asked him if he wanted to touch the keys. James ran away to find his mother in the basement.

Taking the bus home, he asked his mother, "What are white people like?"

"Same as and different than you and me."

"How are they different?"

"Well, for one, they let other people do their washing."

"Does that mean you're more clean?"

She laughed and put her arm around him. He knew that conversation was over. His mother's inner life was like a historic tomb somewhere, far off, locked up and quiet, closed to visitors.

"What you stand there staring at the whole time?" she asked him.

"Just listening," he replied.

Because of this one instance of interest, she started him in lessons the next week, taking on more houses to clean in order to pay for them. Did she believe him to be a prodigy? He didn't honestly think he was. None of it came easily to him. It did end up coming to him; he just worked harder at it than others. And it was this escape route that his mother worked at, the two of them digging out the tunnel day after day. His schoolteachers were a bit alarmed, worried that he was "escaping into a dream world of music." But he didn't understand that. Playing felt more like engagement than disappearance; nothing placed him in the real world more than playing music.

Signora Rosa would do her best to prepare him, as she had others. She would guide him as he stumbled in love through the great musings of Bach. He would work harder at it than most. But he would also have to work differently as well. First, he needed to study for it, prepare for it intellectually, sit down and write the biography of the music, if that's what it took.

She would see him through the recital, rehearsing not just the material but the man he would be when he first walked out onto that concert stage.

"Your audience wants you to be a guardian of tradition. They love us for what they recognize and will love us a little more for the ways in which we challenge that."

That reflex. What did she mean—that he just might become a credit to his people? The Marian Anderson, André Watts, Leontyne Price, Arthur Ashe, Awadagin Pratt gambit? Anything but Louis Farrakhan's fiddle. The kind of black citizen "whose parents expected him to go to college," as Jessye Norman once reassuringly said about herself in an interview. What would his audience be looking for in him: a reason beyond the rainbow? A purely urban American strength, the kind that told the story of what it had taken to get out of the projects amid the ridicule of his neighborhood: “Why you playing not just white music but *dead* white music?” The fact that he had chosen this canon would reaffirm the superiority of that culture; his coveting of that tradition would buy him admission.

None of that changed the fact that he deliberately wore khakis and a sport jacket with his ID tag prominently hung around his neck as he walked in and out of the university buildings. Nowadays he hid the town from the gown. He was caught in another paradox too: he was too black to be white and too white to be black.

Playing the piano as a boy was easier to hide in the projects than other instruments would have been; he went solo to the music studio as if off to somewhere no good, hands in his pockets instead of clutching a flute. Even his teacher told him it took guts; advised him to keep a low profile so when it came time to leave they wouldn’t notice.

What was it about James that made him want to belong to that one percentage point of African Americans employed as classical musicians in the United States? He was never actually called a prodigy, but he was awfully skilled at a young age, able to show off, proving every day that he was different, special. That was important to his mother. She believed in “the ultimate justice of things,” and he was going to be her proof. Going from the New Haven magnet school (the last of its kind to even have a music program) to New York two days a week to study at Performing Arts, he felt intramural if not illegitimate, never the home team. He knew people made allowances for him, that he was some affirmative action baby, lived with their discounting of his talent. But these early years were important. Music can’t be learned brilliantly as an adult. There has to be some early promise. So he had struggled and prevailed at the School of Music, securing himself an audition for one of the coveted postgraduate positions.

But now the stakes were something else altogether. He was no longer hoping to be found but afraid that he would be found out—as a mere striver, a fraud. Signora Rosa was right to point out that his musicality could not just communicate technical proficiency, sensitive phrasing, powerful dynamics—that technique was empirically judged and what each of the contestants would have in common. He needed a persona to carve out; the character would prefigure the art. How would he put across his genial stage manner? An athletic youth who would gray pleasingly, he would be known for his attack, the cutting slant of his phrasing like a killer tennis serve. Productive but not promiscuous, he would gain fame within a narrow if adventurous repertoire, cool Baroque and smart modernist, Bach to Berg.

It had taken over fifty years to figure out things she could teach him right away. More challenging was that she taught in at least two secondary languages: the Italian translated in her head to English but also the touch on the keyboard she was no longer able to demonstrate. When telling failed her she couldn't rely on showing. She heard the phrase, saw how it should go; she knew she would play it beautifully if she were able. Was this what an old man must feel under the spell of desire and the failure of the flesh?

What right did she have teaching anyway, a woman in her condition? She was probably doing him harm, this strange, beautiful, brave boy. He might save her yet; she hadn't thought about a man this way in decades. His size thrilled her; his smell tempted her. She was going crazy finally; she had anticipated the day, knew it must come. A woman her age with such thoughts.

"Go to someone younger; someone who can do you less harm, if not more good," she told him.

Born in Italy, Signora Lotito had mostly trained Europeans throughout her career and felt entitled to make ethnic and aesthetic assumptions about them. She knew this was out of fashion, even considered dangerous by some. Nonetheless, she knew what she knew. The eastern Europeans—they took their inspiration from the chest up. Chopin, the Pole in Paris, sat far away from the keyboard, forcing his arms into straight lines, his head thrown back—his very body a bridge; his notes barely audible past the first few rows in the salon. The Viennese took pleasure in pent-up pressure and release. The Germans felt inspiration from the abdomen, like athletes or singers, their action and voicing tightened into a spring. The Italians burrowed in and dug out: both Apollo and Dionysus. The French melted into pianism, as if the musician's body was a single-cell organism with ten fingers. Steely, huge, aggressively pressing the boundaries of fortissimo: these words described the Russians.

She had never felt confident in getting at the quality of the American sound, but she knew she liked its incongruities, its messy contradictions—the very impossibility of getting at a unity of purpose. It could be ugly and sloppy like its cities, but it could be beautiful like its people.

These days many of the students coming into the conservatory were from Japan and China and Korea. She did not yet know what to say about them but had the vague apprehension that there was something impolite—or worse yet, politically incorrect—about these absolute opinions, as if they revealed more about the thinker than the thought. A colleague at the conservatory had gone so far as to say that one major benefit of globalization was the way it neutralized nationalism in music.

"Everyone is now the same; everyone can now sound the same. Music belongs to everyone and to no one," he had lectured.

"But what is so wrong with saying there is a German sound or an Italian sound?" she had asked him.

"Because, my dear," he had withered, "that is one step from saying that, for instance, the German sound knows better, is better. And we all know where that leads us."

That had quieted her, but she still felt as if he got something important wrong. She had always considered it her job to bring out and preserve what was different and unique about every musician, those qualities that drew on where the musician was born, who had raised him or her. The way an Easter lamb tastes of English grass; a Brunello of Tuscan minerals. Her American students had ambivalence about their own sense of entitlement. Should they be musicians; should they do something more practical? That was the difference between them: in the case of entitlement, Americans presumed while Europeans assumed.

She wouldn't learn to change her ways, but kept quiet about them. It was another way that she was choosing to disappear. Not that it mattered. She had been cast out of the conservatory, semiretired. That was fine with her. She had become bored with her faculty colleagues and their discontent. They equated progress with maladaptation. They were addicted to their own malaise, pressing its bruise to the point of pleasure. As if being contrarian admitted honesty; as if voicing mere complaint practiced a kind of integrity. Of course, she was unhappy too—but it was not a prideful or self-righteous unhappiness.

She had made mistakes; everyone knew that. She had been accused of being inappropriate. That was no surprise to her; weak people learn to love their boundaries, which are made known to them only by others' transgressions. Students no longer came to her; she had a reputation of being "old school," a tyrant, demanding—more than was necessary, more than was healthy. She didn't miss them. She had only one left: this James, who took power from his back, as if he were thrusting himself into the music. Aggressive and challenging, he was more interested in the problems within a piece of music—and far less interested in their resolutions. He liked the fight. She would give him good.

James had amazing endurance; he practiced not just the four to six hours a day most serious students did, but often eight or ten or more. Repetition invites the involuntary part of the mind to respond. Inspiration, she tried to show him, was the end of hard work, not the beginning. Along with her conviction that among all pointless performing arts, playing the piano was the greatest art, she knew it was the least rewarded, the most repetitious, the least ensembled, the loneliest; she wanted her students to accept their likely unglamorous futures as paid-by-the-hour instructors or work-for-hire session musicians.

But what she still had to show him, what he somehow didn't know yet, was how to set the scale of expression. He allowed no concession to technical problems, attacked his Bach with a brilliant variety of timbre and dynamic. But he still had to educate his emotional life. He considered commitment to be character; the artist he wanted to be would simply follow. Nonsense. He needed vision, contrivance, intelligence, choice; he needed to pretend first. James was too impressed with the worthiness of his decision to be a classical pianist. He needed to learn to be less good and more cunning.

Technique is a kind of fakery, a projection of interpretation. It can make the playing flashy, virtuosic, easy, daring. It provides the illusion of spontaneity. It should come across like a secret told. She would show him how to give the piano, with its encyclopedia of chords, the illusion of sound growing by filling in or emptying out what comes before or after, to mimic the action of those instruments to which it thought itself superior: the breath of an oboe or a length of the bow across a violin. He would need to keep his eyes open when making love, to measure the effects of his technique.

"Sometimes we need to feel the effort as well as hear the talent. You push. You build the muscles up, yes. But what does this cost you? You get only stronger. Try to pull. Pulling is exhausting, drawing the emotion out is exhausting. This is not something you can do for twelve hours. Trust me."

He was upset with her, at first, for suggesting he cultivate an onstage insincerity, but he learned what she meant. To pretend is to intend. And that's good enough until your experience and circumstance catch up. For the world to conform to your idea of it. The musical score is not the truth. Playing well brings music into being the way prayer brings God into being.

Signora Rosa felt the current wars differently: not as a virgin wound but like a second- or third-generation scab that refused to heal, opening itself again and again in a manner almost inquisitive before closing over. It did not hurt with any originality but with the tolerance of chronic pain, the cost of living, what it meant to be alive as long as she has. They were was so far away: Afghanistan, Iraq. What did James or any of these young Americans know of war?

Bad memories from her youth and its war sprung at her like a dog at a fence; they snarled with such viciousness she worried whether she was perhaps having a stroke, a violent synapse that surely meant breaking a blood vessel, destroying her neural nets. But, no, she was doomed to coherence, imprisoned by her brain's insistent connectivity, forced to remember with visceral pain the horrors of her life and the banal details of an eternal present.

The good memories were shyer, and she had to coax them out from hiding—almost like a composition releasing its meaning only after years and years of playing it. She cultivated memory with deliberate exercises like wearing her mother's venerable old perfume, which she dabbed behind her ears every morning the way her mother always did. She would prepare farina with boiled milk for breakfast, its white scum clinging to the sides of the bowl, smelling like the wet newspapers she used to pick up and read on the bus home from school. Every crowded place reminded her of the way her mother would stand in the doorways of busy shops to test whether people would bump into her as they attempted to pass.

"Just watch," she would say with equal parts affront and curiosity. "Watch how they bump into me over and over again, just for standing here. As if I was not even here! Bumped into again and again. As if I weren't here at all."

Her life in Italy as a young pianist, before marrying, had been filled with color. Her towels were freshened with sugared lemon juice. Her father kept a parrot to delight the children of his friends. Setting a match to the biscotti wrappers, she would watch them rise to their rapid smoke-out. The hundreds of record albums that cemented her lifelong preference of analog. A closet full of marionettes. The gorgeous 1890 Bösendorfer. Where on earth would that be now? Had her old friend survived? Was it still loved?

Later, her mother had become an invalid, taking to her bed simply because it was too difficult to get up. She was merely arthritic—nothing fatal. It turned out for the best; Rosa was relieved when she realized her mother would miss the watermark events of her youth: her confirmation, her graduation, her conservatory recital.

She began to expect the return of those she loved from the dead. Her mother: forever middle-aged, with a ready bosom to bury her own little face in. Or Enza, the epileptic nanny with the loud laugh and thick ankles who surprised her one day by lifting her skirt and showing her the thick mound of hair between her legs, demonstrating how she could move its lips, a fuzzy puppet or something half alive, a just-gutted fish. The way one thing becomes the whole memory of a person.

She remembered going to the beach and standing in the water to her waist, making up a dance to the song she sang while her father raked the sandy bottom for clams and scungilli. Each time he found a shell he would whistle her over, hand her the rake and let her raise the prize, wet and tight, over her head with a triumphant call to her mother, who would clap from her wheelchair on the boardwalk. When the sack was full, they went home to shuck and eat the tender little clams fresh out of their shells, saving the big ones to chop up into a soup later on.

Her father left her with a lovely image of what a man might be like—strong and able, knowing where to find the goods of the earth and what to do with them—while she could delight him merely by making simple theater in the water.

Then the war came and her father was gone, and she was no longer sure whether men had suddenly become terrible—or if maybe her new longing for them made them terrible. She, like so many others, had made the mistake of marrying young. That calamity, at least, had produced her sweet daughter, that lovely girl who was now a hard woman who barely spoke to her. Her own mother had passed away before her wedding, which was a blessing. She would have been mortified by the handsome and brash Claudio, the way he insisted on the military service with all its bombast, the brass band, the captains with their swords at their sides, their bitter wives at the table and their impatient mistresses at the bar. The way he insisted that the wedding was the groom's domain. The way he would move her to the south, to a tiny farming village. Gratitude was what she ultimately felt for her mother's frailty as she would be spared the travesty of her daughter's life. And the life of her granddaughter, a skinny, ungrateful woman.

While Claudio was away at war, Rosa found refuge not in the volunteer group of women at the church but at her piano. Nothing drowned out the chatter with less effort than the simple playing of scales. Her quest for order was personal, self-reliant, exclusive; this enraged the other hens in the barnyard. Who did she think she was? The outrage was so strong, one would have thought she was spending her afternoons in bed with a lover. In earshot, no less. She didn't mind; she didn't care what they thought of her. She had her family piano, and she could play it loud enough to drown them out.

And then Claudio came back to the village, a survivor of a lost battle, with all the residual fury of the fighting cock in an interrupted match. She could feel the open equation of his return: an empty noose before a crowd. He was ready to be the front-page story, a doomed hero, importing the afterburn of battle into their kitchen. She would become his fight.

Youth was a gift.

What was the point of maturity in a musician? Whose lovemaking is as good at seventy as at thirty? Avoiding that peaking of life was supposed to be the trick of a career, except that pianists were supposed only to get better, more skilled. But instead of a prized vintage wine, Signora Rosa felt like the cellar itself, always cold.

All her senses, in fact, were in retreat. She was shrinking; her eyes were dimming. Smells repelled her. She ate little because tastes were no longer interesting. The fact of food in her mouth, with all its competing textures and flavors, disgusted her. She hated how long it took to chew: her teeth demonstrated their futility before the sheer stubbornness of the matter in her mouth. At times, food simply refused to dissolve, and she would rush to the sink and spit it out. The doctor had given her cartons of a chalky milk to drink instead, insisting that she get her vitamins from a dependable source. It was ghastly, flinty, damp mulch.

Her skin flaked, and her fingers tingled. She touched from the inside out; there was more stimulation from within her body than outside it. But most alarming was the way sound was receding. She still heard with articulation; but the volume had turned low. She refused hearing aids as she was sensitive to the way they monochromed the colors of music.

As she deafened, she enjoyed the power of making other people speak up, the opportunity to pretend she simply couldn't hear them. She enjoyed watching their effort to be heard. There was a young, gooey woman who just recently stopped her piano lessons. The girl molted with flattery; she made her sneeze. Despite needing the money, Signora gradually alienated the girl by pretending she couldn't hear anything she said. "My, but you are soft-spoken," she said to the girl, forcing her to shout everything.

She let the girl's monologue dissipate into a general hum. Signora watched how her eyes played. What was her life like? Could it be as dull as she sounded? What was she like naked under those meticulous clothes? Whenever she asked a question, Signora just shook her head and said, "What, dear? What was that?" confusing the poor girl. Eventually, the girl made excuses and complained of a headache and left early. A note then arrived from the girl: "I don't think I can commit the time to connect with the piano in the way you need me to in order to get the most out of our lessons. So, with respect and admiration, I want to thank you for your time and effort."

Signora Rosa even forgave herself the concerts now, admitting she had always hated the performance halls, where her love for music was buried under the dutiful respect for it. It was like subjecting the spirit to church service. At the concert hall, she felt trapped amid the attentive bodies sitting erect in their seats. As the strangled coughs forced themselves out in staccato beats through the audience, she felt panic rise above her as if shoved into a mass grave. They were being buried alive. What was that phrase she had copied out as a student? Nietzsche: "the ear is the organ of fear."

Arthritic, asthmatic, thick with cysts and tumors (the last one the doctor took out had a patch of fine hair and the stub of a toe), she was still curiously light with life. She was every day inching toward what she had pretended to have been for so many years now: dead inside. Nothing could move her. She was finally going to die. Inside and out.

She barely left the apartment anymore and had even stopped going into the city for her Wednesday afternoon lunches. As if now that Italian cuisine had realized its rightful preeminence over French, the restaurants needed her less. At home, she wandered aimlessly through the rooms, going through the overstuffed drawers in her bureau and boxes in closets trying to get rid of things, deciding what to keep and what to discard. She could spend half her days this way, pacing her purge. She wouldn't get through it all anyway, so she could take her time making piles to give away and then change her mind and sort them back into their drawers.

She enjoyed rationing her time; this had always been what she did best. Sadly, music dominated her life more now than ever just when she had the least affection for it. Her piano took up so much of the front room, she was consigned to move around it, edging its perimeter. Her face reflected in its ebony shine as if in a dark, still pool. No touch of her hand could warm that surface; it was cool from the inside out. The piano allowed for no other furniture in the room except for her lumpy couch on which she took her naps. Getting a good night's sleep was a skill she appeared to have lost.

Sitting before the keys, she bared her teeth. "I'm not afraid of you," she hissed at the 88 rigid, perfectly in-tune hammers—each of them ready to sound out her errors and tolerate her precision. She laid her lame hand on the forbidden keys, the curve of her fingers unable to clench into a fist or flex open. She couldn't simply ignore it even though being inconspicuous was the only thing it desired. At various times, she had hit it, stuck needles into it, tried to make it feel. It always just lay there impassive, and she had grown bored with torturing it, being tortured by it.

At the piano, she played a desultory set of scales with her right hand, like an old woman climbing a staircase up and down on her one good leg, going from room to room trying to remember what she is looking for.

What would she do when she stopped teaching altogether? Read. Read music—in bed at night and in the morning with coffee. Playing out scores in her mind, the way in which she might attack a movement or finger a phrase—or might have once upon a time—reading like the devout in the Bible: for comfort and instruction.

She rather liked the idea of getting this old; it had a certain momentum to it, the way the twilight wants the night.

"Cheer up," she told herself, "for pretty soon you'll have to die."

"*Ma, aspetta*!" Signora Rosa cried out. A wave of adrenaline rushed through her body; there were no arrangements for her burial! Had nobody thought of this? She certainly wouldn't stand for lying beside her husband sometime in the future, in that springtime plot in the Calabrese countryside. Out of the question. Her own family's cemetery was lousy with corpses; no room at that inn. Could it be possible that her grave would not be marked?

That would be the first time such a disgrace had fallen on her family. She had simply forgotten about this; there was no one to take care of this kind of detail. What about her daughter? Where would she go? Maybe Andrea would come up with something. This would have been unthinkable to her mother and father just one generation ago. Oh, how she had let things go!

But, maybe: so what? The earth was already congested with bodies. And all its churches so empty. She would make arrangements to be cremated. Atomized. Gone with the wind. Or maybe not even. Let them figure out what do with what she left behind. *Basta cosi.*

Edging his way around the piano, Dom wondered how the movers had managed to get the instrument into the apartment. He knocked against the beautiful mahogany case: Jonah in the belly of the whale, ship in a bottle.

Signora Rosa called from the bathroom and told him to have a seat. He wished she would take her time so he could sift among the thousand books, the boxed vinyl sets of Bach and Beethoven, the musical scores, the curios, the prints. She had hoarded so many things; the apartment was becoming its collection.

Dom had once asked Signora Rosa if she had actually read all of the books in the apartment.

"Of course not. You miss the point," she answered. "The collector always wants to own more than can be experienced all at once. Possibility must always overtake satisfaction. A collection is one of the only ways to have too much and not enough at the same time, to be consoled by what cannot be known completely."

"Signora, Rosa, you're a theologian," Dominic said with a smile.

Father Dominic and James were the only regular visitors to Signora Rosa these days. She had pushed James to rehearse Dom's choir, and they had become unlikely friends even. The two were so different from each other: James with his muscular physicality and this priest with his nervous, brooding self. Dominic had the opposite of a physical presence, as if he were eating himself alive, right here in front of everybody, disappearing under the cloth he worked so hard to live up to.

Dominic positioned his chair beside Signora Rosa. He cleared his throat, signaling her to begin her confession.

She sat upright and laid her good hand over the damaged one. Dom registered a kind of majesty in the gesture; he was her public or, at best, an intermediary. There were things that would be forever closed to him. She never wanted to talk about the incident. It had to be important. He had only once asked her about it.

"Are you speaking for God's curiosity or out of your own prurient interest?" she answered.

"You answer with a question."

"You know what happened. The story is out there somehow. You can always trust people not to keep your confidence."

"Yes, there is a version out there," Dominic admitted.

"So tell it to me."

"I don't really know what happened. Something about your husband in Italy."

"Claudio, yes. It's easy to blame it all back then, on him, back there. But everyone wants to look at the accident as—"

Dom interrupted her: "The accident?"

"The incident. What the incident has kept me from doing."

"So how would you have me look at it instead?"

"What it has forced me to do instead."

"Tell me about that."

"Father Dominic, let me remind you how this is supposed to work. I tell you things I have done. You administer God's absolution. Remember?"

"Forgive me. What is troubling you?"

She let out a long sigh and set her lips tight against each other. Finally, she looked down at her lap and said, "Maybe I've done bad things as well."

"Yes?"

"Maybe I've neglected my daughter. Maybe I've clung to my hatred of my husband. Maybe I feel bad about provoking him, about not loving him. And, maybe with James . . ."

She halted and furrowed her brow. She looked troubled.

"Signora?" Dom prompted.

"I'm tired now, Father. I must rest."

"I'll come again next week."

"Yes, next week the Schubert. I've marked the score already."

"Signora?"

"You need to work on the Adagio."

"Signora, I am sorry. I think you . . ."

She clucked. "Please hurry." She frowned at him. "Come next week, Father. You know, I have secrets. And I am losing them slowly."

As he left the apartment, Father Dominic took a hard candy from the covered crystal bowl in the foyer. The wrapper stuck to the sticky surface, and he let his tongue separate the last little bits. The weekly sessions with Signora were unlike any of the other confessions he heard. She was forgetting things and afraid not only of running out of time but of living outside of time. Her past was overtaking her present. Confession restored her fantasy of innocence, a starting point from which she could look forward and anticipate a perfect future.

When James entered the chapel, Dominic rushed up flushed and bothered. "I have so much to tell you."

"OK, I can stay afterward; we'll catch up."

James laughed to himself as he watched the priest rush off in a jog that would have been athletic, if not for the little instep.

It was almost a year ago to the day that James observed the priest furtively plastering central campus with handwritten posters advertising an open audition for the church's pianist/organist position. At first, he had no interest in the job, but Signora Rosa had urged him to apply and had primed the priest to look out for him. He figured he could always use a little extra cash, and the ad had promised fifteen bucks an hour. When he showed up at the church in the last fifteen minutes of the audition, Dominic was sitting alone in the gray silence staring up at the rose window. He clearly had expected more candidates.

Father Dominic asked James to sight-read several accompanist scores, but it wasn't until he pulled out the Schütz and Palestrina that the two of them lost their shyness. When James began to play the Bach Cantata "Ich Habe Genug" (I Have Enough), Dominic began to sing along in a confident and graceful baritone, giving the empty church a surprisingly sonorous depth.

The only other white person James knew of growing up in the projects, other than the troubling police, was another priest—a fat, pink, balding man who huffed and puffed when he walked. All the kids called him Piggy Back but tolerated him because he brought them lollipops and helped sick people until one day he was caught touching a girl and got moved away, replaced by a Nigerian priest whose English no one could understand. James was curious about the man whose skin was as dark as his own, and they had become friends; the priest had advised him about academic matters, and James had clued him in on the habits of the neighborhood.

In the meantime, James had found community in the church despite his being irreligious; so were most of the men and women of the Our Lady of Fatima Concert Choir. The singers came from all over the county; some of them had even trained and sang professionally. They came to perform the great choral masterworks the way people go the medieval galleries in the museums, as enlightened and curious secular minds. Still, the choir would fill the church every Advent and every Lent, while the Sunday Masses grew smaller and smaller.

As the singers gathered themselves, Dominic turned to James and said, "Everything has changed suddenly."

James nodded.

"First, it's official. They want to close the church down."

"But you knew that was coming. Still, does that mean they can?"

"Right. We can fight this," Dominic said, as if introducing the idea.

"Next"—Dominic sighed heavily—"Father Carl."

"I know. Funeral's Monday.

"So everyone knows?"

"Small world, you know. I thought you were going to talk to me about Dolores."

Dominic slowed down.

"She's pregnant, right?" James said.

Dominic looked at him, stunned. "How do you know?"

"Come on. You know her; she's been telling her story in all the wrong places. Like I said, it's a small world. Still, only half the people I've talked to believe her."

"How come?"

"First of all, she doesn't look it. Skinnier than ever."

"Well, I think she's pretty early."

"Second, you know as well as I do that she constantly makes stuff up. So long as she's the center of attention. This time, though, she's upped the ante. Then, she keeps on leaving these stupid little hints as to who the father is."

"Really? Not with me."

"No, I guess not. Count yourself lucky; she hasn't named you yet." James laughed.

Dom frowned.

"OK, not funny. But here's the tally as far as I can keep track. Brace yourself: her brother, Marc, or maybe some mechanic boyfriend in Shelton. Sounds made up. Or, beat this, Father Carl.

Dominic looked stricken.

"I know, I know, but just take it easy. She's hinting at everything but saying nothing. She's way out of control. I say let it lay low and see how it all pans out."

At the podium, Dominic watched the chorus assemble into their parts: the dutiful altos showed up like a support team; the sopranos ranged from weak bird-call falsettos to the ancient wobble of their single prima donna; the tenors strained like a saw stuck in a metal pipe; the basses were content to be barely heard like an underground spring. Still, Dom knew what they could do when pushed.

James had talked Dominic into doing Bach at the Christmas concert. The Mass in B Minor.

"I'm not sure we're up for that," Dominic said, worried.

"They'll rise to the occasion. I know it," James countered.

"I'm not just talking about the choir; I meant the congregation as well."

James laughed. "They'll come out for it, I promise. Even if I have to buy every last ticket myself."

"Ladies, let's not sound like little girls tonight. Let's visualize the note. Pretend there is this bright apple hovering right before you, on a string from heaven, as it were. Position your teeth to take one gigantic bite out of the apple. Taste it high in your cheeks. Open your eyes; let your throat hum like a lyre."

The sopranos went for it. Together they had the faces of angels. Dominic loved the wet mink of their tongues.

"That's the note. Find it in front of you. Grab it. Keep it bright!"

He took them slowly up the scale. The altos joined in.

"OK, tenors. Come on, men. We want heroes here, heldentenors. Bright and clear and strong."

To the basses: "Come on, show us how big your chests are. Don't bury those notes. Give courage to them, trust technique to make you sound good. Forget your 'big, grand and important' tones. Keep it bright."

A pleasing, deep harmony emerged, in spite of. Dominic sang along with the baritones, each of them one tone, one note. No one can make a chord alone; the complexity of the music lies only in the relationship of one singer to another.

He nodded to James at the piano to strike an A, and every singer landed on it. Dominic grinned at them and guided them into the Gloria fugue and shouted out, "This is the moment. If you are not already religious, you should be having a crisis of confidence, your singing is so convincing, so earnest."

Two hours into rehearsal the medley of voices began to have a palpable presence. The breathing shallowed; the tide was letting out. The sound began to stale.

"OK, I know it's late and we're getting tired. But I want to get through this piece tonight. It's important for you to hear the whole thing through once. Do I need to say how much Father Carl would have appreciated the effort? If there's a way for him to listen, try stopping him from singing along."

He tapped his music stand with his conductor's wand; his elbows rose.

Dom saw the singers come together, adjust their postures, ready to sound like angels, as if the music were not made by them but somehow drawn out of them. It was here before this choir that he was most struck with the profound sense that people are, by nature, basically good. That the whole is greater than the sum of its parts. No singer can be stronger, faster, louder; the music must be heard as a single entity transparent and articulate. An individual is no more independent of the group than a note from a musical phrase. That was a point of view that took some work; maintaining a communal and benevolent view of the world took conspiratorial effort as much as anyother.

Maybe this was how Dominic could give back. Maybe he should follow James into the conservatory and finish a degree in music, spread the word of a beautiful if amateur faith, become part of the fading quorum who fight for a lessening thing—as the curse of our age in which the worth of a thing (the Church, the earth itself?) is apparent only as it begins to disappear.

Let their bodies dematerialize into the air. Grounded into community, every voice is heard, and every voice sounds better than it would alone, better than it should, joined in the resolve to do and be good.

Make a noise. Mark your joy. Sound your being. Into this best of all possible worlds.

Then, as he did every week before dismissing his choir, he wiped his brow and said, "Ladies and gentlemen, it is an honor to sing with you. Good night."

THREE

A fluffy white bunny. A little felt mouse and a giant pink and green frog that was almost as long as she when stretched alongside it. That was all that remained of her little zoo of stuffed animals. At some point, there had been nearly forty, most of them presents from her father. Dolores hoarded them for years, and it was only in the last three months that she had begun walking discrete bags of five or six plush at a time in plastic grocery bags over to the clothes donation bin behind the Esso station. She would do the same with the boxes of clothes stacked in the closet. She basically wore the same three or four outfits anyway, washing them just frequently enough, she hoped. She knew others felt she didn't bathe enough, but she liked the way she smelled, like an apple half-eaten. Clothes always disappointed her anyway: nothing fit her the way it promised to when she shoplifted it. They were folded neatly in piles like evidence.

Lying on top of the frog, Dolores gently rubbed her hips against the parts where the stuffing had migrated down the limbs, bunching up in places she liked. The frog smelled of egg. Fuzz tickled her nose and made her sleepy. She was often sleepy; all this pretending to go to school and eating of regular meals exhausted her. Sneezing made her sleepy. Pretending that wearing nice clothes was OK even while half the world starved. Pretending that suffering was good for you. Not presuming to understand the mind of God demoralized her. She looked to the spirit for ways in which to feel bigger, not smaller. Pretending who she was on the inside was not how she acted on the outside. Hanging on to that ability, Father Carl said, was the way to stay OK, the very definition of sanity: "You have to pretend," he told her, "in order to protect your inner life, keep yourself from going crazy."

"So, then, denying who you actually are and living in a fake reality—that's sanity?" she asked him.

He manufactured a smile that made his head look heavy, a look that was meant to reassure her that she was just young and naive and would grow out of it. As if her insight was the oldest (and youngest) cliché in the book. She couldn't stand how he patronized her. Behind all his experience, he knew she was right. She still believed that. But all of his arrogance—withholding answers until only he knew she would be ready for them—enraged her, and now he was gone and there was no one around to take it out on. Simply remembering the conversation sent her heartbeat raging. She circled the room and whispered curses at the dead priest. Who the hell did he think he was, God? She called the rectory to see if Father Dominic was around.

Sister Agnes answered.

"Oh, you're back. You know that Father Carl died, right?"

"May he rest in peace."

"Yeah, that's freakin' likely. So junior priest. Is he around?"

"He may be doing his rounds."

"He's on his way here?"

"I'm not sure. He took his daybook with him."

"Does he have his cell?"

"Most likely."

"Good. Give me the number."

"Sorry, I can't do that."

"But what if it's an emergency?"

"Now, Dolores. Isn't it always that with you?"

"Bitch."

Dolores and Sister Agnes hung up the phone in the same moment.

"Fuck her," Dolores said to herself and threw herself on to the frog again. She took its two legs and tied them around the frog's throat, but the knot wouldn't hold.

"Lo," her father used to call her as if it were some kind of forecast, setting her barometer to this bottom to which she always defaulted. There was a compass set deep within her, an orientation toward descent, a drive downward as if the point of any road was its end. She didn't understand it; she just knew it felt inevitable.

"You were robbed of your childhood" went the mantra of her second shrink. "The loss of your father when you were very young, the fact that you had to step up and care for your invalid mother—" But Dolores had intercepted the *et cetera* and screamed, "What the fuck are you talking about? Do you even know what you're talking about? I *want* to be robbed of my freakin' childhood."

She thought about it almost every night, whether she spent it in Father Dominic's car or in the woods or here in her bed with the strangled frog. She thought about killing herself like a kind of lullaby that would promise to calm and put her to sleep. But there would always pipe up another voice, a voice that always had to be different and difficult, that would taunt, "Oh no, you're not gonna get off that easy. You're gonna suffer long as life, right to the bitter end."

That other shrink, the one before the last, the one with the clinic at the university, had said to her, "There is a place for you, Dolores. You will find work that you are good at; that will give you meaning. And you will find someone to love you—and for you to love back."

When she repeated the remark to Father Carl, she was surprised to see the old man's eyes fill suddenly with tears.

"That is close to the truth, actually, but only part of the truth. This psychologist, she doesn't see God in any of this, of course, does she? It takes a kind of breaking down and making over; it's called conversion. But that's not the big thing that's missing from her version. For we are capable of extraordinary things. We are. In how we love! In how we make our way in the world, in how we make the world our way. For each other. And that is what is godlike in you and in me."

She was startled by the old man's sweetness and his power. He really believed. Maybe it was a little bit cruel for him to continue the thought, but people were always making mistakes with her, under- or overestimating what she could handle. Or maybe it was his ill health that would explain why Father Carl went on to say, "I would add that each of us must also find his own way to die."

It was his only mention of death during that whole confusing time, and she fixed on it as a kind of wisdom. That was exactly right; she must find her own way to die.

"Of course," he corrected himself, "you won't really have to think about any of that until you're around my age."

She couldn't imagine making it to even half his age. She knew she was too serious, too intense to last that long. And yet his comment had a clarifying—almost enlightening—impact on her. Death was everywhere—in the global catastrophes that killed masses of innocents and pitched her into spiritual despair. She even shook off the wish that she be one of them, blown up in a market or washed away in a giant wave. She'd have to take more direct responsibility.

She suspected that the pain she was capable of feeling was only partial, vastly inferior to the deeper experience lurking behind her awareness of it. Pain was evident in the way she loved God. Beneath the growl of her sadness was true grip. Pain was like God, then: only ever partially perceived even as it completely overtook her. She could only guess at the complexity of the roots of pain. Her experience of it could always, should always, go deeper. She would always chase it, never know it.

If God loves everyone the same, the only way to distinguish herself was to love Him harder. She knew too that there was vanity in her love for God; she felt Him with a kind of genius. No one could touch it, understand it, take it. Not even Father Carl. That's why they were mean to her; that's why they wanted her gone. They'd be better off too. She knew she was too much for other people; but that only made her more aware that she was not enough for God. "Too much"—they didn't even know how right they were. The more of her there was, the easier it was to get rid of her. She exceeded the suitable quota of selfhood; she insisted on tipping the scale.. Only God could outstrip her, keep her love chasing; only God could accommodate her excesses.

Father Carl was wrong to believe in a heaven; the very idea suffocated her. A life, a consciousness, a self that you could never escape—that was more her idea of hell.

The decision happened one day walking across the long parking lot that surrounded the church. Empty things seemed so vast. It could take all day to get to the gate out to the street. She pretended she was an astronaut walking on the surface of a black moon, tottering on the edges of the potholes as if they were giant craters. Gravity stopped. She had to remember to breathe. Then she could make herself take a step. Small girl, giant surface, small parking lot, giant girl: it was all a mistake of scale. Slow and heavy; the spacesuit weighing her down, saving her life, allowing her to take one more breath. One small step for. One more heartbeat; that happened all by itself. She could concentrate on that. One heartbeat. Forget one day at a time; this was living second by second, getting to what was manageable. She could endure a heartbeat. And one more after that. *Is this what they mean by living in the fucking present?* Hold herself together so that the world could congeal around her. This was her substance. She would not be an insignificant stain on the endless while of the universe; she was walking on the moon! She was a giant, and the world was shrinking; all its eyes were on her. Man on the moon; the ground she stood on had to be solid. Her life was only getting bigger while the world was getting smaller—it would soon be unable to fit her.

The idea of suicide hit her with the force of a revelation, with all the brevity and impact of an oracle and none of the length and ritual of a prayer. An oracle is a kind of prayer in an emergency.

She had a technical problem, though. None of the methods suited. Pills seemed dated, almost recreational, handing yourself over to an experience, allowing chemical changes to transport your mind. She wasn't into the drug scene anyway, mistrusted their shortcut to transcendence. All the idiots in high school did them, as opposed to the other idiots who didn't. And, besides, she could be misconstrued; an overdose could always be accidental. She wanted her death to have none of the ambiguities of her life.

Guns were too mechanical. She wasn't even sure she had the skill to operate one. She would probably mess up anyway and didn't want to spend the rest of her life looking for love with half a face.

Bleeding to death and watching the warm scarlet of her life wasting away appealed to her, but she had read too many accounts of people cutting their wrists open only to be surprised at the resilience of the body and the tendency of blood to clot over the wound as the victim discovered she was too squeamish to continue hacking away at the tender rising flesh. That kind of morbid curiosity was too filled with ego. Head in an oven way too Sylvia Plath. The projects had electric stoves anyway. Self-immolation struck her as too polemical; she didn't have any burning causes to promote. Running the car in a garage would be problematic because she didn't have either; that method was definitely upper-middle-class.

There weren't many buildings tall enough whose roof she'd have access to. Besides, she didn't want to have the opportunity to chicken out. She needed something simple, with momentum method whose outcome she couldn't stop.

She didn't know exactly how she would do it. That's what stopped her—plus the problem of others finding her body, heavy and useless. What a thing to leave behind! It offended her sense of privacy; she didn't want people touching her, dressing her, reassembling her.

Nevertheless, the idea of killing herself had invaded her landscape. She lived under it like weather. Self-destruction, repudiating His gift of life, would be the only way of standing next to God, standing up to God. He would know at last just how seriously to take her. His mistake. The idea of drowning herself, the image of a river flooding over her, was so powerful she had to remember to breathe just thinking of it. It was a feeling her body couldn't manage. Going Ophelia; that would be the way—the image of Hamlet's lost love floating her way into literary eternity was the one thing her loser high school had given her of any value. She loved the poetry of the heroine, its birdlike nonsense so lucid in the woods, the brave and free plunge of the body into a cold—Saint Valentine's Day—body of water. To be of two minds about the value of her life as she invited the river to take it. To make the decision to swim out to the point of no return and then to have the decision taken away.

Dominic couldn't even know whether Dolores was telling the truth. "You believe me, right?" she had asked him that day in the church.

How would the old priest have defended himself against Dolores's charge in any case? Would he have? Would he have needed to do? Would he tell the truth? Was there anything to tell? Was the affair even possible during those last terrible months of chemo treatments or, in fact, after Father Carl stopped treatments? Instead of Carl's buried flesh collapsing in decay, Dominic now flashed on the image of the older priest kissing Dolores's lovely mouth, palming her breasts, his brain sending a signal to his heart to beat harder and rush the flow of blood to his penis. The image was so ugly: spongy tissue engorging with blood. Tumescence. Anger tightened in Dominic's chest and then dropped to his gut as anxiety. The whole issue exhausted him; there would be no way of testing the truth in any case, but he would continue to suspect Father Carl's silence about the matter—as well as his preemptive request for Dom's own silence as well. *Whatever you say, say nothing.*

The thing about secrets is that they always hover about people, just like doubts. Even before Father Carl became sick, Dominic felt an uncertainty come between them. Dom thought it was his own loss of faith and his threats to leave the Church that bothered Father Carl, but now it became clear that there was something else dividing them or, worse yet, binding them together within its deception. How could he do this: not only commit that unpardonable sin but keep the transgression itself secret? Cover it up. He was no better than the rest of them. Becoming a priest was supposed to ensure that, at the very least, a man did no harm. Dominic felt so naive. Everything happened around him. Nothing happened to him.

"One can tell a lot about a person by how they love, Dominic," Father Carl had said to Dominic near the end. "You know, by how open or guarded they are. You can also tell a lot by whether they love at all."

Oracles and mysteries. "Sex," he wanted to tell the old fucker, "usually has consequences. You should have known better." Now he wished Father Carl had just shut up before he died. Dom wished he could go pagan and stitch tight the eyes of the old priest, stuff his mouth with ashes, prevent his spirit from coming home. Just shut up and die already.

Whatever you say, say nothing. The syntax was weird. *Whatever you say*, which might be heard at first as deferential or diffident, became the condition of a command. *Say nothing*. Dominic felt censored, once again.

Answer me when I call, O god of my right! Psalm 4

Give ear to my words, O LORD, give heed to my groaning
Hearken to the sound of my cry,
My King and MY GOD
For to thee I do pray. Psalm 5

I will give thanks to the LORD with my whole heart;
I will tell of all thy wonderful deeds. Psalm 9

Hear a just cause, O LORD; attend to my cry!
Give ear to my prayer from lips free of deceit. Psalm 17

There is no speech, nor are there words;
their voice is not heard. Psalm 19

To thee, O LORD, I call;
My rock; be not deaf to me,
If thou be silent to me . . . Psalm 28

I said, "I will guard my ways that I may not sin with my tongue;
I will bridle my mouth, so long as the wicked are in my presence."
I was dumb and silent,
    I held my peace to no avail;
My distress grew worse
    My heart became hot within me. Psalm 39

Sister Agnes and Dom exchanged polite Good Mornings.

"How was your Thanksgiving, Sister?" Dom had asked.

"Father's lost his mind. Mother's taken to bed."

"Well," said Dom, without missing a beat, "at least you have them."

There was an odd competitiveness between the priest and the nun, a perpetual one-upmanship of personal misery. Sister Agnes was the only Sister of Mercy left at the parish, one of only several dozen or so in the whole archdiocese, a middle-aged woman with tough hands and a severe quietude. There was less work for nuns now that the school had closed, and all the little boys with their blue blazers and clip-on ties and all the little girls with their pleated skirts, like cupcake liners, had been sent off in buses to a surviving Catholic academy twenty miles away—or were "lost" to the local public schools. She had been given a nickname after she had been attacked by two stray dogs mating in the schoolyard; she had attempted to separate them with a broom—Sister Interruptus.

In the fridge Dominic noted the leftover turkey and stuffing from her family meal, an annual souvenir from a parallel life. He had opened the little foil tents and then wrapped them up again. It was a pity. Although he knew she meant them for him, he wouldn't touch the food until she offered, which meant it would sit there until it would spoil. She would also wait for him to throw it away.

When Father Carl was well, Sister had cooked big, wholesome meals—"getting over," she joked with the older priest, "my Irish indifference for the stuff." Now, he was more or less left to fend for himself with the dry pasta and canned tomato sauce she kept the cupboard stocked with, the plastic bags of prewashed tossed salad and the bottled dressing. She over-boiled stock pots of broccoli and stored the paled florets in large Tupperware containers in the fridge. There they sat with the other tubs of assorted cut green peppers, celery, cucumbers, all ready to be mixed into an unloving salad. She would not cook another batch until she thought there had been time enough for him to finish what was there. Sundays, she cooked for him. "There you are, Father, here's your three colors of the Italian flag. White pasta, red sauce, green broccoli. Your *tre colore*," she would trill in contempt.

Sister Agnes dropped five inches of morning mail on the table. Dom grunted a thank-you and sorted out all the junk immediately; he left unopened the envelopes from a local charity, a stationery supplier, the Loyola Press catalog, a mission in Peru. He made a second pile out of invoices, baptismal requests, an updated liturgical calendar and a shorter, third pile of handwritten envelopes to open and read later. There were two envelopes addressed to Father Carl, which gave the dead man an odd present tense. And a postcard from a Mrs. Bouvier, who wanted to know what the parish planned in the way of Christmas decorations now that Thanksgiving had passed: "I want this holiday season to be truly magical for my children, and I'm willing to chair a decorations committee and even bring some overflow wreaths and baubles from home!"

The TV buzzed in the parlor; Sister Agnes had left the radio on upstairs. In his bedroom, the computer was surely dinging with incoming e-mail. Everything had invaded the inner sanctum of the rectory. Consumerism leered at him, licked its lips at him, dared him not to crave.

Dominic watched the early morning sun peek its way under the door from the back garden and worried over the drafts accompanying the light. Last winter he had sealed the space with rubber stripping, but the door warped in its struggle to meet the lock and he had to spend more money with the locksmith than the extra heating bill might have cost.

Sister Agnes busied herself within a hymn; her lips pursed around the sound *roo-loo-loo*. Singing the actual words would have been far less distracting. She aggravated each note with a forced vibrato which Dom could tell she thought beautiful. When distracted, Sister Agnes would stop *roo-looing*, and Dom would concentrate even harder on her pauses, wondering what she was doing.

Backing her way into the kitchen, she noisily slapped at the floor with her wet mop. Without looking up, Dom lifted his feet off the floor as she passed the mop beneath him; he thought he could smell something rise from under her robes as she worked around him. He made excuses for her. Would they be like this forever, living together and married to Christ, the widow and the widower, the virginal bride and the white martyr?

"Don't walk on the floor till it dries," she chided him.

"I'll be here for at least another hour. I've got lots to do."

"Nothing special about that. *Loo-roo-looooo*."

It was unseasonably warm out, in the low fifties, not cold enough for the thermostat to click on. The mop slick on the floor sent the chill Dominic had been struggling to suppress up his spine. He opened the packet that the bishop had given him. He leafed through the independent consultant's report, filled with bright charts and graphs and big PowerPoint outlines. "Take your group through the emotional map identified by the anagram SARAH (Shock, Anger, Resentment, Acceptance, Hope)." Dom groaned. *Don't look back.*

"*Loo-looo, rooooo,*" Sister Agnes knocked her mop loudly against the legs of the table's far side.

Finding the archbishop's "Recommended Sermons for the Closing of a Church," Dom read the potted text under his breath: "This is a heartbreaking moment for us all, one of the most trying moments in our Catholic history that has been rich with trouble."

"But we must face the facts," Dom began to read aloud softly to cover the humming. "Dwindling mass attendance, fewer donations, shortage of priests and nuns, aging buildings that we do not have the funds to renovate."

"*Loo-roo-roo, roo-roo.*" Sister Agnes began to syncopate in some kind of 3:2 Cuban rhythm.

"As it is, the archdiocese is running a deficit of—"

"Enough!" Sister Agnes stamped her mop against the floor.

Dom looked up at her and watched the set of her jaw brace against what she would decide to let herself say.

"Why don't you just tell me? You're going to have to be direct with people, you know. You can start practicing with me."

Dom closed his eyes; against his lids the marbled formica burned red and green.

"Father Dominic, we are alone here. We've lost Father Carl, and we are depending on you."

"The funeral will be Tuesday. I'll need you to order the flowers. DiCarlo has the body. The obit is in both the *Register* and the *Advocate* tomorrow. The *Courier* will probably do something too."

"Father Dominic, I am talking to you."

"The brothers are coming; they'll probably give eulogies."

"How many will show?"

"It'll be a full house, don't you think? In any case, DiCarlo will call today with an estimate."

"We'll cater in the rec hall."

"It'll rain tonight. Make sure Lou takes care of any leaking first thing."

Sister Agnes nodded and continued mopping; she was grateful to have the rest of the day figured out.

Dom took out his pen and began circling the points he would borrow from the recommended sermon. Hating the bishop's language, he began to think about his eulogy for Father Carl. What could he say now? He didn't dare think it through yet. Whatever he said, it would have to be spoken plain. More than once the old man had cautioned him against eloquence: "Beware of expressiveness," he had said. "Your faith is not self-presentation." Dominic knew he must not use the occasion for understanding or consolation. Not yet. Not forgiveness either. Not yet. Any expectation of that would be dishonest. He trusted all of it would come. Almost always too late, almost never on time.

Sister Agnes hummed her way up the stairwell, its steady anxiety dependable as a respirator.

"Sister Agnes, I'm going out but can't find my keys. Have you seen them?" he yelled up to her.

"Go and ask Saint Jude." she hollered down the stairs.

When the judge sentenced Dom, he made sure to stipulate that the five-hundred-dollar fine was not to be paid out of the parish coffers. As if. His driving license would be revoked and set up for review at the one-year anniversary of the DWI charge. And while the six weeks of community service would be somewhat redundant with the work the priest did anyway, it would still be enforced.

Dom would be asked to spend another ten hours a week at the AIDS center. "Consider it an exercise in humility of the soul, Father," the judge said with a trace of a sneer. Dom asked that the forty-eight hours of mandatory jail time be suspended until after the time of Father Carl's funeral, which would need to take place in the next two days. The judge wondered whether being imprisoned in Dom's conscience would be punishment enough. If he agreed to enter an alcohol abuse program, the court would suspend incarceration. "And not," the judge added, "as a group leader or counselor but as just a regular who gets up and calls himself an alcoholic."

The bishop's office had called to schedule a follow-up visit—no doubt he had received the police report—but Dom erased the message. He would see all the Church brass at Father Carl's funeral, and he didn't have the wheels to get to Hartford in any case. And now he would have to figure out how to get the five hundred dollars to pay the fine. Father Carl kept a small petty cash fund in the rectory, accumulated and maintained by the occasional ten bucks taken out of the weekly Sunday collections basket. He didn't dare touch the fund because it would mean both acknowledging that it existed and continuing the weekly skim to keep it whole. But dire times demanded dire practices.

In debt, outlawed and horny, it was lucky Dominic had not become a Jesuit and taken the three vows of poverty, obedience and chastity. Even so, there were expectations established in seminary; a place he was fond of the way a soldier is of boot camp: a place to have survived and be stronger for it. When he first arrived there two decades ago, he handed over all his earthly possessions (so little really: some clothes, some books and records, the only token of his childhood). Quarantined during his monastic period, he believed that the spiritual life was fragile enough to require isolation from the outside world. His success would be measured intangibly: "You will be judged on your love," wrote Paul Claudel with damning imprecision.

While he wasn't expected to take a vow of poverty as a priest, he had never really known anything but. The car he (once) drove, the clothes on his back, the books on his desk: none of it was his property. Not much of a salary to speak of, no pension; all his material cares were taken care of by the mother church, modestly. He needed nothing, "for the forms of this world pass away," sayeth Corinthians. On the other hand, he never had to worry about doing without either; he even had a small monthly stipend to treat himself to the occasional movie, restaurant meal (or compensated female companionship). He admitted the hypocrisy. Poverty was in effect an aesthetic choice for priests, a political act of anticonsumerism; he knew enough not to confuse which side of the soup kitchen he stood on. Dom's poverty was a righteous, voluntary poverty, a denial of luxury. It was not desperate and option-less poverty. At best, all he could have was sympathy for the poor.

Celibacy, the promise to never marry, the promise to serve the people of God as a minister of the sacraments, was the tough nut. The ultimate "gift from God." The big sacrifice that constituted his sentimental education. The beauty of Saint Augustine, who implored with a saucy wink: "Lord, Make me chaste. But not yet."

When he was fifteen, Dom used to help a neighborhood girl from his school babysit for a local family. Grace was beautiful and even mostly nice to him, giving him sufficient grounds to plan an insidious seduction. He went to the library and checked out the Rolling Stones' LP *It's Only Rock 'N' Roll* for the way it choreographed the cynical strategy of his lust. The opening three rockers would get them steamy; then, the fuzzy blues would buzz around them like a fly. They would cling together almost to avoid the sound. The music emboldened him. He managed to put his hand on the swell of her waist, his nose against her damp temple, his thumbs under her sweater. His left hand found her skin soft and excessive as he reached down below her buttocks. She let him reach under her skirt and squeeze; he braced her breasts against his chest. He moved to her left breast. Was one in fact heavier than the other? She was unequal in her parts, spilling out at him variously—variously and suddenly until the cumulative embodiment of all that was Grace became powerfully clear to him: hips, ass, neck, bosom, hair. As her composite image accumulated itself, tightening itself around him, Dominic felt himself dissolving. As she became whole in his arms, he atomized until he spilled out, leaking down below his shorts. She felt the ooze against her bare leg and screamed ("Oh, my God," of all things) and ran out of the house.

Later there would be the dozens of prostitutes who had serviced him orally (he was thus technically a virgin), but they figured only in the haze of guilt and self-loathing that compromised his better version of himself. One never regrets the life not lived as much as the life not owned up to.

Over the years, Dom had seen as many working models for celibacy as he had for sobriety. The way priests bent the rules and rationalized around them fascinated him. Many even had unofficial "wives" who worked in the rectories and did everything but spend the night. Then there was Paul Riley, the senior seminarian assigned to be Dominic's mentor. Paul was working on his Ph.D. in physics, but the way he had studied philosophy and theology made him both scientist and priest; he straddled the two cultures and saw neither as a closed system, exhausting the possibility of knowing deeper and further. Paul focused his study on a sense of wonder—the sentimental awe some feel about scientific observation and others about divine presence, as if reverence were mere projection, without an object, purely subjective—not so much moved as impressed by a personal capacity to be moved. He had ingested his Darwin, Marx and Freud but tried at the same time to instill in himself the spirit of the Holy Trinity. He came to seminary, he said, not to be an ideologue, but to "steep inside the mythology."

"The priest of the future will be more of a theater director, using great texts to compose a useful and helpful tableaux," Paul wrote in one of his essays. "We have to hearken back to the originality of the radical Jewish carpenter who taught us to love our enemies, eschew consumerism and to love the shit of the earth. We have yet to deal with the universal symbolism of a political prisoner who was crucified for his vision of a better world."

One late Sunday afternoon, Paul came to Dominic's room and invited him to go for a walk, impromptu. He and Dominic spoke only Latin on their walks, demonstrating just how few words were really necessary. That day, though, Paul's silence burned as he led the way along the foothill trail, nearly jogging to reach the peak first, a slab of granite that advantaged a beautiful western view. Bright and breathless in the sunlight, Paul reached down and grabbed Dominic's hand to give him a boost up. Only he didn't let go. Dominic tried to remove his hand from the grasp, but Paul held firmly and gazed directly into his eyes. This violated the code of *tactus*, the modest lowering of eyes, the control of visual contact that the brothers in the seminary observed with each other. Winded and confused, Dominic just stood there as Paul stepped forward and put his arms around his waist, surprising him with the brusque stubble of his chin against his neck. Dominic shook his head.

"OK, buddy." He laughed. "Forget I ever asked. I'll just let you stew in your own morbid squeamishness."

"Morbid squeamishness." The phrase bothered Dom not so

much for its accusation as for its manipulation. Paul could walk away proud of his virile healthy anticlericalism even as he went around breaking codes of ethics they had all agreed upon. Paul would get to live within the myth of vital, hypocrisy-breaking, open-minded life force, while Dom would have to sit inside an ambivalent moral orthodoxy.

Dominic was pissed off by the dishonesty of the moment and avoided Paul for the next few days. What he had regarded as the man's holiness was really narcissism. Paul was truly brilliant of mind and spirit, but his dream of Catholicism was overly utopian, filled with rules of discipline that existed only to feel the joy of breaking them.

A loss often insults before it hurts. One morning a week later, Dominic walked into the library and was surprised to see the top of Paul's desk cleared, its chair upended and showing its underbelly, white numbers marking its place on the floor plan. Its four legs stretched stiffly upward like a cartooned dead dog. He felt afraid, as if the young man had been wiped away without a trace. As if Dominic were to blame, even. If only Paul hadn't dared to propose; if only Dominic had dared to satisfy. If only people were vague and good and undemanding; if only people acted like Dom.

If Dominic's poverty was merely symbolic, his failure at celibacy was actual. The women he paid to comfort him counted, despite the cold and brief nature of the transactions between them. He knew that most priests found their way around celibacy and that it was unrealistic to think that they wouldn't. The unexpected cost, though, was the talent in priests to lie and to live in denial and the instinct of the Church to look the other way. Allowing people to behave badly while not being held personally accountable would have the disastrous consequence known as the Scandal, the kind of evil that depends on a large-scale bureaucracy in order to survive. But, on a local level, most priests would suffer more fundamentally as men of God, like cheating husbands living with a split libido. Neither here nor there.

Asking a healthy body to deny its sexuality is as naive as asking a dead body not to rot.

Just as poverty had robbed him of negotiating his way in the real world, the vow of chastity had prevented his forming adult relationships with women. He wondered if the Church felt about its priests the way the military did its soldiers: that they were indispensable, noble, committed, necessary, protected—loved, even—but ultimately disposable, sacrificed for the greater good.

In the end, though, it was the promise of obedience that gave him the most trouble. It was one thing to surrender his possessions in poverty, another to surrender his body in celibacy, but still another to surrender his will to obey that of God's as seen through his superiors. He loved his congregation, those few still devoted to the church, each of whom attended Mass weekly and donated money they could ill afford to give in order to keep it going. He loved keeping the integrity of the liturgy and serving the sacraments—even as he was convinced that no one person can act as a spiritual guide for anyone else. No one can be that entirely. Still, it was those few who only came when in need or in trouble, like Dolores or her mother, that reminded him why he was a priest. But he had managed to consistently piss off the bishop, in his blog, in his sermons, in his published writings, in his very ministry.

By these measures, he was a failure as a priest. He was sure he wasn't alone. Young seminarians are trained to live up to the very high standards that would paradoxically ensure a kind of mediocrity. Where were they now? There were several he had run into, and they each had become who they hinted they would be as young men. The majority who needed to play it safe. Get ordained. Settle down into a kind of clericalism. The sorts who kept the Church standing still if not falling behind; who cared for a bureaucracy whose only interest was self-perpetuation. There were the careerists who were in charge. The workaholics whose social life was no different from their ministry. And there was the rare genius, the true celibate who didn't even require the prohibition, the gifted one who knew what it was to sacrifice his will. The holy.

But he also knew now that his passion in seminary was kind of an artistic lying; it was he himself who was found wanting. The thing that depressed him most about losing his faith in God, if that in fact was what was happening, was not the disillusionment itself, not the threat of going to hell, not losing his livelihood or his way of life, but the fact that his anguish itself was anachronistic, centuries too late. Wasn't Christianity a much more efficient operation, ignorant of all this trepidation? He suspected that he might be inventing or at least exaggerating the crisis to evade the middle-aged flatness of things, the diminution of astonishment in a world not lit by God. Despite its ascetic temperament, his dedication to an ideal god was in itself a kind of voluptuousness. Decadence was at the heart of his devotion to sincerity, in his denial of the self in pursuit of the absolute.

Who would have thought back then, with the enormity of the troubled world and the work to be done for it, that Dominic would have been measuring diminishing returns, when what remains to do would be undone by what may no longer be done.

At the 6:00 Mass, Dolores stood last in line, the seventh to take Communion. Without looking at Dom, she accepted the host on her tongue with curiosity as if taking a litmus test. She evaded Dom's eyes, which kept him wondering. Afterward, she lingered in the back of the chapel while he cleaned the altar. There weren't any altar boys left except for Sunday services, and he took his time hanging up his vestments, digging the wax out of the wells of the candlesticks, washing out the cruets and chalice. He could feel her sitting there watching him. He couldn't ignore her forever; she needed him. He would be gentle with her, forgive her manipulations.

Descending the steps to the chapel, he called out to her: "You're up early. You feeling OK?"

"Yeah, yeah. I'm good. Listen, I just wanted to talk to you." She sidled up to him nervously. She was wearing too much perfume, the kind of scent that cloyed the way cream is quick to clot. He needed to get her outside into the fresh air.

"OK. You want to go for a walk?"

"Sure." "OK, but let's get out of here. How about Lighthouse Point Park? We can walk on the water."

"You mean by the water? You said 'walk *on* the water.'"

"Did I?" he laughed. "Well, I could try, but I know even *that* would fail to impress you."

She laughed.

"What's on your mind, Dolores?"

"I don't know. I wanted to apologize?" She looked up at him.

"Is that a question? You want me to answer for you?" Dominic put on his expression of patience and empathy. A priest should be there to make people feel not just absolved but understood, reciprocated, loved in a specific way, loved for their particularity. He was like each of them as he was like none of them, except for their common faith.

"No, no. I guess I missed you. I wanted to talk to you, outside the church, not in the confessional."

The truth was Dominic had missed her too. She was like an enzyme; one had to react to her. Not even Dominic could make an abstraction of this girl, Dolores. She was inside out; her life was spilling out of itself.

It was affection that made him think he could be tougher with her.

"You expect too much from the Church, Dolores, asking it to save your life. We cannot and will not do it for you. You have to save yourself."

This surprised Dolores; she had come back to apologize for hurting his pride as she had for so many who tried to help her and failed. She tried people, tired them out, made them all feed inadequate: the teachers, counselors, therapists. Her troubles deprived the community of consensus or plan of action; she destabilized the construction of any narrative around which to build their compassion. No wonder so many people hated her, rejected her, wanted her out of the parish. It takes a village to destroy one like her. In forcing others to reckon with her, she targeted their greatest vulnerability. In Dominic, she had zeroed in on his vagueness, the vapor of his goodness. He was most terrified of ending up, coming to some point. The substance of his faith was its own confusion. She knew she could get to him.

Dominic saw the brief register of hurt and rushed to console it. Could this girl afford to change; could she possibly care for a child? What would she do outside her role of benign freak? How would she gather herself in from unpredictability and settle into some manageable life? Who would find her, recognize her? Keep her from burning out or evaporating away? This was his work. Maybe Dolores was his life's work.

They walked out of the parking lot and waited at the corner for the light to change.

"Oh shit," she said, as a white van rolled to a stop before them. Marc Alfano rolled down his window.

"Hi ya, Sis. Father," he said and lit a Marlboro Light.

"Marc. Twice in two days. Are you stalking me or something?" Dominic asked. Dolores stepped behind him and pressed against his back.

"Taking care of business, Father. Just wanna make sure I get my cut," he said.

"Marc," Dolores implored over Dominic's shoulder.

"Somebody's got to look after her. Might as well be me pimping her."

"Motherfucker!" Dolores screamed and lunged at the van, banging her fists on the side and falling onto the ground. The van peeled away.

"What are you doing?" Dominic screamed at her. "You can't be throwing yourself around like that."

He put his arm around her shoulders and walked her back to the rectory. He felt extraordinary calm as he fetched cotton balls and oxygen peroxide and dabbed the scrapes on her knees and knuckles. He wet a washcloth with warm water and soap and gently washed her face and neck, behind the ears. He applied Neosporin and covered the wounds with Band-Aids. He made tea for them both and put cookies on a plate. They sat at the kitchen table together. She licked the honey off her spoon seriously and slowly and then stopped to stare as if she expected the spoon to begin speaking.

"You're a nice man," she said after a silence. "Is that why you became a priest? Or did becoming a priest make you that?"

Before he had a chance to answer, she blurted out, "I'm feeling the creep of atheism, Father."

As if reading his mind.

But he didn't really believe her. Her world, terrible as it was, was never godless. It had a monster of a god.

"You know, Dolores, atheism is just another mind-set, a kind of orientation, a commitment to a reverse faith in reason. The problem with having no one to please but ourselves is that we grow bored with our own pleasure. That's the real ingenuity of the Church; it understands that the goal of reaching the perfect self is impossible so it externalizes the challenge, leaves it to a great and remote God to set the impossible standard we can't help but disappoint."

"So, you're saying God is a myth?"

"No, I'm not saying that. I'm saying it doesn't really matter. We need to believe in what God winds up being for us rather than pretending to know who God is. The more imagination your faith practices, the more alive and convincing God will be."

This talk was precisely the kind of thing the bishop had slapped him down for. He was incorrigible, he knew. Disobedient. The Church was right to distrust him. He wasn't doing it any favors. But he might be helping Dolores, and that was what mattered to him. People would come to his church because it was a safe place to be naive, to be witnessed, to be able, without embarrassment, to ask the urgent question, "How to live?"

"I can keep a secret, you know," Dominic said to her.

She stopped and looked at him. "I know. I guess that's why I told you."

"You haven't told me everything."

She looked scared. She lowered her eyes and then blurted it out quickly: "It's Father Carl. OK? Happy now?"

Dominic stopped short.

"Or not."

Dominic slapped the table. "Dolores, stop playing with me!"

"I'm not. I'm not. I seriously don't know for sure."

"Don't you want to know?"

"I don't know. I don't know." She began to cry again.

"If it's Father Carl, that changes everything. I'll have to think about what to do next."

She grabbed his arm. "No, no, no!" she screamed. "You can't do anything!"

"Dolores, this is really important."

"No!" she shrieked. "You have to protect my secret."

"Dolores, think about others that might come after you. This has to stop!"

"Think about ME, right now!" she jumped up and yelled in his face.

"Ok, OK." He shrugged her off, "Relax. We'll figure it out together."

They both quieted down.

"Tell me how you feel," he said.

"Wonderful. And awful."

"Do you think you can care for this baby?"

"I know I can love him?"

"You know it's a boy?"

"No, I just feel it is."

"I can try to help you."

"How?"

"I've already researched local pregnancy programs, funds we can appeal to."

"You know, they want to send me away," she said and looked away.

"Who does?"

"My brother, the Church. Even Father Carl wanted to, even though . . ."

"How about your mother?"

"She doesn't even know anything about it. You can't talk to her. She's crazy, you know."

"What do you want to do?"

"I want to go now."

"Let's both think about what you want, what you need—and how I can help."

"I'm going to name him Little Dominic." She looked at him hopefully

Dominic was quiet. He felt flattered and touched and irritated. He didn't want this symbol lingering behind him when he left.

Dolores was still staring at him.

"Do you miss him?" he asked her.

"Who?" she asked.

Dominic looked at her; there was something different in her voice suddenly, a steely quality that was nonetheless bright. She was hard to negotiate; he was never sure whether she was crying wolf or howling like one.

Dolores squared her shoulders. "I'm not letting you off the hook, you know. The abortion thing. I could get you in a lot of trouble."

Dominic looked at her; he wasn't scared. He needed to reach the point from which there was no turning back.

"So, tell me, just how well do you think you know God?" she asked him.

She was being rude. Dom surprised himself by immediately responding with a question of his own: "What do I love when I love God?"

"What does that mean?"

"Actually that's not me. Saint Augustine wrote that. You might want to try a little bit of his *Confessions*."

"Typical," Dolores spat, "you know ever since I was a little girl I've been disappointed in you people. Every time I've asked for help in finding God I'm told to look in books. It's really disappointing to find out that you think the only way to get to God is through books. Show me the God who comes out at night with the stars—or even as the stars."

Dolores stood up to leave. "It's no wonder they're gonna close you down."

Failed Prayer Number Seven
We are to blame, aren't we? Just like all the little gods in our history, You atrophy with our inattention.
Do You, in fact, need human love to exist?
As we become smaller, as our belief in You becomes smaller,
You become smaller.
We become smaller.
Are we in fact killing You?

There was so much to do. Thankfully. On his plate before the 5:30 Mass: think through Sunday's sermon, administer the sacraments to the sick at the assisted living complex. "Not even doctors still make house calls," he thought resentfully. See the roofer about the leak. Attend the first of the three weekly meetings with the lay staff. After Mass, choir practice and the AA spiritual workshop. But first, the eulogy for Father Carl: *whatever you say, say nothing.*

Was this still love Dom felt for the old priest? Still? Even now? Father Carl had been so many things to him: mentor, counselor, spiritual guide. But was he also a real shit, a predator, a pedophile? Dominic might never know. But, with the obligation of the eulogist, he would still need to paint a picture that acknowledged the strength of his character, acknowledged his weaknesses as charming eccentricities, et cetera—but how to get at him as a man?

Though fastidiously neat and clean, Father Carl was not fussy about his looks. He got his hair cut monthly but let random grass sprout freely from his ears and nose. His eyebrows were bushy and thatched, like a robin's nest housing the blues of his eyes. His affect was warm and open. Even when he got sick, the creases and rings under his eyes curved upward, giving his old face a bright and friendly cast.

What else? What nothing might Dom still say?

While carrying himself gracefully, almost athletically, Father Carl sat like a slouch usually, his long legs hinging open from the waist. He carried his own vial of salt in his pocket, always worried there wouldn't be enough to cover his meal with a fresh dusting of snow. He came home from conventions and meetings with laundry bags filled with miniature hotel shampoos and bars of soap to give to orphanages.

But now Dom was forced to acknowledge boredom with the old man in the end. All that "wintering" of the spirit talk; Father Carl had never taken Dom's spiritual crisis seriously. Together, they would fight it, wait it out like a virus. And he was right in a way. Father Carl had served as a check on Dominic's panic; the old priest's resolve would not tolerate the younger priest's confusions. It had taken Father Carl's dying for Dom to finally admit the failure in his own prayers.

What could he say about Father Carl in his eulogy other than acknowledge his congregation's love for him. The weekly visit by the widow Lara, that small woman shrinking into her widow's black, babushka kerchief, as if further miniaturized by her own benevolent witchcraft—bringing her offering of the plastic C-Town shopping bag filled with backyard tomatoes and the tough leaves of dandelion tied at the stalks with rough brown cord—all of it was a sacrament. Likewise the little wooden birds offered by the retired barber, whittled from blocks of wood salvaged from the bins behind the Home Depot, painted by hand in colors that loved their forms, as if they believed that the bird in the hand could be released, become plural in the bush. Or the recently divorced father of two who mowed the church lawn on Saturdays. Or the cooler of fresh fish (striped bass and porgies, mostly, from the Sound) gutted, cleaned and dropped off every summer Sunday afternoon by the electrician with a powerboat. Or just the presence of those dozen or so people who still made it to the 6 a.m. Mass every morning.

How had Father Carl never tired of all these people, each of them keeping him at their beck and call? He saw them as truly powerless and lovely, God's children, having no illusions about their importance, having nothing compelling to sell or buy. Hungry and searching, they didn't need much; there was no burden of good taste to commodify or demonstrate. And he was kind to them. He even put up little bells on the door so that the rectory would jingle like a candy shop when visitors came. He would stare at strangers in an elevator and murmur a blessing over them—as naturally as Dom might a judgment.

Unguarded yet safe. Open and secure. Father Carl was a church with its doors always wide open. And oh! how they loved him—with an honesty that was at once timeless and anachronistic, convinced purely and wholly of the significance of the children they brought to him to baptize, the fuzzy little warm heads they laid in his big hand to anoint with oil. He laughed with joy at the babies who screamed, grimaced, smiled, burped, farted, pissed or slept through the sacrament. How physical he was with his parishioners: the long hugs at weddings, the formal feeling at deathbeds.

He had that way of making Dom feel portentous and clumsy, exasperating. If sincere and productive, Dom's ministry showed effort. He talked too fast, exciting himself to the very edge of coherence. He sometimes misused words, favoring zeal over precision. There was something performative in the way Dominic ministered the Liturgy. In some ways, his faith had been stunted by his early calling, like a nine-year-old prodigy who mimics the romantic ache in Schubert without any firsthand knowledge of it. The return of the prodigious son.

At first, Dom tried to avoid the dozens of family parties celebrating christenings, Communions and confirmations, weddings.

"You go to these things, Dominic," he had scolded him, "like a big smoking humidor, reeking of incense. Lighten up!"

The old priest had urged Dominic to see what was still "gorgeous" and "radiant" about those taking the sacraments—the gleaming innocence of the seven-year-olds lining up for Holy Communion. The corruption (Father Carl would call it an enhancement) of their youth with a big idea. The girls in their little white wedding dresses, the boys in their first blue suits presented to the congregation as archetypal citizens, with sudden knowledge of good and evil.

Dom always felt jealous of how many people loved Father Carl. Now he realized that he really envied Father Carl's ability to love them back—and how they felt sure of that love, trusted it, especially when they didn't deserve it. "You are a good priest, Dominic, but you care with the specialization of a scholar. There is a way they can enter your life, Dominic. Just give them the chance. They want to know you're human, that you suffer too. That your life is hard too. They want to be sure you're not too overly blessed—that you were not somehow forgiven hardship by devoting your life to God."

"Still," Dom thought uncharitably, "it was under Father Carl's watch that the church buildings had started to crumble, parishioners began to defect and the archdiocese fingered Our Lady of Fatima for closure."

Before he died, nothing Father Carl ever did completely alienated Dominic. Nothing, that is, except getting sick. It was not the sorrow or panic or anger the diagnosis provoked in the old priest that troubled Dominic but the strength with which he bore it. Month after month, he underwent radiation and chemotherapy. He lost weight, lost his hair, the light in his eyes and, it must be said, his appeal. This is what shamed Dominic; he had abandoned his good, old friend in the end—not physically, he was there by his side till the end—but spiritually. For the first time in their relationship, it was the younger priest's occasion to minister to the elder's faith. But Father Carl would trump him once again.

"I do not look at this illness as the condition of my life," Father Carl had spoken from the lectern that Sunday after he was diagnosed. "This cancer—this illness and its treatment—is not what my life has to endure. It is my life. It is how I live now."

No one could ask for a more dignified response. The man even regarded his cancer as if it were a spiritual lesson from which his congregation would be able to draw. No one could ask for more exemplary, integrated and soulful leadership—or a more irritating one, as far as Dom was concerned. Perhaps it was this: the old man was vain; he did not know sweet humility. He put his dignity onstage. Maybe that's where it belonged; maybe dignity is exclusively and merely a public thing. But the whole matter confused Dominic, especially his own response: so mean, so un-Christian! He realized he was also jealous of Father Carl's faith, spiteful of his self-satisfaction and certitude, envious of the comfort faith provided for the older man instead of the torment it inspired in Dom. This had been the first serious clue to Dom that it was time for him to consider leaving the Church.

During the social after the last Mass Father Carl was able to celebrate, Dominic scowled over the jelly donuts and panettone as the well-wishers lined up. Dolores was there too, the Cassandra of the coffee clutch. Dom knew he was wrong to feel so resentful. The affection of his parishioners sustained the old priest, but Dom only felt scorn. Their comments tripped him up like cracks in a sidewalk. Father Carl's jokey patter made him sound like a train conductor. That's what happens when your secrets are kept by telling lies; you become vapid and repetitive. He saw that now. Father Carl was a little too good to believe. He was in no position to ask people to be honest with themselves; in that, he had lost the advantage of surprising people.

Dominic overheard a woman say, "Well, throughout all of this, Father, your strength, your courage—you have been an incredible example to us all."

"How nice for you," Dominic had muttered. Father Carl wheeled around and glowered at the younger priest. He dropped his cane, and the room went dead with silence.

Dominic hadn't even realized he had spoken it aloud.

The bishop had not even bothered to list the problems. There was no reason to. It was no mystery why the Catholic priesthood was in decline. Dom himself was a rarity: an American-born priest just over forty. The Church had more recent success recruiting in Africa and South America than enticing young Americans into seminaries. Yet another unattractive service job left to guest workers. American priests joked about their stats at annual archdiocese meetings as if they were dodo birds at a sustainable environment convention. Catholic ordinations in America were down nearly 70 percent over the last thirty years. Dom was certain that those who made it did not have proper testing of their discernment. No one had helped him test his readiness, his rightness.

Not so long ago, he would have been revered by women, adored by children, fussed over by nuns, deferred to by men. Now, he faced constant public suspicion, worked around the clock without a living wage, had his needs barely met by the Church administration that prescribed them—and he would be worked these sixty-five hours a week till he reached seventy-five or so. He had no private life outside his vocation to speak of and no privacy to live it out should one emerge. He felt constantly judged by his parish. His bishop cared nothing for him. He had no money. He had many relationships in which others shared their intimate secrets with him; it was presumed he would have none himself to share. There was no real fraternity among priests he knew; there was no conversation around these issues. And now the world had come to regard even his hard-won celibacy as something warped rather than sacramental.

The extinction of priests was inevitable anyway, almost preordained. God himself had witnessed the winnowing of the clerical instinct among his faithful: a complete disinheritance, like the dying dance of the Shakers. Maybe it was a good thing; maybe it was an act of nature for the clergy to self-select out of existence, the final irony of intelligent design.

It was a miracle there were even any Catholics at all, those hordes of faithful who flirted with the Church's prohibitions: premarital sex, abortion, birth control. But he knew that only priests were meant to observe orthodoxies. Even his most pious had only two or three children. Dominic did not see them as hypocrites; just practical as well as practicing Catholics. And the ban on women and gay priests: as if there were leagues of them to be turned away! He himself worked hard to balance between the traditional and progressive sides of the clergy, scoring for both teams. Not that it mattered much; Dominic himself had long abandoned ecclesiastical ambition. He worked for local good, local change.

There were, of course, activist issues around which Dom and the Church agreed: raising the national minimum wage, AIDS counseling, building mission churches in Nicaragua and Guatemala, missions to aid famine relief in West Africa—but these addressed all the big obvious wrongs in the world. Who else but the Church? What made Dom queasy was the arrogance of the Church's position on personal matters: birth control, premarital sex, gay rights, abortion. Why was the Church so disgusted by intimate matters? Why did it recoil at the very idea of biological self-determination? Was it really the domain of these sexless, old men to watch over the laws of propagation? Was there some cosmic joke that left them in charge of the future of the species' sex?

Dominic had come into the Church in its moment of crisis—and that crisis itself had lodged him, nestled him in its wavering bosom of deliberation. On that infirm ground he had found resolve. The Holy Father himself, Pope Benedict, struck Dominic as being a closet atheist. There was too much intellectual willfulness to his theology to pass. While he largely blamed atheism and its attendant moral relativism for many of the world problems, the pope leaned toward learned skeptical temperament. He strove "to live a faith that comes from the Logos, from creative reason, and that, because of this, is also open to all that is truly rational."

Maybe the Church had gotten away too long with being a total belief system. Faith ought to be personalized, tailored. Dominic, while always having a great respect for the systematic defenses of the great theologians, loved his own faith precisely because it was indefensible, because it would not, could not, *must* not be reasoned with. And a rejection of reason is a very powerful gesture toward freedom.

Reason loves its own limits; faith is the pursuit of the mind beyond itself. Reason finds intolerable the premise that we may be ruled by cosmic laws that we are incapable of grasping; faith submits willfully to that very premise. Reason, with its confidence in objectivity, simply doesn't have the self-awareness of subjectivity.

There isn't enough daylight between the life it governs and life itself.

Dominic was not and would not be—and could not be—didn't want to be the—a—possessor of the truth. Things fall apart, inevitably. The very survival of personal belief lies in the fact that faith, unlike ideas, does not need to formally stabilize in order to survive. What might be seen as true today may no longer be tomorrow, but it will not shake his faith, for it is built on questioning. In fact, the swing of his doubt had more momentum than that of inflexible conviction—as if a pendulum descended halfway only to begin the arduous climb back up from its middle point. His faith was nothing but the management of doubt, the stuff of thought itself.

Was it his fault the parish was closing, its buildings decaying, its people squabbling and defecting? On his watch? He wanted now simply to grow old without becoming an elder; he was disgusted with his own whining. What would Father Carl have said about his constant need for personal fulfillment—as if that were something more than or different from serving God? Dominic was ashamed of the egoism of his disillusion, as if God's existence were up to him, clapping in the audience, shouting out with the others "I believe! I believe!" as the pencil-point light of Tinker Bell once again danced about the stage.

Even God was acting like a real paranoid, with all the vigilance of someone who is hell-bent on proving his own significance, constantly demonstrating signals of his own overstated worth. Why stop with the church closing, the buildings falling apart? Maybe a monument shouldn't commemorate forever. Maybe the Catholic Church was losing its usefulness, of interest only anthropologically, reduced to local cults, dressed up for the opera stage. Maybe the Vatican would be visited some day the way people visit Machu Picchu or Angkor Wat.

Faith in practice is a kind of useful modesty, a sweet humility, a being put in one's place, a substitution of receptivity for knowledge. He struggled to reach up to it; the failure to do so was familiar, even consoling. Not so much suspension, then, more strenuous than voluntary—but the illusion of levitation.

Maybe what he was experiencing was not a loss of faith but a boredom with the myths of redemption.

He was not sure he could go on living a life on his knees.

He was weary from a life stood on its toes.

Dolores pinched her nipples. She palmed her hip bone. She arched to exaggerate the curve of her back. All she ever wanted was to get smaller, to invert things in order to feel bigger within, to escape this giddy, changeable flesh.

"Skank and Bones" was what her brother called her. "Nothing but." Which didn't stop him from looking at her that way, the way that made her hate him so much she wanted to cut him. But what was she? Still only a butter knife. She couldn't hurt the way she wanted to. If she was dangerous, it was only to herself. If she could, she would cut away the little flap of flesh around her waist—even as her belly grew out. She would only extend outward. This was how she would care for the fetus growing inside her.

Father Dominic had remarked that it looked as if she were at last eating right. Asshole. Looking at her body, judging it. He had nice hands, though, golden and strong. She wanted not so much to be touched by them but to become them and touch herself.

She patted her belly, breathed in deeply. She imagined she could still smell Him a little as she parted her legs. She wanted to believe He loved her that much, to put this little life inside her. On a Thursday the archangel had blessed her. Passing through her like a heavy wind. Out of the mountain's hollow flank.

But she felt a little resentful already of the fetus's ambition to live on its own, without her. Later. This baby already knew enough not to trust her. She couldn't save him. He would come into this world so disadvantaged: a mother who might disappear at any moment. Come into this world knowing that. What kind of freak might he be: three ears, a missing spleen, unable to look her in the eye? Who would love her poor little baby, predestined, pre-fucked-up? Maybe all that would make him do great things. All that rising-of-the-human-spirit crap. She would merely be remembered, the martyred mother. She was even a little jealous. For her body to live on, thrive, be in the world without her aching inside it: this was always what she had hoped for herself.

She tried to feel pregnant, as if she was giving birth to this baby instead of merely producing it. That is the biggest thing people don't understand about the mystics: they simply believe the world is vested with the powers they imagine.

She was not to blame for her belly getting bigger this time, her breasts getting fuller. She oozed into it. Her body was making a baby. That was all. And she was going to let it. She was going to make it.

When Bruno Simonovic, a local contractor, and his wife invited Dominic to dinner (after many failed attempts) for the Saturday after Thanksgiving, he couldn't say no. There was no credible way of excusing himself, and, besides, he had many favors to ask this man. James and he had begun to list the projects in the old church needing desperate attention and the names of the local contractors who might volunteer their work. The church's foundation needed shoring up; the potholes in the lot were a liability. They could get rid of the asbestos. Install storm windows. The roof. If they just fixed the place up a bit, people would come back.

They wouldn't want to see the disintegration of the place in which they were confirmed, in which their babies were baptized. Dominic could orchestrate a whole grassroots campaign which the bishop could not ignore.

But Dominic arrived late, losing an hour at the local single-screen movie house. He hadn't even bothered to check what was playing. He just walked in midfeature at the last bargain showing and sat down in the back where he could gaze over the blue heads of the women with their teased hair in the celluloid light glowing like so many haloes.

Dinner, in the meantime, had gotten cold. The children had been fed already but were told to sit at the table while the adults ate. He felt the place stiffen with his presence—in the way the son corrected his posture at the table; in the way the teenage daughter repeatedly stole glances at Dominic's collar; in the way their mother refilled his plate before he had the chance to clear it. Bruno was terse, disappointed; he seemed to regret hosting the dinner in the first place.

They were decent people, second-generation Serbo-Croatians. He couldn't remember which side of the hyphen they came down on. The year before, both Father Carl and he attended their older daughter's wedding reception, a large party held in the "Blue and Gold" room at the local catering hall, a tinny mini-Versailles in which there was no wall that wasn't covered with a gilded mirror to judge him. At the wedding reception, Dominic drank at least a dozen watered-down gins and tonic in smallish bar glasses as well as most of a bottle of red wine. Bruno reminded him at least three times that he had paid for an open bar, encouraging the priest to get him his money's worth.

So Dominic drank and drank until the effort to keep up the smile on his face got easier. He watched a few of the older couples dance the fox-trot, finely tuned but without regard for each other, like parts in a clock. Dom began to slap the men on the back and accept the dance invitations from the women. And all of it came back to him, the steps his mother had taught him as a little boy in the kitchen after supper: the Lindy, the cha-cha, the waltz. The fact that he danced almost too well was yet another confusing thing about him, suggesting other things that might have been.

At the end of the evening, a bottle of homemade grappa was placed at each table while the bride's father stood at the microphone and announced that he had booked the band and the banquet room an additional hour. The guests applauded, the dancing resumed, a bit sloppier; the groom's hands lowered to grope his bride's ass during a slow dance.

A group of men, ties loosened and sweaty shirts untucked, balanced their drunken bodies against each other and sang some sort of political anthem loudly over the band. And that was it. They were charged by another group of men, and then chairs were being smashed over backs. Dominic had seen this before—several times, in fact. He stood up and tried to project some of the gravitas of his station, but stumbled into the crowd himself. He locked eyes with Bruno and nodded. They identified the chief offender. Dominic locked his head from behind. When the drunk reached up to loosen the grip, Simonovic rushed him, punching him hard in the gut. Dominic could feel the blow come at him right through the man. The man went loose in his arms like a soufflé falling. Simonovic grabbed the man's ankles; Dominic lifted him by the armpits, and together they carried him outdoors, down the steps of the hall, and laid him on the sidewalk. Before walking away, Dom had taken off his coat and laid it over the man.

Since then he and the contractor had had a begrudging respect for each other, but Dom could see his campaign to fix the church would not win. He reached into his coat pocket and took out his Marlboro Lights. He had a cinematic appreciation for smoking as a kind of transition, the registering of a mood, like getting a beat before a good line.

"You smoke?" blurted the ten-year-old son, looking at Dominic in amazement.

"God doesn't mind; only my doctor." Dom squinted like a cowboy and then winked at the mother, who rushed into the kitchen to dig up an ashtray.

Simonivic dismissed the children and gave Dom the bad news. The front steps were crumbling and couldn't be repaired again. They needed to be rebuilt. The rafters on the porch overhang were leaking, and he suspected rot on the inside.

"Once you open something like that up, Father, there's no telling what you'll find inside. On the other hand, don't look, and the whole thing might just fall down on someone's head. And we don't want to read about that in the *Register*, Father."

They would have to remove the heavy terra-cotta tile over the sacristy, customize their replacements while trying to age-match the original glaze, strip down to the plywood beneath and fix the problem. He could minimize the cost now and just concern himself with the trouble spot, but the roof was old—seventy-five years old after all, a good run. He would have to think about replacing the whole thing sooner or later. An estimate could be drawn up, you know, "special for the church," Bruno said and looked down.

"Or is there another way? Can we ask the men in the parish to pitch in, put in some weekends, get the work done? Under your supervision, of course."

"That's not easy, Father. It's tough: insurance, the union. We'll see, Father. We'll just have to see—especially, you know, given the bishop and all," he said, wiping his mouth with a napkin. "Father, if you don't mind, I won't open a second bottle. Kids, time for bed," he said and stood up from the table.

Dom wiped his mouth with the cloth napkin.

The little boy was at his side, tugging at his coat. "You want to see my rabbit?"

"If it's OK with your dad, I'd love to see it."

Dom followed the children to the basement to a corner of the boiler room where the little white rabbit sat in a straw-strewn crate. The kids opened the chicken wire gate, grabbed the bunny by the scruff of its neck and deposited it in the priest's lap. Dominic felt genuine surprise at the way it sat there heavy and twitching, at the way a living thing could be so panicked and so still at the same time. A captive heart wary of its own beating. A rush of tenderness overwhelmed him as he petted the extravagant ears and thick fur of the rabbit, stroking deep within its fear and trembling.

Failed Prayer Number Eight
We believe in prayer that we will be loved back just for the asking.
There is no one person you can ask to love you back
Or to love you as much as you want.

Too early to sleep, unable to pray, Dom felt the evening dig into its own hole. He thought to drive himself downtown, but then remembered that his license had been revoked and the car impounded. Just as well; a drive would only depress him more—nothing is bleaker than the main streets of a college town at 10:45 on a winter holiday weekend, when the pizzeria shuts down and the last shot at dinner is microwaved in shrink-wrap at the Exxon station Milk 'n' Things. The temporary couples at the ice cream parlor at closing time. Every night that same emptiness.

As he hit the streets around the church, he felt he didn't have the right socks on. They were always too thin or too thick, too hot or not warm enough. He was half hoping he would run into

Dolores, fellow creature of the night. He wasn't sure why except she could always be counted on to stir it up. He was afraid that he was not equipped to help her. He could barely orient a walk on a city street with her; she refused to accept the easy cues about people (their uniforms, builds, gaits) but wanted to probe who they might be, what their lives might be like. They had once gone to an art gallery together, and Dolores couldn't help watching "all the beautiful people looking at beautiful things." She said that she couldn't even begin to know the pain she saw in their eyes, in the way they ambled across the galleries and tottered before the paintings. She wondered how each of them managed to have sex, what their mouths on other mouths might be like. She wanted to take on the essence of every person she met, like trying to see all the colors in the world at once; he feared that she would wind up seeing nothing but go blind staring at the brilliant white light of all the colors blending, canceling themselves out.

Maybe the Church was completely wrong for Dolores. She didn't need one indivisible God so much as maybe three billion individual glimpses of God, each person making its own god, each instinct toward a wholeness to match itself against, a personal god to set a goal that transcends the ugly chaos and endless banality of daily life.

That wasn't it either. He worried about her; the fact that he didn't know how to minister to her—or even care for her—confused and excited him. She needed a way to imagine the future; he could help her come up with that. She should be living up to her beauty. Knowing love, her body knowing love. She should not be like him.

A fire truck raced up the street, and Dominic flinched against the instinct to hit the ground and curl up into a fetal position.

He took a deep breath. At State Street, he stepped into the crosswalk, hunching his shoulders forward to make himself look more estimable. His short peacoat, a black woolen cap pulled low over his ears, black work shoes—all of it gave him a macho malice, he hoped. Over the years, Dom had become a willful pedestrian, stepping out into the traffic when it suited him, staring down the oncoming cars, daring them not to slow down.

A battered white van rumbled down the street. Dom did not made eye contact with the driver but glared disparagingly at the front grille of the vehicle. He put his head down, shook it slowly side to side and continued to amble across the street with contemptuous ease. It was a game of chicken. The van didn't brake, and Dom didn't move any faster. Though his heart raced, Dom didn't pick up his pace. He could feel the hot breath of the grille at his hip. As he reached the curb, Dom exhaled slowly, letting his breath collect itself as if into a blank cartoon caption.

The van slowed to a stop as Dom stepped onto the sidewalk.

The driver rolled down his window. Dom couldn't make out his face, but he heard a man's voice call out slowly, "What, so you think you're special?"

He turned and walked on. He knew that voice.

"I said, do you think you're special or something, Father?"

Marc Alfano. Was the guy stalking him?

Say nothing, Dominic coached himself.

"What's the matter, Father? You look lonely. You need to hook up. What's wrong; can't find my sister?"

Dom turned the next corner down a one-way street where the van couldn't follow him; nonetheless, he glanced nervously behind him. Nothing. He stopped and breathed in deeply till the winter cold chafed his lungs. He felt lightheaded; a paleness ringed his vision. Zipping up the hoodie under his coat, he headed down the small curving street lined with the small houses that were filled with working-class families and transient graduate students—past the various front yards where short winter shadows leave no privacy despite the Dwarf Alberta Spruces, rosebushes pruned to a winter blunt, shell shrines abandoned by their garaged Madonnas. Lace curtains drew tight across a window like a shawl around an old pair of shoulders.

The little comforts always depressed him. Their inadequacy seemed almost deliberate. Living a life of faith, he realized, was largely a problem of scale.

Across the street a second-story, big picture window lit up. He walked toward it, attracted to its bright rectangle glowing in the dark. Leaning into it is a lovely young woman. She forms a round circle with her mouth and breathes gently on the surface of the window. For a second he imagines she is blowing kisses at him. A moonglow appears on the glass. She moves a few inches and sighs another halo onto the window. She repeats this several times. He smiles at her; she smiles back, he thinks. The window pulses backward like jellyfish in an aquarium. A man comes up behind her, whispers something in her ear and kisses her neck. Dom can see her laughing. She reaches up to the cord to lower the shade but pauses to watch the way her polka dots dance out their light and close in on themselves with the pop of a bubble.

FOUR

Saturdays confused James. He would spend the morning at the local Catholic church rehearsing the chorus with Father Dominic, who challenged his local amateurs with polyphonic Renaissance works. Often it was awful; sometimes it was sweet. He had to hand it to Father Dom, though: it was always sincere. This year, of course, was the year of Bach. After rehearsing the choral parts of the Mass in B Minor that morning, he and Father Dominic had gone out for a quick lunch and made a list of things that needed to be done to save the parish church. They joked about their status in the world, devoted to endangered things, rehearsing their own obsolescence, the two anomalies.

Occasionally James would find a local chamber orchestra to play with, groups who sought out black musicians. Once in a blue moon, he'd be invited to give a concert in a local Baptist church, where he was always welcomed enthusiastically. Usually, though, James would go off to his weekend job at the mall, where he would change into his white tuxedo and ascend the stairs onto the lucite platform hovering between the escalators. For four years straight, he had climbed to sit at a gleaming white baby grand, riffing off songs by Billy Joel and Burt Bacharach, turning into some sort of mascot duck, being stuffed with its own down.

"Thank you very much," he would ape Elvis at the vague shoppers bundled in their winter coats being carried up and down the escalators like luggage on an airport carousel, waiting for someone to claim them.

"This next song was written by my uncle's asshole," he would mumble pleasantly into the microphone, confident no one was listening to anything he said. "Para espanol, oprima numero dos." "The rain in Spain falls mainly in the plain." Vamping jazzy riffs over "What a Wonderful World" and "What the World Needs Now" and "We Are the World." As the afternoon waned, he would liberate himself from actual songs, forget their beginnings and endings and simply pastiche his way through the chord changes vocalizing the terrible clichés of his life: the brutal and absent father, the strong redeeming love of his mama, the love white bitches have for black cock, the plight of the artistic soul raised in the mean streets of the projects, the implicit racism in the conservatory, the very anachronism of that racist complaint—and not least of all, the illegitimate resentment against the charge of affirmative action now that he could no longer take advantage of its opportunity. Tatters to tuxedos. Potato:tomato. His riffs would press at the edge of dissonance and non sequitur—but it was no good. He had perfect pitch, which in some ways was a liability. He was troubled by music whose harmonic relationships he couldn't intuit. He craved the wholly formed in his music, a rational even if unpredictable sense of cause and effect.

By the end of the day, his mouth would go dry. His jaw ached from smiling at the faces that were, for an instant, distracted by him: the old ladies who cooed, the occasional toddler who bobbed on the stairs, the teenage girls who completely ignored him and their boyfriends—wearing ass-crack jeans, untied basketball shoes, Jay-Z T-shirts but never passing for black—who threw gum wrappers at him. But it was black people who made him feel most unseen, there where he was most visible.

His biggest fear was that one day he would see his mother arrive on some senior outing, making good on her obligation to get out, "do something social." He would hate to see her shaking her head at the stores, aiming only to buy something practical, like a flashlight or a new mop, items she'd never find in that mall. On the escalator, she would claim her own stair, while the others gathered two at a time, running commentary on their silly asses in her head, picking up on the black Liberace twinkling to her right, satisfied that at least her boy wasn't such a fool. She had done better to imagine him as something more than that at least. James hoped that maybe she wouldn't even recognize him sitting there in his white monkey suit; he certainly didn't recognize himself. Maybe she would just feel pity for a stranger rather than outrage for her blood. Then she would do a double take and drop her mouth open as she made him. She might even climb over the escalator banister, "showing off her goods to anyone looking" just to come and smack him upside the head. He wouldn't put it past her. She had wanted something so much more for her boy.

Back on campus, he couldn't shake the feeling that just maybe he was hiding out there. Giving the shake. A clean break, a scholarship kid—but none of it was free. What did he have to give, give back, give up? He had left home, cursed and cursing. Here, where he lived like a kept man, his meals ("Had my mother cooked meat, I'd have chosen to stay" was the inspiring verse of one of the Goldberg canons) lay in wait for him, his needs anticipated and met and fallen short of. Here, where the mornings had no start time, he was up before dawn. Here where he had a room to himself, he watched the elegant deadness of the 1920s' Gothic towers; he traced the squirrels chasing each other across the slate roofs. Through his suite of leaded glass windows he watched a raven land on a telephone wire. The black bird was far too heavy for the wire, which swung under his weight—how could he have misjudged that? The raven spread its wings and landed on the ground with a clumsy reluctance, as if flight and fall were part and parcel.

The dirty secret of any social charity is that the beneficiary always ends up resentful—for all the right reasons: for being singled out as a special case, the token toward the quota; for the slot taken that others feel more entitled to. While never experiencing any overt racism, James knew he had to work double time to compel the school to overcome its own contradictions: the self-congratulatory welcome that contains within it the skeptical conviction that he won't, in the end, succeed or thank them. He has to be that good.

Signora Rosa had made it clear to him she had no time for his feeling special. She had lost patience with him, seen through him. "You are not serious, James. What are you doing here? Why did you come here? To feel sorry for yourself? To make me feel sorry for you?"

"Because I want to learn."

"Do you? How can I be sure you are serious?"

"I will work harder."

"Not just harder. Better. With no sense of entitlement or revenge. None of that matters. You come here like a pretender to the throne. But don't you know the king is dead? Why have you come here?"

He felt a bit nasty, challenged. She was mean, the kind of lady who might have scared him as a child, warning him not to touch anything in her shop. He felt his chest go up and his hips go back and his head cock sideways, and he said, "'Cuz my mama dun tol' me you wanna know 'bout somethin', aks sum one who know."

That it was lost on her relieved him. He had wanted to be funny, but it came out hostile. Was this how he was heard, pressed hard against the blackface accent like a mime against glass? Amphibious, he was a reptile in a shallow pool, camouflaged. He dried off salt white. His jive came off even more disingenuous than he intended. He was a racist himself, after all, a primitive and a sophisticate, a sample of folk art—as well as its collector. Once again, he dove for the antiquated—more Dust Bowl residue than contemporary street; even his sense of humor was out of step.

It was just 4:30, and already dusk was settling around him. James ended his practice by running through the chords of the Variations, quieting his fingers over the piano keys gradually as if putting a child to bed. Before the mirror in his bedroom, he stripped down to his underwear to prepare for a workout he had downloaded from the Internet designed to keep marines in shape when off-base: 400 Jumping Jacks; Push-ups and Mountain Climbers pyramid up to 15 and back to 1. 100 Grappling Push-ups. Rest 30 seconds. 25 Shootfighters and 25 Bootstrappers. 40 Striders and 40 High Knee Jumps. Rest 30 seconds. 20 Striders. 100 Walking Lunges. 100 Alternating Flutter Kicks and Good Mornings. 90 Sit-and-Tucks and Crunches. 100 Russian Twists. Rest 60 seconds. Repeat.

After alternating pairs of wide-grip pull-ups and close-grip chin-ups to failure at the bar, he grabbed a shower, lolling his neck from side to side beneath the hot water. The rigor and exactitude of the workout satisfied him; he loved the deep set to his chest and the heaviness in his limbs. He put on a clean pair of khakis and a pressed white shirt, his arms filling out the sleeves. In the darkening, suggestive light of his living room, he flexed his muscles and watched the blue shadows in the folds of the cotton. He waited for Vanessa. They met online, through a dating service. He had not time nor interest in hooking up at bars. He wanted to love one woman, for as long as it was good.

Tired from her day at the law firm, Vanessa would kick off her heels, and he would see how her skirt stretched across her ass. Her corporate get-up was crazy sexy to him. On his knees he would nuzzle against the weave of her suit, tell her how out of his mind he was for her; how he was jumping out of his skin for her. He would undress her slowly, gaze at the impossible slope of her breasts from her tight and muscular shoulders. He grinded his teeth and growled softly to keep from taking a bite out of her. Together they would try to make the evening stretch out against the urge to speed it up.

"I don't like classical music, really," Vanessa confessed to him soon after they first met. "It's just all too stuffy, too pretentious."

He knew what she meant, of course, but was astonished that she knew he could be offended without taking offense. And went ahead anyway and said it. All the same, he recognized that she was talking about the culture of classical music—not the listening or playing experience. The entire industry was based on false pieties that betrayed the actual joy of music, snobby dichotomies that postured high over low art. Many of those illusions had passed away in the 1950s, anyway; classical music has been kept barely alive on a respirator ever since: royalty in a coma, visited by its graying and dutiful children who, racked with guilt, listen to its overwrought complaints and accusations of neglect.

James knew better than to defend any of this; he didn't care about "the future of classical music" either. Instead, he simply went to his piano and played selections for her. In fragments at first, so as not to bore her or scare her with too much. In fragments, the way lovers always play themselves for each other in the beginning. In fragments, suggestive and resonant, parts of a whole, leaving room to want more.

He told her the stories of the pieces he played: how they were written; what they meant to him. He wanted to play them so she could love them as much as he did, trusting that her soul would take as much delight as did his, playing for her as he did for himself—loving her. In bed, their limbs entwined, they listened to records and compared different interpretations of his favorite compositions. Vanessa liked this enough, she said, and she agreed that it was beautiful—but only when he showed her how. She would never choose to listen to this stuff on her own; none of this would make it to her desert island.

"But you—you I would take to my desert island. You and your piano," she told him, wondering how she might fit in.

She loved the tender way he played, the gentle and fierce attention with which he taught her to listen. He was a quiet man; he didn't talk much. He wasn't prone to abstraction or analysis. But before this music, he was like a piece of kindling eager for a fire. He seemed to urge himself at the piano, disappeared into it. The way he played this Bach—it was as if she were summoned before it. She didn't care whether he would someday play professionally. When he was at the piano, she heard the heart of a lion; he presented himself with the clarity, the aggression and the self-knowledge of a hero.

"What I like about you," she teased him, "is that you don't obsess on your inner life, the pain of it all—like most artists, saints and other perverts. But it's there. You just sound it out."

She heard his playing like a taste on her tongue, the running of cool water somewhere and then the drying of mown grass there and ice cream over here.

She had done well in choosing a boyfriend for whom touch was everything.

Signora Rosa was surprised to see that girl again. So thin. This was skinny on purpose. This was washerwoman thin, wringing-shirts-all-day thin. This was like someone who might have worked for her family long ago, though she supposed it was considered stylish now.

"Mother, how are you this morning?"

To think: this girl with the sleeveless blouse, showing off those stringy arms, calling her Mother.

She could play along. "Oh, I'm lovely. Thank you."

"Do you need anything?"

"No, I have everything I need."

"More than you need, actually."

"I beg your pardon?"

"Come on, Mother, we talked about this. You said you would get rid of all this stuff, and now you've unpacked it all over again!"

"Yes, I need to look at everything again. I need to reexamine everything."

"Seriously. I can hire someone to come and help you clear all this up."

"Please don't bother. My daughter will come and take care of everything."

Andrea looked at her. This was new.

"Mother?"

The old woman picked at her hem.

"Mother, don't you recognize me? It's me, Andrea."

The two women looked at each other.

"Nonsense. My daughter always wears a bra."

Andrea laughed; she was being played with. The lapse had

been convincing but ultimately didn't have the blankness of true dementia. As always, her mother never gave her the option of a simple response. She was both relieved and annoyed at being played with.

"Very nice, Mother. But you better be careful. Remember when you used to tell me not to make funny faces because one day it would stick? Well, you better heed those words."

She was silent.

"I guess I'll just have to come back here someday and take care of all this myself."

"Well, maybe you won't have to wait long."

This girl, her daughter. Is it possible she truly dislikes her as much as she thinks? She had only wanted to protect her when she was a child: so delicate and vulnerable, something needing to be saved. She was always a tiny thing. Only nibbled. Still so. Her body now, so hard, dangerous as a weapon, a well-maintained machine, and those hard suits she wore—not so much a suit as a sheath.

Andrea picked at a group of photographs that had scattered on the floor and under the piano. On top: a photograph of herself with her mother at a family wedding a few years ago. They were both smiling; Andrea had her arm around her mother, but the tension between them was visible—as if they were about to be shot. Her mother wore a flowered print dress with panty hose and rubber-soled loafers. Andrea wore a black suit with a very short skirt, stockings held up with a visible garter and her Blahniks. Was it possible there was only a single generation between them? Her mother, with her wars and immigrant saga, appeared to be centuries older. They wore different oppressions: Signora Rosa was heavy with history while Andrea, in her American middle-aged adolescent fantasy, was trying to beat the very next minute.

The second photograph whitened her. "Who's this with you, in this picture? Is that him?"

She had never met her father—her mother had left Italy without knowing she was pregnant on that November day in 1960, which she described as a late Indian summer, the roses in their freakish bloom, the yellow leaves tired of clinging to the trees.

Signora Rosa looked at the photograph. His hair had already grayed by that point but was still thick and wooly. His mustache, though, was inky black. How could that be? Did he dye only that? She looked closer. She recognized the suit. His fit. He was always too cheap to buy a new suit. He relied on just two wardrobes: military and business. She looked closer still at the way the shirt stretched apart at the buttons.

"What year was this taken?" her daughter asked. She could hear her voice getting shrill. "Mother, what is this? Why didn't you show me?"

"Why should I have shown it to you? What is there to see, anyway?" she yelled back at her daughter. "Who needs to have this conversation? I don't need it. Let me tell you something—you don't need it either. What is there to see anyway? Only an old man who cleans his teeth at the dinner table with his steak knife."

What was there to see anyway? Go to the arraignment, see if his enemies could get it together to take him to trial? War crimes; they should only know. Would they be bothering her at this point?

"So this is my father, huh? Oh my god. That heinous creature, my father. So, this is what he looked like."

Signora Rosa shook her head.

"Mother, will you testify? Will you tell them what he did to you?"

What was there to see anyway? After all these years. How could anyone expect him to be able to pay for everything he did? Why give him the satisfaction of seeing her like this—a survivor who had to make do with how he left her?

What was there to see anyway?

A man who was sentimental but unkind. Whose nephews refused to visit because he would seduce their wives. Who cooed at his baby daughter, bringing himself to tears because he was so moved by his own capacity to love her.

A man who took a pillow to a little baby's head and laid his weight on it—just to see what would happen. And she had let it happen too, this sacrifice of her little baby boy.

What was there to see anyway?

Andrea could hear her mother shut down, as she always did when she tried to talk about her father. She knew it was time to drop it. Parents don't change. She couldn't take him on. Not now. She couldn't take on any man.

Andrea took her mother to hear a concert, despite her protests. A pianist with a concave face and sad eyes walked onstage with military assertion. She played the piano as if it were forged, a brass instrument. Her pianissimo played not so much to the note but to the space before and after it, the tension of expectation and release, the satisfaction so delicate it nearly disappointed.

Andrea never understood this kind of devotion—her mother's—the virtuosity of the virtuoso, the working away at a piece of music, reaching an interpretation that is a kind of platonic ideal—the love of the thing itself is a kind of mutilation, a teasing or torturing of the adored—so as to make it what she wants it to be, thinks it to be, forces it to be, wills it to be. Is this the essence of love itself?

She remembered the wistful sounds of the student musicians passing through her childhood home. How serious and eager to please her mother they all were. How privileged they imagined themselves to be. She listened hardest to the interruptions in the playing; in the cinched silence she tried to hear what instruction her mother was giving, imagined what she might be saying to them. How her reprimands seemed different than the ones she knew so well. To this day, she grew impatient listening straight through a piece of music, hating the confidence of a musician who dared to finish without correction, thinking she was good enough simply to play on without regard to her imperfections.

She had defied her mother by refusing to play the piano or any instrument. She would not be judged dull and adequate when compared to her mother's master students.

For the priest, Signora would lay a spread usually. Make tea, unwrap the biscotti in the tin. But she had forgotten he was coming that day. He surprised her. She would not have recognized him but for the collar. Once settled, she was offended by the sense he gave of being in a hurry. As if he were busier than she! He came to hear her confession, but all she wanted was to control her memory—deny the things she wanted kept away and recall the things she wanted close.

They sat on her little lumpy couch. She went silent with regret. She should never have bothered with this priest—even going so far as to introduce him to her daughter. Why did she need to take care of him?

Finally, Dominic asked, "Your daughter, Andrea?"

"Yes, I know her name."

"She called me," Dominic said. "She was very kind, talked to me about her magazine. I may even try to write something for her."

"Don't waste her time. Make sure it's very, very good. She's too busy."

Dominic had called Andrea just that morning and was surprised when the editor readily picked up the phone. They were polite with each other. Andrea even thanked him for looking after his mother. Dominic wanted to make sure that she didn't think he was calling in a favor. He agreed to assemble a number of essays that might serve as a kind of proposal for her magazine. She told him that she could only offer him work on spec.

He was feeling very encouraged until she had the gall to ask him one "off the record question."

"Don't take this the wrong way, Father, but I've been curious about something. I'm having a little trouble squaring your intellectual probity with your faith. I mean, really, can one be a real, thinking person and still be a true believer?"

That wasn't a good start; he doubted they could survive that opening.

"Be good to her," Signora continued. "Lord knows I wasn't good enough."

"I'm not sure I understand, Signora."

"I don't know why, but—yes, it's true—I've always hated her. I don't understand how. I know it's bad, but I cannot bear her. I want to punish her."

"What for?"

"How should I know? It's not rational, but it is real. I want her punished. She is too professional, too successful. And yet somehow still so desperate. She needs my approval. Just like my students. Everyone needs my approval. And she hasn't earned it."

"What must she do to earn it?"

"Sometimes I'm not even sure I know what they are anymore."

"Signora?" Dominic waited.

"My secrets. You should go," she waved her hand at him. "I have to sort through my papers."

Dominic cleared his throat. "So, our James. Pretty heady stuff."

She was silent; she would not be led into pointless conversation.

"Do you think he's that good?" Dominic continued. "You think he should go for the fellowship?"

"Why do you have to ask?" This irritated her. "Do you doubt my judgment?"

"No, no. I'm sure you're right. It's just that . . ."

"Just what?" she said sharply, pleased at the way she made him flinch.

"Well, I just don't know if he's that sure of himself or what he wants."

"He has four months to get sure," she said. "What's he not sure about? If it's because he thinks he's not good enough, well then he's probably right. But he can be good enough."

"The school hasn't been exactly encouraging. James is not even so sure he wants it anymore. You know, we talk, he and I. Maybe playing for fun, for our chorus, is enough for him."

"That is just fear talking."

"Signora, maybe you should just think about . . ."

"It's funny how everyone calls me that—Signora—how I've insisted on it. Such a grand name for someone as little as I. Thank you, Father for your blessing; I am tired now."

"Start your day with Bach," she advised James. "Pablo Casals did so every day for seventy years. He knew. It will ground you." But she hadn't exactly meant the Goldberg Variations. That piece was secular, not bound to liturgical obligation and thus burdened with its own solemnity.

James loved the way he felt after playing Bach—not necessarily complete, but finished. He loved the illusion of journey the

Goldberg gives—a journey without destiny. Bach had to think of everything. He was like a librarian in a hurry to fill all the empty shelves, anxious to reach the end in which all time and space got taken up.

Virtuosity in Bach delights not so much in answering its own musical questions (like Mozart) but in puzzling out the possible ranges of resolutions. Contemplative, sober, evenhanded, Bach's rapture is careful and self-contained. Not pleased with itself, the way playing Mozart or Handel made James feel. Not incomplete, unsettled or unpleased with himself the way he felt playing Chopin or Schubert. Playing Bach, he felt not so much lyrical as experienced.

Bach reaches conclusions but is never conclusive. His compositions have a general infrastructure that is scalable, allowing for an infinite capacity for asking questions and posing problems. The courage to ask such difficult questions rests on the confidence that they may in fact be answered—even as he recognizes that the more complex the structure of understanding, the more is revealed as hidden and inaccessible. In this way, as musical historians have noted, Bach writes theology.

"And the angels were amazed," Signora Rosa would say to him when he played a variation particularly well. "You know that quote, don't you? To me, we are better amazed by what is possible, by art that lets us into the process of its making. Why waste time on the ineffable?" There was still time to learn, still room for James to grow. He would come into his own.

Playing the Goldberg Variations in the early morning, James felt the hot breath of another mind on his fingers. The centuries shortened between him and the composer, as if the Master watched over his shoulder with approval—with affection even, maybe. Bach believed in the triumph of spirit over matter, composing music that sounded like it certainly needed more than two hands and ten fingers.

James could play the Goldberg with competence, voice all the notes, control the pace and markings. He had gotten there with Bach, one on one, mano a mano, as if there were a score to settle. But was this competence as good as he would ever get? Was this beautiful noise he made just a version heard against the ideal? He couldn't believe that after all this time there was still more to learn, to variegate; there was still time to change.

Signora wanted him to write it out, a biography of the Goldberg Variations, to sketch out a plan for playing it. He didn't really understand the point, but he liked the diversion of it, the excuse it gave him to spend time away from the piano and still call it work. At his laptop, he liked the blank light of the screen.

He wanted to write about music the way Signora spoke about it, approach words the way she would musical notes. It wasn't only her diction or the foreignness of her accent that was strange to him; it was the way she chose words as if she was not so much translating as transplanting, repotting rare orchids into a strange soil.

"There are never enough markings on the score," she said. "Not everything occurred to the maker. So we have to wonder after his intention, mar perfection with our speculation." She told James that it was a musical truth to make stuff up, to imagine. Ask any musician, translator, dancer, reader, builder, interpreter of texts.

It was also a truth to invent oneself. Who would he imagine himself to be as he walked on that stage?

He had many false starts, just as he did at the piano. Wanting to get at the experience of playing the piece, he tried telling the story of its life. He wondered if the true value of experience is in the narrating of it later on, the urge to tell someone, to be witnessed.

He started with a title page:

THE GOLDBERG VARIATIONS: A LIFE

"There is something of the heavens in it," wrote Sir Thomas Browne in an epigraph that appears in the Schirmer edition of the Goldberg Variations. At once, even before he looks at the first note, the pianist's expectations are not only heightened but cautioned. We are put on notice to recognize something of divine origin here—except that there is also something suspect about the statement. A little detective work reveals that Sir Thomas Browne published the remark in 1642, a century before Bach set the piece to paper. So we learn that the cosmic dimension so commonly attributed to the piece has been retroactively applied, first, by the American harpsichordist Ralph Kirkpatrick in 1935. Nevertheless, the damage has been done. We have been set up.

In fact, the Goldberg Variations has a much more modest provenance. It wasn't even called by its name until 1802, fifty-two years after Bach's death, in a biography of the composer written by Forkel. Bach himself published the Goldberg in a series of keyboard music as *Clavierübung*, or "Keyboard Practice," a plain title for these exercises "consisting of an Aria with diverse Variations for the Harpsichord with two manuals."

Forkel tells us of our debt to Count Keyserlingk, Russian envoy to the Elector of Saxony, who brought his estate's harpsichordist, Goldberg, to study with Bach in Leipzig. The count, who suffered from chronic insomnia, asked Bach to compose some clavier pieces that required Goldberg "to spend the night in an adjoining room so that he could play something to him during this sleeplessness." The music "should be of such a soft and somewhat lively character that he might be a little cheered up by [it] in his sleepless nights."

Bach, wishing to satisfy his patron, decided on a set of variations and was "handsomely rewarded . . . with a golden goblet filled with a hundred Louis d'ors."

There is, of course, much scholarship that disputes this lore. There is no documentary evidence of the work being commissioned, no official dedication on its published title page, no evidence that the then-fourteen-year-old Goldberg had the technical expertise to play the piece competently and no record of the golden goblet in Bach's estate inventoried upon his death in 1750.

But the mythology survives nonetheless: a divinely inspired music for an insomniac count, a model of exquisite solitude, a piece of work to be performed through a night of the soul, on demand, for as long as it would take a count to forget his worries and fall asleep.

Apocryphal or not, the tale belies certain ambiguities about the work and its historical legacy. How is it that a piece of music, designed to soothe an insomniac's restive nights, has evolved into the very standard of musical intellectualism, an icon of artistic profundity, a masterwork of such complexity as to have bewitched musicians for centuries, a map of the logical and conceptual capacity of the enlightened mind and, for many, a keyhole peek at the very nature of divinity?

James swiveled his chair away from the desk. Whose voice was he ventriloquizing here: the host of *Masterpiece Theatre*? It was nearly impossible to write about this music and not sound like the stuff of concert programs. He walked over to the piano and struck its first couple of notes. The Goldberg Variations. They are what Dr. Hannibal Lecter listens to as he sups on human victuals with a nice bottle of Chianti. Juliette Binoche plays them on a piano rigged with explosives by the Nazis in *The English Patient,* assured that the "piano would be safe if one played Bach on it." The Goldberg Variations. Aren't they what Woody Allen thought his next-door neighbors in Coney Island did in bed Saturday nights?

The opening notes of the Aria, a sad and stately sarabande, calmed and stimulated him. In their embrace, James thought of nothing but new beginnings, first steps, the dawning mind of Adam and Eve—newborn but not infants. To his ears, the notes sounded virginal as if a new grammatical tense were being invented. The beginning and the end. The resistance of the eyes opening in the morning and the pull to close them in the evening. Was this what Bach was after, especially since the piece was written for an aristocratic insomniac, a man whose days did not sufficiently exhaust his nights?

And the beauty of that last phrase, rolling out like a mother tongue, so maternal in its legato swaddle. One couldn't help but rock to it, be rocked by it. It is a phrase that might as well never end, gives us the illusion that it will never end until we are pulled away groggy and well fed.

Upon repeating the Aria, James added the trills and grace notes, the cocky flourishes the second time around the block. These ornamentations delighted and disappointed him. He would rather play it simply, as if for the first time again—but there is no avoiding the loss of innocence the second go-round. There are only so many primary things one can know a first time, know originally, to experience as discovery. The rest is boasting, questioning, ornamenting, darkening, variations on a theme.

Bach called the thirty variations between the Aria and its repetition at the end "an ungrateful task." The pianist cannot help but be excited by the form: the first articulation of the main theme, as if stating one's identity. Then to have the courage to journey out from it, to test its identity by torturing every latent idea in it, putting it through every worthwhile variation.

The thirty variations teach that not just origination but interpretation is progress. Among the Variations, nine are strict canons placed regularly at every three pieces and arranged systematically in ascending order of the interval between two canonic parts. "Three" is an important number; between the arias, the variations are divided into ten groups of three pieces—beginning with a canon, free-style variation and variation in duet. The last variation is an unusual piece called a *quodlibet*, built upon several melodies. Two folk tunes are traditionally heard here, one lyrical:

I have long been away from you,
Come here, come here, come here

and the other comical:

Cabbage and turnips have driven me here,
Had my mother cooked meat, I'd have chosen to stay.

Many scholars have over the centuries found thematic significance in the complex structure of this piece that never fails to yield opportunity for analysis. In 1984, David Humphreys claimed that the unifying structure of the work is its allegorical scheme, which represents "an ascent through the nine spheres of Ptolemaic cosmology." Another reading traces aspects of Quintilian's classical rules of rhetoric in the music.

James left off and went straight to his stereo.

His romance with the Goldberg needed to reckon with the history of all the famed pianists who had tackled it. James studied the great recordings—the reverent precision in the harpsichord of Wanda Landowska who reputedly chastised a colleague by saying, "You play Bach your way, my dear, and I'll play him his way." And all the pianists who followed. Rosalyn Tureck's sober rendering. Kipnis and Arrau, who played more expressively and romantically, amplifying the original dynamics of the piece, and, to come full circle, those more recent performers who would subvert the pianism of the instrument itself in order to simulate the character of the original harpsichord.

"Art should be given the chance to phase itself out," wrote Glenn Gould. "We must accept the fact that art is not inevitably benign, that it is potentially destructive. We should analyze the areas where it tends to do least harm, use them as a guideline and build into art a component that will enable it to preside over its own obsolescence." For years, James was obsessed with the Canadian maverick pianist, for the aesthetic model he presented; for the way style was indistinguishable from proficiency; for his mathematical yet capricious sense of time (there is a difference of thirteen minutes and eighteen seconds between Gould's 1955 and 1981 recordings of the Goldberg); for the way he spurned live performance in favor of the manipulated precision of the recording studio; for the way he vocalized along and conducted himself, his nose nearly touching the keys; for the way he treated the pieties of art as religious heresies needing to be snuffed out. Gould was a charlatan and a genius and had perpetrated the perfect hate crime of the preemptive interpretation, a kind of terrorist act against the original to make it his own, to set the standard, the mother of all future interpretations—that which must always be reckoned with every time a pianist sat down at the keyboard. Every future version would have to refer back to Gould's whether in homage or disdain or correction.

Except that wasn't how it turned out. Angela Hewitt, András

Schiff, Murray Perahia, Simone Dinnerstein and many others recorded gorgeous, rational, nonideological versions in the next room as the hysterical howls of Gould faded into legend.

Just come from the filth and disorder of war, Claudio told his young wife that he was disgusted at the way she kept house. "It's filthy here. I'm away putting my life at risk, and you can't even keep the house clean."

"How can you tell?" Signora Rosa retorted. "We don't have enough to let get dirty."

That brought the first smack across the face with the flat of his hand. She was surprised by the rightness of the sting. It hurt just the way she anticipated it would. She didn't feel chastened by the blow so much as adjusted—turned around by the force of it so she could see her life from another side. It was the first of many; the random force of his anger gave her a new appreciation for the kind fall of the piano hammer, useful and controlled.

Claudio made lists of things she would need to accomplish every day: Sweep the floors and scrub the mortar between the tiles until it was white. Slaughter two chickens for Sunday's supper.

She campaigned a counterattack. She did sweep the floors, diligently even. Then she rolled back the carpet and distributed the dust under its span with the care of a monk creating a sand mandala.

She replaced the carpet carefully so he wouldn't feel the slight padding beneath. Every day she repeated this.

She did slaughter the chickens but made it look like the handiwork of foxes during the night. She scooped out all the edible meat and bones, leaving the scraps of the carcass behind.

It wasn't until she added the cracked and emptied eggshells to the scum beneath the carpet that crunched beneath the heel of his boot that he discovered her. Finding the mess, realizing the care and deliberation in it, acknowledging the sly and satisfied look on her face, he grabbed her by the hair, dragged her out of the house by her left hand that just that morning had finally mastered the counterpoint of a difficult piece, spread her fingers on the grained surface of a tree stump and drove the flat end of an ax onto it.

Opening her eyes a half hour or so later, she found herself being cared for by the other wives of the village, who suddenly found sympathy for her reduced state, for the loss of the instrument that allowed her airs. She was no better than they now, and for that kind of misery they could find love.

Despite her best efforts to put these memories out of her mind, they came rushing at her under their own power. The past was overtaking the present; things that happened to her long ago became more vivid than the events of this morning. What remained to live would sound out from that trauma—all of her something ready to spring into action, a hammer against a string, demonstrating her, describing the possible boundaries of her tether, breaking through the membranous circumscription of her life—birth, losing her virginity, giving birth and now, the final circle like the dust of pure and dark pigment.

When had it happened: the moment when she went from having too much reality to not enough?

Signora Rosa dressed up for the priest. She applied lipstick and put on a dress. White gloves stretched to her elbows. When she greeted him at the door, Dominic was overwhelmed by how much cologne she had doused herself with.

"James is going to win, you know. He knows the Goldberg inside out," she said.

Dominic nodded. "That's quite a turnaround from where you were last week."

"Oh, I can always change my mind because I am absolutely superior. Can't you tell?" She laughed. "That way, I require no consistency or self-knowledge—or at least none that I need show. You"—she paused—"you can't get away with that. You are too humble."

Dominic smiled. "It's my training."

"No, no, no, no, no," Signora chided. "It's your lack of presumption, your naïveté. You are always going to be tested, and you are always going to be unprepared."

"You believe in God, Signora. Why do I surprise you?"

"I do believe in God. That's why you're here. You are easy to like because you are so flawed."

"Thanks, I guess."

"Like James."

"How so?"

"He is too good to believe. Much too good to believe. Except that he is not." She grew suddenly pensive. "He's not good enough."

"But you just said that . . ."

"He's not good enough, and I have always known it," she said stubbornly.

"Why do you encourage him, then? You had many opportunities to tell him the truth."

"He had the audacity to pretend he believed in the music, that he was an artist. I wanted to see how long he could fool himself. He might still believe it, for all I know. If this were a just world, he would make it. They would all have to believe in him, the conservatory, the musical directors, all of classical music—because they were determined to. His success would mock them."

"But he's not good enough."

"Worse than that. And better. He might have been stopped, come to his senses, but what good would that do?"

"You could have stopped him from wasting his time."

"Waste of time? Do you want to know what was a waste of time? Jesus dying on the cross was a waste of time. It couldn't be stopped. And it came to naught. What did it accomplish—his sacrifice, his assisted suicide?"

Dominic stood up.

"Sit down," she said sternly.

She took off each of her white gloves. He couldn't help but stare at her fabled left hand. The skin was browner and tougher, looked more like leather. Her fingers were short and bent, and her fingernails were clipped neatly. He had the sense that her hand had been preserved, petrified. He sat down.

She struggled to take off the wedding ring from her finger; it dropped on the glass plate of her coffee table, rang a note and then fell over, reverberating in quickening spirals before coming to a rest.

"Hmm, a perfect C," she said. "The trouble with James is that he believes he is good enough, or worse, that he doesn't need to be. His aspiration—that needs to be disabled. Your aspiration is just on the other side of achievable; it will always lead you on."

Dominic swallowed hard. "And you, Signora? Which side do you live on?"

"I knew I wasn't good enough, really, but I couldn't accept my own mediocrity. This hand, well, in the end, is a relief. I would not become mediocre."

Dominic reached out and put a hand on her back; it was bony and brittle.

"You know, that's why I practice. I practice the piano. I practice my faith. I practice my self, my selves really. That's what I try to teach my students. Not to be but to practice being."

"What might you have liked to be?" Dominic asked.

"It wasn't a lie, Father. Claudio did do this thing to me, but I pressed him to. I made him hate the piano and my devotion to it. I taunted him. I dared him. I told him that if he was so threatened by the piano, he should make sure I couldn't play it. If he were a real man, he would take care of the problem. I knew that he would. I used Claudio and made myself a tragic figure, a sacrifice, but I kept my secret behind the secret. People accepted my story, and I was saved from fulfilling my promise."

Dominic hung his head.

"I made sure that neither of us got what we wanted and that both of us got what we didn't want. Now, that's a marriage!"

FIVE

Sunday morning Mass was ill attended, particularly for a Thanksgiving weekend. No sign of Dolores. Mrs. Rogers had marched in halfway through his sermon and sat noisily in the front pew, dragging along her daughter, Patricia—a pretty young woman engaged to a man who had just suffered a serious cycling accident that left him a quadriplegic. After the service, Mrs. Rogers knocked on the sacristy door before Dominic was out of his vestments. She marched her daughter before him.

"OK, Father. Tell her not to ruin her life. Of course, it's a very sad thing, what happened, but it's no reason she should ruin her whole life. She's a baby."

The young man himself had encouraged Patricia to rethink the engagement.

"This is what he told her. He said, 'You didn't sign on for this, I know. You can bail out. I would totally understand.' That's what he said. He basically handed her a free pass, but she won't listen!" the mother screamed at Dom. "She wants to stick by him."

Dominic asked the young woman what she thought.

The young woman hesitated but then squared her shoulders

and, without looking at her mother, said simply and strongly, "I just love him, Father. That's the only thing I am sure of. That hasn't changed. So why should anything else be different?"

Mrs. Rogers let out a sigh that ended in a kind of roar. "Tell her, Father. Tell her how hard her life will be. Tell her that she'll never have children! Tell her that she is not going to hell by making the right decision here. Tell her God wants her to!"

"Well, I don't think that's the point."

The mother glowered at Dominic. "Well, thank you, Father. You've been a lot of help," and stormed out of the church.

He took a deep breath and looked at the young woman. "What will you do?"

"The right thing," she replied.

"You've thought this through?"

She hesitated. "I don't need to. I know what I want."

Dominic walked back to the rectory, let out a big sigh, bolted the door and readied himself to face Father Carl's eulogy when the doorbell rang.

Dominic was tempted to sneak into the library and pretend he wasn't there. Wasn't he entitled to settle into the solitude of a chilly November Sunday morning, at least until the evening Mass?

He peeked through the curtains of the window. Dolores stood at the front steps of the rectory. Dom found himself smiling. He had been worrying about her. He was glad to see her hair brushed. She appeared to be wearing makeup. She looked pretty. His mood lifted. He was truly glad to see her.

"Hi. What are you doing here?"

"Well, I've come to help clean up," Dolores said brightly. "I'm good at that, and anyway I have those nesting hormones raging all over the place."

"It's the holiday weekend, Dolores. I'm all set, thank you. You know Sister Agnes is back early anyway. She's preparing the chapel for the funeral. But I'm sure she'll be happy to hear that you're willing to help out."

"You've been all alone? What about Thanksgiving? What did you eat?"

"I did the blessing at the shelter. I had a fine turkey dinner there."

"Oh. Well, that was nice of you."

"I do it every year."

"Makes Thanksgiving feel meaningful, I guess."

"Yup."

"I guess we have much to be thankful for," Dolores said and grew thoughtful. She was chastened by this evidence of Father Dominic's deep need to serve. There was always so much to do.

Dominic stayed quiet. He looked at her closely; he was learning to wait and watch. It didn't feel right, though. He was her priest, not her analyst.

"Maybe I could just pick stuff up." She brushed past him and began to push a broom around the foyer. The insolent slap of her flip-flops on the tile floor irritated him. Why was she wearing those in November? She was always hopelessly unprepared.

"I'm working, Dolores. And I don't think it's appropriate for us to be alone here."

"Really? Why?"

Coyness crept through the inept application of makeup on her face. He could swear she jutted a hip saying this. He waited. Dolores looked confused; she began to cry—softly, perhaps deliberately, as if there were nothing else she could think to do. Father Dominic sat down on a bench. Dolores sat beside him and crossed her legs and sobbed.

Dominic leaned his head against hers; the tired scent of a fruity shampoo fought through an overlay of cigarette smoke.

"Come now, Dolores."

"It's all just too awful"

"Tell me what is too awful."

"Everything."

"Dolores, that's too big. Let's break it down. Tell me specifically what hurts you so badly. You know, your emotions are feeling big right now also because of hormonal changes happening in your body."

"Why do I even come here? I mean, can you even imagine anything worse than what happened here?"

"Are we talking about Father Carl here? Dolores, you have to come clean. Make them face up to it. We can do a DNA test. I'll go the distance with you. Are you up for that?"

Even as he said it, Dominic felt squeamish; was he really turning Internal Affairs on Father Carl? *Whatever you say, say nothing.*

Dolores ignored him. "And as if that wasn't bad enough, the lying. To cover it up, to move these pervs from parish to parish to commit their crimes again and again—it just means you people don't learn from anything. Your evil just goes on and on."

"You people."

"I don't mean . . . I mean, I do think you're different. That's why I'm here."

Dom heard himself ready to give Dolores the same reply he had been given: "You can't condemn the whole Church for the acts of a few. We should be angry and seek justice, and it is right to do so. But you have to realize we also do good. We cannot forget that. You must find it in yourself to forgive those you can't understand."

But the rhetoric stank like a bad taste in his mouth. The cant must come to a stop.

"Dolores," he said, "I have no excuses for those terrible men. All I can do is do my part to see that they do no more harm. But, anyway, let's talk about your pregnancy. I've made an appointment with the clinic for you on Wednesday. And I'm going to take you."

"I don't think so. I'll go. But I'll go alone."

"OK, but I want a full report."

She nodded and said, "But that's not why I'm here."

This time she had done her homework; her project, it seemed, was to document the species' doom. She kept her cool while reciting the numbers on global warming, the casualties of the war, the extinction of species, the souls lost to starvation—but her knowledge only brought home the pointlessness of caring, the inability to actually do anything to help.

She began sniffling. She rubbed at a smudge on her left heel. The dynamics of her temperament moved like weather on a mountain. But he was prepared. Dominic gave her his handkerchief; he had learned from Father Carl to pocket a clean one every day for just such an occasion. He looked at her and noticed the little mole above her right eye and saw in an instant how she might yet become beautiful.

"You have a big heart, Dolores. A very big soul, but you mustn't lose yourself in it."

She looked at him and quieted herself. She started a laugh.

"What's so funny?" Dominic asked her.

"Nothing," she said and looked away. Sometimes she'd just suddenly fill up with feeling for a stranger. She'd look at a man, a stranger on the bus or another eating a bowl of soup alone in a diner with the spoon in his hand licked clean, and she'd be filled with love. She would want to nibble alongside his loneliness, pet his head as it lay against her breast. There was not enough love in the world to convince every person of his own beauty. The love she was capable of was too big to bear, as if it could dissolve her.

She was liquid with love. If others knew how powerfully she could love, they would drown of her.

"No, really," Dominic said with a paranoid edge, "I want to know what's so funny."

"Everybody, even you, wears, you know, underwear."

"What does that mean?"

"Nothing!" she screamed, surprising both of them. She felt chilly; she closed her eyes. A teardrop squeezed out of the corner of her right eye. All this feeling for others, when she couldn't even stand herself.

"I just have to do something. Sometimes I feel like I just walk down the street—and all the people that pass me? I can see their pain, and it just like *pours* into me. I take it from them; I absorb it all."

"Dolores, unfortunately they will continue to suffer—no matter how much you do," Dominic said.

"Fine, so what? Just get an abortion, just kill yourself?"

"I'm not saying that."

"But how do people even live? How do they get up in the morning, smell themselves and move into their day? How do they eat and just live? How is it all possible?"

"Do you really believe you can change the world?" asked Dominic.

Dolores looked at him sharply. "Don't you?"

"What is it you feel you have to do?" he asked.

"I don't know. Something to make it stop. Make myself stop disappearing. Just walking around like a ghost taking in everything. Everything passing through me. Wasting me. You know Father Carl said I was 'too proud' of my love, my sense of pity. He called it *narcissistic*, and I can't tell you how pissed I felt."

"Why?"

"That he would use the same fucking word as one of my shrinks!"

She got very quiet.

"Dolores?"

"I don't know. Everything."

What would he tell her? "Befriend Jesus Christ? Our Lord will save you?" It all seemed so facile: the great theological systems of Catholicism were almost comprehensive enough to counter every native dread of human life. Almost.

The work to believe was so hard. She might not be up to it. One must have hope in order to have faith. How many times had he invoked the posthumous words of the poet Czeslaw Milosz?

> If there is no God
> Not everything is permitted to man
> He is still his brother's keeper
> And he is not permitted to sadden his brother,
> By saying that there is no God.

And is there anyone left to care whether we believe or not? Whom would we anger by saying so? In the end, all the research proving a chemical or cellular predisposition in the brain to believing in God seemed to miss the point. It doesn't take a damaged brain to learn to love. The gradual and low-grade trauma that accumulates in a single lifetime is reason enough to turn to God.

He stood up and laid his palm on top of her head. A spark of static passed between her hair and his hand.

"Oh," she gasped and reached out quickly to grab his legs and buried her head in his crotch. He had to press into her to keep from falling over backward. Her hot breath instantly aroused him. She looked up at him. She seemed suddenly beautiful and fragile and corruptible; she had this uncanny way of squinting that made her eyes get bigger.

"I know what to do," she said and began moving her hands up the back of his thighs.

He stepped back.

"Come on, let me," she said.

"No," he said firmly.

Immediately, he knew his resolve. Notwithstanding this responsiveness of his body—was it yet another betrayal?

Dolores stood and flung her arms around Dom's neck. Her clutch was so strong, he felt he might have to hurt her to get her off him. He grabbed her shoulders and sat her back down.

"I am really sorry," she cried out. "I'm so stupid."

"You got confused. It's OK."

"You confuse me. Everything confuses me. I ruin everything."

"Why?"

"I should be alone. I can't take it all in, all the pain in the world, all at once. Only God can do that—and he deserves every minute of it, too."

What kind of future could be imagined for such a girl? Would she grow into the woman who showed up at community meetings all alone in an empty row because no one wanted to sit next to her, the crusading woman, friend to no landlord who moved from job to job almost as frequently as from apartment to apartment; the lover-less wreck of a beauty with diminishing options whose poetic despair at the world had calcified into embittered evangelism which she flogged at the open mike of weary city council sessions and regretful poetry readings?

"People don't like me," she said. "And I don't blame them. I'm a freak. I remember when I was a kid, there was a cat who had her litter under our back stairs. But she left behind this one failing kitten, just left it behind to die. I wanted to save it so I made it a little bed in a shoe box, stuffed it with cotton balls, got a dish-towel for a blanket. I got an eyedrop bottle and squeezed out little drops of milk for it. It never took it. It just mewed weakly and stared at me scared. Panting so hard. When I realized I couldn't save it, I wanted to kill it. How dare that little cat refuse my help!"

Dolores started to shout. She stopped herself, cocked her head and looked Dom straight in the eyes. "So I stepped on it and I killed it."

Dominic sighed at her. Her timing was impeccable; she knew how to test his love just at the moment before it was convinced—like an animal retreating to higher ground before a flood.

"That's me. The Savior who can't be saved."

"Listen to me, Dolores, most people can't think beyond their day at work. You want to take responsibility for everything."

Dolores began to weep again. Dominic took her hands, offering guidance, which is as different from advice as it is from wisdom, the only way he knew how. "It's OK to feel so much pain. You are not alone."

"Aaaaaah!" she screamed and threw his hands away. "You'll never stop being such a goddamned priest, will you, not even for one freakin' minute!"

Her mouth curled. "This is why nobody should fall in love with a priest!" she said and started to walk away.

"Dolores, just wait a minute!" Dom shouted. "You . . . you show up in a whirl and then you storm out. Let's slow things down. Being aggressive is not the only way to get to people. You need to tell me . . ."

She put two fingers against his lips. "Do you have what it takes, Father Dominic? That's what it really comes down to, you know."

Dominic watched the very bones in her face shift. Her eyes lowered and grayed. She would destroy herself, maybe him too if he let her. The ability to destroy is what guaranteed her centrality in every situation. She needed others to feel her life as she did: urgent and outsized, naive and corrupt. Like any predator, she was sure of the slice of her claw, the venom in her bite. They never failed her; she kept them vital in practice.

"I see your doubt, Father," she sang mockingly. "Which is not good. How do you expect to guide us with that?"

Dominic braced his shoulders as if to hold up the sky. She could undo him; he was exhausted by the pressure to be responsive to her need, whole before her despair, orthodox in his guidance, agnostic before her sexuality.

Her voice suddenly softened. She put a palm against his cheek. "Are you as tough as Father Carl? Are you smart enough, strong enough to know what to do with me?"

"Dolores . . ."

She looked at him. "Still want me to flush my baby down the toilet, great and holy Father Dominic?

She clucked.

"Fucking hypocrite."

Dolores kicked her toes hard against her bedroom doorjamb—once, twice, three times until the pain had time to register. "Shit," she cried out and hopped on her good foot. Warm blood rushed to the new center of pain. But it never lasted—and it was not even a half minute before she felt the shame of Dominic's rejection like a pain in the gut.

I know what to do.

Had she actually said that?

"Fucking idiot!" she screamed at herself.

"Dolores, your language," her mother chided from the living room.

As if she even knew what to do. As if anyone who knew what they were doing would say such a thing. And he had rejected her! How mortifying was that? He was probably repulsed by the idea—she couldn't even seduce a horny priest. She had never been very good at knowing when to touch someone and when not to; when to be touched.

Such a freaking nube! She had only taken the lead once before. One late summer night, she had started talking to some guy in a McDonalds on Whalley; the way he held his Big Mac with his two hands killed her. His third and fourth fingernails were ragged while the others were nicely manicured. His bald spot was perfectly sweet and round, like a halo. She wanted to kiss it. His wore zipper boots and a wedding band. He had a little ketchup in the corner of his mouth. He said he was being bad; he had already eaten dinner but was still hungry. "Who knows; KFC might be next," he said. They began imagining details about the lives of the other customers coming in and out, tried to decode the movements of the drug deals that were going down in the men's room. He ordered a Quarter Pounder and wondered if he would fit into his suit the next morning. She shared his fries. He went to his car and made a call on his cell phone. When he came back she noticed he had taken the ring off, leaving a pale and pudgy band around his finger like a raised rope burn. He bought them each a milkshake, drove her to the top of East Rock, parked his car and took out his penis. It was hard and red and angry—she was a little afraid but also very curious. The hard-on it was called, and it looked as if it were a difficult thing to bear. The man seemed different too; he had been funny and interesting but became single-minded and serious, as if the whole of him had been panicked into his erection. The penis seemed so needy; it looked ready to have a tantrum. It jerked to attention when she touched it and passed her thumb over its head, which was already wet and sticky. The man moaned. "OK, baby, just blow me," he said, and she had no idea what he was talking about but figured he knew what he liked so she leaned over, pursed her lips together, took a deep breath and let the air out gradually, moving her head slowly side to side like a fan.

"What the fuck?" the man said, pushing her away. He looked at her in shock and then started laughing. "Holy mother of God," he said. "How old are you anyway?" He put his deflated dick back in his pants and dropped her off at the base of the park. Handing her twenty bucks, he said with a chuckle, "Hey, stay off the streets. You might have done a lot worse."

The memory was so mortifying that just recalling it made her blurt out a little Tourette's yelp. How could her experience be so inept, immature and inadequate when her desire was so deep, the profoundest thing any grown up-could feel, she imagined. How she longed for the close crop of Father Carl's white head between her legs, his gray beard rough against her thighs, his deep voice humming. She might have even healed him with love; that's how strong she felt it.

And then there was Father Dominic. She felt bad about lying to him. There had been no cat. She read that story somewhere. It didn't matter; the story could have been true. She might have done a thing like that. He took her seriously. She could see that. And that was what she wanted. That's all that mattered. And, anyway, maybe she was talking about herself; maybe she was the one being left behind and stamped out.

Father Dominic was being so sweet; one might almost think he cared about her. But she couldn't fool herself. He was a priest; it was his job to care for people. It had nothing to do with her. She knew he would feel relieved when she was gone. He must feel that her pain, while extreme, was not unlike that of others. And there was that element in his caring, as if he couldn't wait for people to leave him alone and go away. Other people seemed to be his problem, but she had the hunch that maybe it was Father Dominic who was the one who should be walking away. Only God could understand how extraordinary was her suffering: how the only thing that could save her would destroy her.

"Some people just can't be saved," Father Carl had said to her when his cancer was advanced and the doctors stopped treatment.

The night of the encounter with Dominic, Dolores got no sleep at all. She dragged her tired body out of bed into the slushy light of winter before dawn. She would have to creep out of her room so as not to wake up her mother, who was snoring in her chair. Peering at herself in the mirror above her bureau, she inserted the nose ring into the hole that had nearly healed, opening it up again. A little bubble of blood colored the pressure on her sinuses. A tear formed in her eye, and its suggestion made her cry.

Her mother stirred in the other room, and Dolores quieted, fantasizing that suddenly her mother were able to get up out of her chair and come to her and know to say exactly the right thing. She would know how to say the thing that would set it all right because she was her mother.

When she was younger, Dolores's mother used to take her to the cemetery to visit her father's grave every second Sunday after Mass. They made a day out of it, packing a lunch, washing the plastic flowers, picking weeds and the odd scrap of litter. For her, it was a day in the park.

But that was a long time ago. Who knows how long it's been since her mother even left the apartment?

Dolores stood before her mother reclining in the living room. How selfish and wasteful sleep was (when there was so much to feel, to see, to hurt). The television flickered soundlessly like an aquarium. The terrible beauty of things off-time, the streetlight out the window, the theatrical cast of the trees, the prospect of her night crawl—all of this softened her hostility toward her mother into pity—pity at her great breasts sagging onto her belly, at the number of chins doubling up to support her head, at the bubbling purr of her snore.

Her mother's hands lay on the arms of the chair—palms up, a supplicant's silence. Dolores saw intelligence in them, as if all the inert energy in that massive body surged into her mother's brief and elegant fingertips. As if wanting to be released. And she thought how easy it would be just to do her right there and then—take a pillow to the face and snuff out all that unwanted, useless life. How easy it would be, really, to crush her, to give her mother what she wanted, to give her what she lived for.

She kissed her mother's oily forehead. As her snores halted and her breathing shallowed, Dolores left the apartment.

After the 5:30 Mass, Dom jogged across the parking lot to the recreation hall, where a group of men was already waiting on the steps. One of the windowpanes was broken by a stone that had been thrown through it; the plastic garbage bag he had hastily covered it with sucked in the wind. Abandoned scaffolding sat against the wall, stripped of optimism. The building moved him in the way it held its own against nature's reclamation, its see-saw of decay and promise, somewhere between wasteland and construction site. He kept seeing it half-alive, half-dead: tarnished, toothless with loose tiles, caught in the flux of incompletion: the not yet done and the done with.

Ronnie had a large carton of Dunkin' Donuts coffee and was already pouring the coffee into Styrofoam cups. To a man, they took it black.

Ronnie handed Dom a cup of "Saint Dunkin' ". "There he is, the man in black. Showing up late like this, Father, we're starting to worry that you don't really love us." Ronnie gave him the cup and roughly grabbed his shoulder.

"I'd leave the key under the doormat, but everybody knows you can't trust a drunk," Dominic replied.

The eleven men laughed and filed in after Dom, making an effort to neutralize the damp funk of the room, opening the windows that would open, unfolding the aluminum chairs and arranging them in a circle. Dom started his benediction. Out of the corner of his eye he spotted that worrisome splotch of black mold growing under the broken window.

This was his primary ministry now, his penalty for the drunk driving charge: an eight-week therapeutic workshop, "Men in Recovery." Dom knew most of these guys from the regular AA meetings held in the rec hall; he even loved them, with the kind of allowances made for an extended family.

That was the big joke about Alcoholics Anonymous: it's where everybody knows your name.

Ronnie had first made contact with Dominic in the confessional: "It's been many years since my last confession."

"How many?"

"Can't even remember."

"Why have you come now?"

"I was a devout kid, you know, even considered becoming a priest."

"But you grew up," Dom said quickly.

"Yeah, I guess, you know."

"So why now?"

"Because it all gets harder and harder. I've taken to the bottle some, cheated on my wife."

"Yes."

"So, I've come—first—for forgiveness."

"What do you mean by that?"

"Father, you're asking some tough questions today. I don't know: first confession and then Communion."

"Not so fast. The sacraments are the markers for a life as a Catholic; not just steps toward self-acceptance. First, you have to study and reembrace the Catechism."

"OK, OK. I mean I don't want to do this . . . insincerely or nothing."

"Good. It's very important that you understand that. Read the Gospels. Study the Catechism. Then you should find a priest to work through and test your readiness."

There was a pause. "Would you be such a priest, Father?"

Dom hadn't answered, and Ronnie never followed up.

Ronnie had become the ringleader of the AA workshop, sponsoring new members; he had never missed a meeting and usually began the "sharing."

". . . You know, all those clubs. The Elks, The Moose, The Mongoose, whatever: I couldn't wait to get into those meetings—with all their 'refreshments,' if you know what I mean. At eighteen, I was like, 'sign me up.' "

The men in the group nodded their heads knowingly.

"Of course, by then, I'd already been drinking for ten years."

Chairs scraped against the rough wood of the floor. Everyone laughed. Jimmy slapped Ronnie on the back and asked him where he could get an application for the Mongoose Club. They were witnessing each other; the white gospel, importing the rhetoric of teasing and self-deprecation they had learned in the bars; they had rid themselves of alcohol, but they would never unlearn the social structure.

Dominic had heard this story before; had heard all these stories before: the hitting of rock bottom, the jackpot. The alcoholic's state of mind had two possibilities: either suicidal or homicidal, the point at which one can't get drunk or sober.

Paul said, "I'm still dealing with the hangover. I was drunk for thirty-plus years, so I'm just getting around to forgiving Nixon, Ford, Carter and Reagan. Hopefully, I'll be dead before I get to Bush."

At the end of the seventy-five minutes, Dominic asked whether any of the men who hadn't had the chance to speak felt compelled to share.

"Nah, I gotta go," Frank said, "my wife she's giving me crap. 'Another meeting?' she shrieks at me. I say, 'What, would you prefer I went to Liffy's and knocked back a couple?' "

"Well, I'm done with that shit," Robbie said.

"You signed?"

"Signed, sealed, delivered." Robbie nodded.

"So, you're a free man," Frank said.

Robbie sat still.

"Bittersweet, though," Frank said softly.

"Yeah," Robbie said. "Saw her Friday night. She brings my kids over on the nights I work late, puts them to bed and waits for me to come home. So she's sitting there drinking my Coke, you know, eating my chips, watching my cable, and I say 'OK, thanks, you can go now.' "

"Yeah?"

"And she says, 'What, are you trying to get rid of me or something?' So I say, 'Well, I tried like a madman to change your mind and keep you but, yeah . . . , now I'm trying to get rid of you.' "

Frank patted Robbie on the knee, and the men sat in silence in their circle.

They hadn't had a new member in quite some time; the group needed one. A new set of stories with a confirming theme: the unpredictability but the certainty of the "mystery of recovery."

"So, anybody hear from Vinnie?" asked Luis.

"Oh man, I've been worrying about him," said Frank. "Must be out there homeless, at this point."

"He's not homeless," Ronnie said, offended.

"No? Then what's his address?" Frank asked.

The circle quieted again.

"Shall we pray?" Dominic asked, finally breaking in.

"Before we break, Father, how about an update on Father Carl?" Rocco asked.

A mineral taste rose in Dominic's mouth. He heard the old man's voice rebuking him, "Dominic, don't you see the essential humility these men bring? A generosity of spirit in regarding each other." Starlight. Starbright, whatever.

"Father," Ronnie asked, "how's the old man?"

Dominic lowered his head.

"Jesus, Father," Ronnie said, "weren't you gonna say something?"

The men looked at him; Dominic asked them to bow their heads and join him in prayer.

"You know," he said, "maybe the appropriate thing is to repeat something Father Carl used to say: 'When we talk about serenity, when we talk about peace, the mystery of recovery, we are NOT talking about a lack of chaos, relief of stress, avoidance of adversity. It does not mean the end of trouble. Serenity is not experienced as a kind of absence—but as a kind of presence, a "set" of the mind, a base degree of sanity you come to rely on.' "

The men grumbled in affirmation.

"The Lord be with you."

"And also with you."

The men folded the chairs and stacked them against the wall. Dominic could swear he heard the splintering metal of hinges as he walked over and examined the black mold on the wall. The spidery figure had horns. This was definitely some living thing; it might take more than a rag soaked in bleach. He made a mental note to call someone.

As he locked the door, Dominic remembered asking Father Carl's advice the night before he took over the workshop. The elder had replied: "Just remember, don't beat them up. Everyone's an addict. Everyone has his addiction. They should count themselves lucky that they know what theirs is."

"Really? What is yours, Father? What is it you had to kick?"

"My faith."

Given the bishop's warning, Father Dominic logged on with some anxiety. Instead of his blog he checked into a private chat room—an invitation-only site for the dozen or so priests in the Northeast hosting these Men in Recovery workshops. It was one of the few opportunities for fraternity in the priesthood. He wrote:

> Comment #89 by FrDom at 9:04 p.m.
> So, tonight, I was asked, "Where are the new drunks?" Where are our people, Brothers, our natural parish, those blotto sheep that are falling down in the sewer? I see them on the street: why aren't they finding their way to God? Or at least coming in for a free meal or two in the soup kitchen? How is your work with alcoholics this week?

> Comment #90 by SJlife at 10:37 p.m.
> I still have a lot of trouble with the word itself—*alcoholic*. I heard the confession of a man the other day who actually drank more than most guys I know. But he refused to call himself an alcoholic. The word seems reductive. It lacks agency. It externalizes the demons,

like moving in with a police dog. Its vigilance operates from the outside in. It still gives the drink way too much power.

This guy, a real hotshot in the community, very successful, fit as a fiddle, runs the marathon even. Drinks a fifth of gin every night. Every night! And wouldn't admit he was alcoholic until he showed up three weeks ago—and then only when his wife left him. He was vain even in the way he regarded his failures.

Alcoholics always exaggerate. About everything except how much they drink. They expect things to go wrong, make them helpless. So they can be ruined and start over. You know what they say about nervous breakdowns: "mission accomplished."

You think you are fighting off the demons except that it seems THEY already know how you will die. They already have an image of you in storage: floating in a jar in some laboratory, eyes shut against a future, limbs curling into a fetal position. All homunculus."

Comment #91 by FrDom at 10:55 p.m.
Demons. Strange for us to be internalizing the devil so literally, especially now that we've theologically neutered him.

Funny thing; I guess I want sobriety without a higher power. To me, the tough part was not so much day by day but day after day.

Comment #92 by SJlife at 11:08 p.m.
Lord make me sober, but not yet.

Here's a story for you. A real cautionary tale.

True Confessions. OK? Last week, I was flying home from this eight-day retreat. It had gone very well, but I was good and tired.

The stewardess came by with her trolley and asked me, "Can I get you something to drink?"

And I just said, "Yes."

It was weird. Didn't feel momentous or anything. Four and a half years of sobriety. Gone. Just like that. So I paid her five bucks for one of her little airplane bottles of Scotch, so tiny it almost didn't feel real, Monopoly money. Then I poured it over the ice in the plastic glass, and I drank it. Like a day hadn't gone by. So then I went and hunted the stewardess down and spent ten more bucks. At 35,000 feet above sea level, whiskey looks good even in a ribbed, plastic glass—amber and elegant and lit sharp in the ice cubes.

This lady in the seat beside me, who had been nice and quiet up till then, introduced herself. Normally, I give off the "don't approach" vibe when I travel. I was in disguise, wearing a big sweater which hid my collar, and so she didn't know I was a priest. She talked and talked, and as I was feeling all nice and warm inside, I listened. She asked, and so I told her about me and my family. Turns out we're both from Rhode Island, and so we talked about growing up there, and then she did something that stunned me.

"Can I ask you a personal question?" she said.

"Like what?" I asked warily.

She turned in her seat so she could face me squarely. She looked me right in the eye and asked, "Why are you so sad?"

I don't know what happened, but I just went waterworks. Tears streaming down my face. She put her hand on my arm and squeezed it, and I started bawling like a little baby. Just shaking.

She stroked my back and took out a tissue and wiped my cheeks. She was the essence of compassion.

And then she did it. She asked me if I "had Jesus Christ in my life." If I was ready to be reborn. And I just went bananas. I actually got really pissed off. Who did she think she was, introducing ME to Christ! Like some stranger walking up, ringing your doorbell, offering to give you a tour of your own house. As if she even understood Christ, with her saccharine, evangelical, megachurch, feel-good, fundamentalist puppet god.

I was enraged. I had been evangelized. I had been slimed. I started screaming at her, "Who do you think you are? Like you even know anything about Christ!" The stewardess had to come over and tell me to quiet down, I was so out of control.

I asked for another drink, but she actually cut me off!

I changed my seat and sat there fuming; I really wanted nothing but to go back there and tell her off again. She sat there so calmly reading a Bible she had taken out of her bag. As if it existed for passing the time, for solace!

Comment #93 by JfrJ at 11:17 p.m.
I love that you got evangelized. That's like bringing a glass of water to the river to convince them both.

But let me play devil's advocate, though, Father. Don't you think people deserve their own version of Christ? Whatever works?

Comment #94 by SJlife at 11:18 p.m.
NO, NO, NO, NO, NO. That's the whole point! There is no other version. That's what the Catholic Church is all about. It took two thousand years of power struggles, military crusades, institutional

warfare, millennia of inspiring art, music, architecture, literature, philosophy, science, and it is NOT OVER yet.

What is it, the Gallup poll? The one which says nine out of ten Americans believe in a god who loves them? I mean, what are we looking for here, a pension plan? Money in the bank? We can't simply define God as anything you need Him to be. It's not only about your comfort level or awe before the Creator, or whatever way you decide you need Him: great watcher, fulfiller of unfulfillable needs. He is not there to fill in the blank.

Fundamentalists are our real enemy here, worse than atheists.

Comment #95 by FrDom at 11:37 p.m.
Take it easy, Father. We're on the same side here. Let's get down to it. What is it that made you want to drink? Can you get to that feeling in that moment when you said yes?

Comment #96 by SJlife at 11:55 p.m.
I don't know; it's hard to get to that. It was just so easy. Blink: I'm back. And even though I loved the taste of the Scotch going down, its effect on me felt strangely, I don't know . . . impersonal. My desire for it seemed bottomless, insatiable and anxious. Was there enough gas to fly the plane? Could there possibly be enough Scotch?

It's like AA has it all wrong. We alcoholics have not a failure but an abundance of will—the deadliest weapon, the urge to self-destruct. The dread behind drinking is that we'll wake up to learn we've survived.

I don't know. Maybe I was out of line. "I'll pray for you"—that's all that lady would say when I freaked out on her.

Comment #97 by JfrJ at 12:05 a.m.

I cry on airplanes. All the time. In the toilet. I do, I don't know what it is. About 3⁄4 of the way through the flight, I make my way to the toilet and make like a big baby.

Monday morning's newspaper carried Father Carl's obituary, the listing for his funeral at 10:00 a.m. Tuesday and the news story that named Our Lady of Fatima as one of the parishes the archdiocese planned to close within six months. There was no denying it. Despite all the phone calls of support, Dominic knew the end was near.

There were practical things to sort out; things to attend to before they were forgotten altogether. He needed to polish the beautiful candlesticks and the host plate—forged from the melted gold of the wedding bands of widows who lost husbands in the two world wars of the last century. The censer, the bell, the cruets, the chalice, the carefully evolved accoutrements of the altar: he would clean and polish each of them perhaps for the last time.

Father Carl hated Vatican II, with its vernacular flattening of the Mass. He hated turning away from the Tabernacle to face the congregation as if they were an audience. Dominic would chant the funeral High Mass in Latin to honor Father Carl—he had called it "groaning," and few priests had relished more the cadence of lament, delivering it with the confidence of praise, breaking through language into ritual. Dominic would revive the tradition this Sunday, just as the parish itself would begin its end. The breath of truth would be spoken here. He would draw the pews back to their original rows, in defiance of the "theater in the round" design. The congregation would once again sit lined up before the priest who would face away from them, marking the vanishing point, staring into the dogmatic, low-key, cool air, slow heartbeat of the Mass.

He would arrive early wearing black pants, his lace-ups and the banded black shirt with collar. In the bad breath of the neglected sanctuary, he would shawl the amice around his shoulders. Then he would kiss the bunched-up alb and pull it down around his head to his waist, belting it with the cincture rope. Next he would cross the stole across his breast. Then he could pin the maniple to his sleeve. Last, the chasuble. He would be robed, perhaps for the last time.

In honor of Father Carl, the choir would sing the evening compline every night at nine o'clock for a week. The church itself would listen to the choir singing plainchant out of sight, hidden within its bosom. How connected Dominic felt to the intractable fact of its timeline, the sheer unlikelihood of its survival, art out of prayer like light out of darkness. The physical calm that came over him as he listened: animal still, like a horse in a dirt field. He felt it like an absence, in the cavity of his abdomen, even in the space between his toes. The bath had gone cold; the magic had staled.

The Mass would run out of its beautiful words: *Alleluia. Hosanna. Amen.* And then he would hang the vestments up, and there would be one more exotic thing lost to the world, one more sacrifice to the corroding grayness of enlightened taste—this great truth that was supposed to last forever, or at least beyond any time able to measure its end.

The answering machine beeped red, and Father Dominic cued it up to hear Dolores speak a long message, each of her sentences curling up like a question.

> Father Dominic, I just wanted to tell you—oh, by the way, it's me, Dolores . . . but you probably figured that out by now. Like

you know my voice. Huh, which is pretty obvious anyway since I just said who it was . . . Whoo. Anyway, to say I'm, to basically apologize for the way I, for what I said, the thing, that terrible thing I said about you? I didn't really mean it, you know, I don't think you are that, and also I shouldn't have put the f-word in front of it. Oh, God, what am I saying? What I mean to say, the point of my calling you and leaving this message?—is that I didn't mean to say all that to you. I did because I got so angry; I mean you made me so angry. I don't know how you could suggest . . . how you think it OK for me to do what you said. I mean, who is it even worse to be—for you to put me into that position, or for you to be in that position of telling to me to do that awful thing? I mean, what if I told on you? I almost did tell—"

The answering machine cut her off midsentence, and she began a second: "Wow. Did I really let myself go on that way? The machine gives me just ten seconds more to finish up. Phew! Let me tell you why I called in the first place. OK, here goes."

The machine beeped her off again. Next message: "OK. Let me just leave this very short message this time to say I am sorry for making your life so difficult right now. I know you have a lot of stuff going on. But you know so do I too. Bye, uhmmm it's me, Dolores."

End of message.

The church filled up quickly with townspeople and the wreaths sent from various civil societies of the greater region honoring the dead priest, marking their community stature; several deans and officers from the university, the VFW, the Knights of Columbus, the family, the Elks, the mayor's office, the chief of police, a consortium of small businesses from State Street, the local insurance and tax companies, both the office of the district attorney and the local public defenders. Dom surveyed the spoiling flowers with a certain distaste. There was easily a few grand worth of floral arrangements here. What a waste; why not just donate the money to the Church? This made Dom feel small and parochial, like a Judas resenting the oiling of Christ's feet. The poor will be with us always. When would he stop believing there was something he could do? He could only manage one person at a time. That had to be enough.

The parking lot was fuller than it had been in years. The police department had closed off the main intersecting streets to traffic, the first time it had bothered doing that since the president's last visit to his alma mater. It was a mild first of December with a consoling winter light that paled the white bricks of the church. The pews filled. Dom looked out at the crowd and felt refreshed by their number; it was like an opening night.

In how many funeral parlors had Dominic watched family and friends honor the dead by laughing and weeping, consoling themselves by pretending the dead could overhear the flattering remarks, the jokes, the teasing affection? As if the dead were peeking just there behind the curtains, listening quietly, smiling to themselves, nodding their heads, watching our every move, perhaps pre-knowing our every thought—even if we turned away till at last we forgot them, or remembered only what they meant.

The chapel itself seemed buoyed; it was used to the dozen or so regulars that showed up reliably every day for Father Carl's 6 a.m. Mass. They had already come to that morning's predawn service, and they were here again a few hours later. He had always envied the way they went off after Mass to go to their jobs, hard and serious, their certain place in the world: their industry, their gift for endurance, the toughness of their faith. Day after day, they showed up before dawn, their faces dark with the need to be exhorted, as if their prayers were a protest against their very purpose.

This morning, they huddled together in the back row in an unlikely solidarity; the church was too crowded to let them sit scattershot as usual among the pews in the front half of the church. Before the procession, Dominic shook each of their hands and thanked them for coming. He knew each of their situations; he had listened to their confessions for years now. They nodded back at him; he knew their faith to be a very private thing, local and personal. They cared more for the fate of the weekly soup kitchen than they did for the affairs of the Vatican. Where would they take their sweet humility once all this was gone?

He scanned the crowd for Dolores, not sure whether he was hoping to see her or not. No sign yet.

Dom had not bothered to raise the heat for the occasion. People would be forced to sit close to each other. The heat of their bodies would warm the usual chill of the chapel. There were some complex dynamics at work here. Divorces, remarriages, hires and fires. Respect for the dead forced a civility over the room; sadness took the edge off a lot of these resentments.

The night before, Dom had met with the family, Carl's two brothers. George was the younger brother, a youthful sixty-year-old, a successful stockbroker who wore a bespoke suit that shamed the off-the-rack best of the local brass. Broad-shouldered, George came at you with a bright smile and a firm handshake that was instantly familiar and yet aloof at once. He could see something of Father Carl's ease and strength here as a kind of bearing, a rearing; the Giulini brothers had been trained to get what they wanted.

The same was true for Father Carl's twin brother, Joseph, who had come at Dom sideways to reaffirm how important it was to give some testimonial. He was the director of a good regional repertory theater about ninety minutes away and had from time to time come down for dinner with his brother.

Dom looked at these two men and wished he could study them; they could teach him something, he felt. The whole lot of them, in fact: the two wives, first marriages each, elegant, helpful and alert, who saw to the details of the funeral luncheon like generals in a war room, the four nephews and two nieces. Dom noted the ease of their being together. How Father Carl had been loved. How natural they seemed together. The Giulini family was compelling; they made him feel like he wanted to be part of it, let him feel as if he were. Then they would bury their brother.

What would they say if they knew about Dolores?

All eulogy is suspect.

The hundreds of eulogies he had heard—had said, performed. Some of them were polite, routine, evasive, a white sheet taking the form of the body it had been laid over. Others he had heard so lovely in their contradictions, part lament and part celebration. Eventually, as time passes, we know what happens next—to legacies, to reputations, to those left behind. To secrets. The dead don't get to know. Dom understood that testimonials are most suspicious when they appear most deeply felt, those that sputter and stop and fall apart and wash away in tears. He knew in his heart that true grief is overcome, inarticulate. Silent. *Saying Nothing*

Carl's twin walked up to the lectern. Dominic watched him, did the negative calculations: a bit trimmer, nose bent slightly to the right, but the similarity was alarming except for an essential physicality that Joseph lacked. Even in old age, Carl had a heavy-limbed and deliberate walk, while Joseph was more skittish and jittery. Carl also had a ready smile that could redress any awkwardness; Joseph's expression was watchful and suspicious. Standing before the crowd, Joseph took a moment to collect his thoughts. He looked up and said, "Good morning." He sounded so much like Carl that the room itself shifted. Several sniffles could be heard in the congregation.

Joseph took a few folded pages out of his inside coat pocket and read:

> Each of us has lost someone special today. A friend, a brother, a counselor. I have lost my fraternal twin, a measuring stick, my other half—excuses to my wife. I want to tell you about the man, but the only thing I can think to say is how he was what I am not.
>
> You know, in lots of ways, he was a tough son of a gun, our Carl. A tough judge of character. I remember once he said to me about all his nieces and nephews—and sorry to say this to all of you sitting here, but he said, "You know they're each of them nice enough but, I don't know, do any of them have any fire in the belly?"
>
> I replied, "Well, I'm not sure how to answer that since I'm responsible for half of them." But the point is he didn't love us less for our failures, only wanted us to be more.
>
> But let me tell you about the boy, about our dear little Carli. You always felt Carli knew what he was doing, knew that he wanted to be a priest.
>
> I never knew a more religious man than he, and I speak about this as a pure atheist, true, but maybe a little bit of an envious atheist. I felt a personal lack of religion as deeply and intuitively as Carli felt the presence of his own. It was one of the first and clearest distinctions between us. Or divisions. Or perhaps destinations. As a boy, Carli was the first to sign up for altar boy service—he counted the days the way I would later for my driver's permit. He said to me that he knew he wanted to be a priest from that first day up on the altar. He had the calling. He almost

couldn't help that. Nonetheless, he was the first kid in the seventh grade to go on a date.

At this the congregation laughed, grateful for the break.

And my parents, bless their soul, were about as happy as anyone could be. To have a son become a priest—there just isn't a higher honor for us Catholics. Especially for my mother. Having a priest for a son said we were a good and blessed family. She loved us all—equally, I believe that. But she adored Carli. Revered him and his faith.

I didn't get his faith. The more Carli was drawn to the Church, the more I withdrew. As a teenager, I just found him weird and wanted to separate myself in every way possible. He went off to board at a seminary high school. As a young man, I condescended to that, just didn't get his life. Now, an old man with my own mortality in sight, I envy it. Was there a better way for him to live his life? Wasn't he more faithful to the original idea of what his life was for than many of us can claim?

I regret that my inability to understand his choices in life made my love unavailable to him at times. But that was a two-way street also. There was something about Carli's faith that allowed him to shut out anything unnecessary to it. More than making him who he was, his faith more importantly helped him decide what he wasn't, what he needn't concern himself with, decide what was unnecessary. I am hurting to say I became one of those things.

I want to leave you with one last thought. Just before he died, I asked my brother for a favor: I wanted him to hear my confession. He agreed. I got inside that box right over there and kneeled down. He slid the grate open. I told him it had been fifty-eight years since my last confession. He said he knew and that they'd been waiting. I laughed, but then I told him about everything. I

> just talked and talked, and he listened. I cried, and I believed that something happened there. I felt relieved, a little bit humbled, a little less complicated. He told me to forgive myself and others; this is what he understood it was to love God. I told him I loved him, and he returned the sentiment.

He put the papers back in his pocket and for a moment looked a bit lost, as if surprised that there was a room filled with people looking up at him. "I guess . . . that's it," he said and made his way back to his seat.

It was time for Dom to say High Mass; that was a privilege always given to Father Carl, he felt the loss most poignantly in the first reading from the Book of Job:

> Oh that my words were written!
> Oh that they were inscribed in a book!
> Oh that with an iron pen and lead they were graven in the rock forever!

The Liturgy had its own diction; its text registered more like behavior than syntax. The touch of the crystal cruets to the golden chalice. The gentle rustle of his vestments. The transubstantiation of the wafer translucent in his hands as he raised it above his head. "Take this and eat of it." It was always going to be his parish; he was always the heir apparent. It was meant to be a peaceful passage of power, a son burying a father. Everything had seemed right about it. But it was just like God to show him the illegitimacy of his ambition at the very moment he intended to realize it.

The physiology of the funeral service had always intrigued him: the emotional high of the eulogies, the readings, the public posturing: the kneeling, standing, bowing during the Mass almost automatic and then, finally, the private prayer after Communion, after all the takers had returned to their seat. Like little children who are consoled after taking a scare, resolved to be good. They were all quiet. The chalice shone on the altar. He had been very careful not to spill a drop. In the quiet, Dominic had trained himself to hear the collective buzz of the private prayers, like the reading rooms of public libraries, giving purpose to the height of the arches of the church. In the chalice, Father Dominic found and ate the remaining few hosts himself and let them seal against the roof of his mouth. He cleared the altar and walked back to the pastor's chair.

As he lowered his eyes, Dom listened to the muffle of the congregants nestling into their pews. An alert silence fell over them, each of them fed, renewed, ready to be rediscovered. Still and expectant like books lined in a library. The collective heartbeat slowed down to a murmur.

Dominic dropped his own head into his hands, into the ritual darkness of prayer, and he listened to this new grief for his mentor, the person who had drawn him forward, who had worked to pull him toward a legitimate faith and who might now see that he had been wrong, that he had overestimated the younger man who could now grieve for both of them together: the convinced and the unconvinced, the good faith and the in bad faith, the future and its illusion. What, in the end, had Father Carl felt for Dominic really? Less a love than a kind of marshaling, a tough love, a shepherd's lonely love.

Dom felt his throat tighten and pressure build in his head. He had come to bury himself, perhaps.

He could hear people giving in to the discomfort in their knees, giving each other permission to settle into their seats. A few coughs landed on him like rocks onto a road. Dom walked slowly to the front of the altar. He cleared his throat, adjusted his robes and looked out at the expectant faces before him. Father Carl haunted his eulogy. *Say nothing.*

> When I see us all together today, I do so with a kind of nostalgia. And affection. I don't want to be a scold today. Today of all days. I am quieted by you, by the feeling in this room, a kind of reverence. By which I mean not only the usual connotations—awe and love—but something much more controlled: obedience. We are here together with every good intention; we gather with formal intention, to commit to a ceremony.
>
> Which is something Father Carl would have appreciated because to love him was to love an institution—by which I mean both his stature and the Church that he stood for. He was very much an orthodox Catholic, strict and unwavering. What the Church thought, Father Carl thought. He was truly a messenger of God.
>
> Father Carl's sense of justice was fundamental. He believed in several nonnegotiable principles, tough and simple:
>
> Do unto others as you would have them do unto you.
> The poor must be housed and fed.
> No one must interfere with another man's right to earn a living wage.
> Women and homosexuals must not be ordained.
> Children must be protected from harm.
> Life must be protected, from the unborn to the convicted to the dying.
>
> These are the things he believed in. These were the things he wouldn't argue. He was the real deal, ladies and gentlemen. A Christian soldier. He raised his faith the way a father would a proud and stubborn child: tough, unsparing yet indulgent at times. Life is nothing but experience, guided by doing the right thing. There is no other formula. Just do a good job at living.

> Father Carl's faith was very deep and very private, yet he made a gift of it to us. He became more and more institutional, which is to say that the Church and in particular we, his congregation, had the luck to have Catholicism embodied for us by this man. But we must not despair. We must remain Roman Catholics in the way he taught us to be.

Dominic heard the click in his mouth. He was going to choke on his own words. He felt the turmoil in his gut, and a cool sweat spread across his brow. That bottle of wine the night before. He was starting to sound specious; this obsession to perpetuate the myth that the old man had to appear to die beautifully, with a spiritual simplicity, as if with a will to be born. He had to finish up.

"Father Carl believed in this church. In this parish. In you. I would like to end by quoting something he said to me near the end. '*Say nothing.*' "

He heard the voice of the old man. He paused as he decided what not to say and what to say.

"He said to me that the Church will always be. You, I, the bishop, the cardinals—the pope himself—all belong to it. It does not belong to them. It will always be here. This building does belong to them, though. And this will not always be here. There is a lesson in humility here. If the Church were to lose all its possessions, its buildings, its people, it would still exist. And as far as your work as a priest, he would tell me, you are not meant to complete or perfect it, but neither are you allowed to stop working at it."

The doors of the chapel opened, and Dolores walked in. Half the congregation turned and looked. The bishop crossed his legs and fingered the part in his hair. She was holding a handkerchief to her nose. She took a seat in the second-to-last row.

Despite the fact that he had said too much, Dominic knew that he had evaded the big question. What Father Carl had said in the hospital, at the end, was intolerable.

"Is there something you want to tell me?" he asked the old man.

But there was no confession of any secret sin, no coming clean, nothing about Dolores. It was fear of death that drove Father Carl crawling onto Dominic's lap like a hurt kitten, unblinking, unthinking, wild with pain from the cancer which spread like a block of lead through his body, growing sadistically within him from the bottom up so that the only thing left that worked was his mind, fully grasping the extent of the pain, to wonder at the wickedness that would deserve such pain—tracing the path of the cancer as it colonized each of his organs, imperially, one by one, squeezing everything hopeful out of him, a river of doubt rising till it lapped at the bridge of his nose, catching his breath against the panic. *For the waters have come up to my neck*.

Father Carl had been utterly convinced of an afterlife, the only sure reward to which he felt entitled but, in the end, renounced it: "I'm not ready. I don't want to die. I'm not ready," he had said to Dominic.

Dominic held the old man in his arms, trying to quiet him, scared like Adam in the garden.

"I was nineteen years old when I entered the seminary. Nineteen! If I were nineteen today . . . No, I couldn't imagine it."

"What do you believe?" Dominic asked him, knowing that he wanted, in the terrible end of it—resenting the lack of choice—to exchange redemption for one more day of life.

Dominic closed his eyes against the image and vowed to say nothing. He looked at the pew in which Father Carl's family sat together, anchoring themselves in these final moments with their hands folded in their laps—working so hard to reconfigure in their minds the treachery of letting go, the dread of sliding away, the pull of the other side. What it would take for them to get up and walk away, make their way down the long aisle, chins quivering and eyes tearing as they avoided the gaze of the witnesses lined up in the pews they passed. The betrayal of moving on, the gravity of going forward.

Dominic looked at the casket placed with the head toward the altar, a position saved for the clergy, facing his people as he did in his life. All that was left of an unpropertied—childless, yet—priest: the selfishness of the body having to be carried off like a child on the backs of the living to its tomb. The sheer weight of this stiffening thing, obstinate and cold and silent. Why leave this behind?

In the end, during the last rites, Father Carl had come around. Dom had wanted a deathbed confession, a coming clean. What he got instead was a deathbed conversion, a shedding, a white-hot moment of truth, a panicked realization of self-delusion, a jump off the cliff to sudden, meaningless, clarifying death.

"What do you believe?" Dominic had the courage again to ask the old man. It was so hard, those last days, when the old priest was too weak even to swallow, except maybe swallow his own words. He would go out in orthodoxy.

"In our Lord, Jesus Christ, the only begotten son of God. In our Savior."

It was as simple and essential a statement as the remaining breaths the man had to utter it and more evidence that it was going to be necessary for Father Dominic to leave the Church.

And finally the words that haunted Dom: "*Whatever you say, say nothing*," spoken as his eyes lowered like a heavy curtain over a proscenium.

If I do not remember thee, let my tongue cleave to the roof of my mouth (Psalm 137).

Are you tough enough to do God's will? Dolores had asked him. Can you deliver Father Carl to Him?

He hesitated but added, “Father Carl is with Jesus now,” and shuddered with the shame of it. The eulogy tasted like ashes in the mouth.

“The Mass is ended. Go in peace.”

Dominic gave the nod to James at the organ.

The hymn flared out cold and gray, a familiar anthem often heard but rarely listened to. One sang it the way one might enter a monument: cold and hollow, coercive—not the song itself but its echo. The very pores of his skin closed against it.

Was there a time he didn’t know this song?

PART TWO

SIX

"You are the first to arrive," the maitre d' said. Andrea heard it as an accusation.

"I'd like to sit," she said with impatience.

He tipped his eyeglasses to the bridge of his nose, looked down at his reservation book and marked a diagonal line across the little box next to her name with his fountain pen.

"Half empty or half full?" Andrea thought to herself.

Seated, she searched through the dozen or so pens that clicked against each other in the well of her tote bag. Unbanding her Moleskin notebook, she read her notes. "Father D: Sexlessness. Life with a vow of celibacy; the defrocking; the coming out, as it were. Beginning a sex life at middle age."

Her mother had invited the scribbling priest to reach out to Andrea, which should have been enough to disqualify him immediately. They had talked on the phone some months ago, and she had skeptically read the sermons Father Dominic posted online; his glosses on Scripture were poignant and surprising enough to track the contentious commentary on his blog. Now his church was closed—but despite everything, he still wrote his blog, posted from the public library. She surprised herself by checking in with him online every morning; there was equanimity and provocation in the voice, a daily tottering toward balance. In any event, there was enough there to get her to agree to this breakfast.

She also admitted something prurient about wanting to meet the man. She hadn't been this close to a priest in at least twenty-five years, certainly not since she had become sexual; she wanted to see whether she could discern any crippling effects of his celibacy. "A lifelong prayer," he had called it, "a disciplined wanting that satisfies more than any kind of having." Sounded like garbage. Andrea had checked out his picture on his site; Father Dominic had a boxer's nose, crooked smile, sad eyes—he was handsome, masculine, a little rough even. And while this was most certainly a business meeting, Andrea couldn't escape the irony that in what was probably the closest thing to a setup her mother had ever fixed, it would have to be with a priest.

She had to admit it was a stretch for her to take him seriously—especially as a writer. She was not only skeptical but impatient about all things religious. Faith-based intellectual activity was automatically discounted by Andrea; she had a tin ear for the pieties, the certitude—all that confidence in the depth of the "mystery." At the same time, she might confess curiosity about a man who presumably would not want anything from her. And she knew her women readers would find such an author attractive, a byline from a celibate, sexy guy, the possibility of his awakening in bed, the fantasy of initiating him, the validation of any woman's irresistibility.

But he was now more than fifteen minutes late. That was not good; she had expected more from him. What kind of person allows himself to be late for meetings? What kind of priest, for God's sake? With someone as busy as she? Presumably he didn't get to meet someone this connected every day.

She had asked her assistant to book the table yesterday. "They say you can have the table but only for seventy-five minutes," the girl had told her importantly.

"Tell them if it goes any longer, they have my permission—requirement, even—to shoot me dead." What did they think, she had all day? Not to mention the fact that she and her department probably dropped a hundred grand in the establishment every year; they could afford to kiss her ass a little.

The restaurant was off the lobby of a four-star hotel, and Andrea watched the tentative guests arrive at their tables. Despite the fact that she was in her fifth decade, she still paid too much attention to the age of people, measuring their accomplishments against hers at their age. Her career was under constant siege; she needed to be as inflected as a paranoid. She watched them settle into their oversized armchairs, their personalities hardening. She loved the vulnerability of early mornings. Her own habit was to jump out of bed and throw the covers over the sweet spot in which she had lain, as if to protect her body heat for a while longer.

Several of the men still had wet strands of hair dampening their collars; she could almost smell the new day's makeup on the women. It was all vaguely erotic to her: people so fresh, all but entirely ready, just come downstairs from their nonsmoking rooms with their bedsheets curled up, damp towels thrown on the bathroom floor, yesterday's underwear bundled in a drawer, the stray sock lost under the desk, the better clothes carefully hung, the Dopp kits strategically unpacked; the disarray both public and private arranged to accommodate or trouble the maids. Sweet almost. She loved going on business trips herself—a little bit temporary and a little bit lonely, harder to reach, eating less well, off schedule, deserving of treats, tempted, vowing to be a better person once she got home . . .

"Good morning, Andrea?"

She frowned at the time on her Cartier watch and offered her hand.

"I'm so sorry I'm late, the traffic was awful and—"

"Sit down," she said briskly. He looked older than his Web site had suggested, a little puffy. She was disappointed at first sight; he was not what she expected. Maybe it was the civvies: knock-off Joseph Abboud, she guessed, looking at the thick weave of his sport coat, the mock turtleneck, the coordinated pocket square, the worsted wool slacks. At any rate, there was something itinerant about his getup—business casual, the kind of outfit put together by a salesperson, some jock with a queer eye at the Men's Wearhouse or some other midpriced haberdashery. The clothes screamed "transition" at her—design for a recent divorcé at a weekend sales conference or white-collar ex-con at a resort, looking to start over, make a new impression. Credit card debt.

Her cell phone rang, and she recognized her daughter's number on the screen. "Excuse me."

"What is it?" she whispered into the phone.

Dom listened, trying to write in the missing pieces of the conversation.

"Forget it. Call me later, sweetie."

"Sorry about that. Now"—she turned to him. The phone rang again.

"No, just ignore it," she shout-whispered into the phone. "You don't have to answer. Ella. Stop. Listen. Stop. Listen to me. Just put the phone down. Connie will be there in, like, seven minutes to take you to school. That's the next thing that will happen, OK? OK. Love you."

"Is everything all right?" Dom asked. "Do you need to go?"

"No," she barked. "No," she softened, "it's just my daughter. The babysitter was late but on her way. She's just waiting at home."

"By herself?" Dominic asked.

"She's ten anyway. I told the doorman not to . . . At any rate, I don't think I need."

"I'm sorry, I didn't mean . . ."

"Have a real breakfast," she commanded, and, as if on cue, Dominic heard that damning rumble in his stomach, rebuking him for the vindaloo and the martinis the night before in a midtown Indian restaurant. Drinking more than he wanted to, he had stumbled to the men's room and had a philosophical moment. If, like Augustine, he believed in the authority of the senses, there was nothing wrong with the indulgent way in which he had dined. In fact, he put himself up to another test. Paying the bill, he pocketed the pen. Outside on the sidewalk, he felt weak with guilt. This was not the way he had been raised. He didn't steal things. All night long, he anticipated the tap on his shoulder, the police waiting on the corner, the air conditioner falling from a window to crush in his cranium.

Nonetheless, he struggled with the choice between the artichoke and goat cheese frittata and the crepes with strawberries and crème fraiche. He decided on the latter with a double latte. Why not start the day with dessert?

"So," Andrea said, "we have a lot in common."

"Your mother for one," Dom replied. "I mean, that's why I'm here."

Andrea was appalled to see Dominic pull out the white soft dough of his rosemary ciabatta with his fingers, roll it slightly between his palms and pop it into his mouth. The hulled crusts lay on the tablecloth beside his plate like disinterred artifacts. She was amazed by the childishness of the act. She herself hadn't eaten white dough in a decade.

"Well, yes"—she blinked—"but also the religion thing. You do know, of course, that I'm a lapsed Catholic."

"By that, you mean a kind of regression or deterioration, that you've slipped back to some inferior state. That's what *lapse* infers."

"No, that's not what I meant," she said, reddening.

"Because if you did mean that, you would be right. We do have a lot in common. I mean every Catholic is in some sense 'lapsed'—some say even the pope."

She leaned forward, intending to take control of the conversation. "Let me cut to the chase," she said. "I've been reading your essays, sermons . . . whatever you call them online. I think there is something there."

Dom swallowed his dough ball quickly. "Really?"

"Yeah, I mean you're not our standard fare. And we'll have to somehow coax the reader out of his atheistic knee-jerk cynicism, you know, but there's something in your voice I like very much."

"So this knee-jerk cynicism of your readers. Will they extend their political correctness to us godly types? Seems to me the mainstream media just discounts any sort of conversation based in faith. How are you going to get them to overcome their revulsion—to our insularity, our irrationality, their own xenophobia?

"You have to admit, the conversation often makes it very easy."

"Well, maybe I'm still bristling over your comment on the phone that I can be either a man of faith or a man of the intellect, but I can't be both."

"I'm still asking you that same question. Maybe I'm asking you to prove me wrong."

Dominic smiled. "Now, I'm listening. What would you like from me: something like a rereading of my sermons from the outside? A meditation on what happens to a life of faith once it's been de-institutionalized?"

"No. I would like to know about not having sex for twenty years—if that's technically true—and whether you plan on getting back in the game."

Dom reddened. What was the use of learning to blush this late in the day? He folded his hands on the table. "I don't know if I want to do that."

She wet her finger, reached across the table and began to press up the crumbs from his ciabatta, which clung to her like metal filings to a magnet. She dropped them onto her own bread plate.

"What? Have sex or write about it?"

He coughed and turned it into a chuckle. He was surprised by her sudden brashness—as he was by his own—but he was not impressed with it. She had now begun to wipe the tablecloth clean with her open palm; the gesture was pedantic in its impatience.

"I'm not even sure I exactly know what you're asking me," he said and looked squarely into her eyes. "And I'm not sure I owe you an answer."

This time it was she who blushed. She had been too brusque with him, even a little sadistic.

"Oh, of course, I don't know, I was j-just. Don't misunderstand please."

"No, I think I understand perfectly well. You want me to be your magazine's freak show, right? Watch, everybody, how the man of the cloth takes off his clothes."

She was confused by his sudden sternness. She had just told him of her Catholic past; he had to know that she was nice on the inside. Why was he treating her like a total stranger? She felt like a stunned teenager who is confused that the celebrity she stalked was not at all like he was on TV.

"And now you have this sudden stammer, right? Dom said. "Just to let me know you're not dangerous."

"Wait a minute."

"No, I get it. It's a good story. From where you sit. The celibate priest reenters libidinous society, you know, like some returning astronaut or something, isolated, in containment and observed."

Andrea tensed and issued a sudden battery of sneezes, a serial of five pneumatic fur balls: *choo, choo, choo, choo, choo*—paced perfectly in little, equidistant volleys.

"God bless you," Dom said and fished out the clean handkerchief from his pocket, an old habit he had learned from Father Carl, "and I mean that unofficially."

He picked up his brand-new briefcase (already scuffed) and slid his chair back from the table. "Look, my decision to leave the Church was the most difficult thing I've ever done. And I want to do some hard thinking about that and maybe write about it, yes, in due time, but we've gotten off to a really bad start and I don't think—"

"Stay."

"I won't be your real-life 'forty-year-old virgin.' I'm not that anyway."

"I'm sorry."

He looked at her.

"I want to work with you," she said to him. "I know I've blown this first meeting, and I'm sorry."

"You think that because I've been celibate maybe I don't have any balls, pardon the expression, and that you can toy with me."

"No, no, I've, I've been . . ."

"It's OK." He smiled. "It's fine. I've been here before."

"We both think we know too much about each other." She smiled back.

"Speak for yourself," he replied.

"I'm really not who you think I am."

"You're not that different."

He was so rattled by the meeting, he had gone to the bathroom immediately afterward, and flushed the regrettable pocket square right down the toilet. He was out of his element. The life of the priest, while rife with irony, is unprepared for the cut of sarcasm. He was unfit for the kind of banter she was so good at. All his conversations came to a point, the same point, the ultimate point.

And here she was urging him to say the very something he must not say, whatever he said.

She was more forward than he had expected, but he was proud of his ability to meet her straight on. She had challenged, engaged, pacified and then evaded him. All this he found a little bit sexy. Perhaps he had misread the cue; perhaps she was actually flirting with him a little bit. If he had wanted to flirt back, Lord knows he had seriously flubbed it.

Dominic relied on the fact that people knew very little about him; he hated that he was becoming increasingly transparent. What could possibly be the utility of learning to blush now in middle life? His face, his walk, his self-presentation, his mumble, his accent: these were things he didn't so much give away as things that gave him away. Without the collar, he was less in control of how other people saw him. He was terrified that people would size him up before he could take his own measure. This whole writing thing—what in fact did he want out of it but to gain control once again of his self presentation?

She had e-mailed him immediately. He picked up her apology at an Internet café where he stopped in to post the next column on his blog. The next day, she posted a comment and e-mailed him another invitation to meet. She even offered him a contract for a single piece. The price per word astonished him; he was worth something on the street after all.

For their second meeting, the magazine put him up in a boutique hotel with suggestive if inadequate lighting. The bathroom was mirrored from floor to ceiling, which had titillated at first but seemed lurid the following morning. One really wanted to be given the choice. Walking around the city into the wee hours, Dominic stumbled in and out of the busy bars on Third Avenue, pretending to search the crowds for friends, stealing furtive glances at all the happy people. He played the ninety-second game he invented as a teenager in which God would make him invisible, allowing him to stalk the street, eyeing every passing girl with impunity. He could have his choice, but God, his pimp, gave him a scant minute and a half before being made visible again. The girl Dom chose would automatically fall deeply in love with him and—oh, what pleasures awaited them both! In the end, though, ninety seconds always passed too quickly. Every time a woman left him behind it was a diminution of possibility, a loss in his life never to be recovered. The thousands of impulses he never acted on were just like dead skin cells invisibly shed, lust dust. In loss began possibility; that was his contract with God.

Wretched celibacy was the only souvenir from his dormant priesthood, and, indeed, while his body was perhaps regretfully chaste, his mind had become entirely pornographic. Hitherto, lust had always been indirect for him. He had always loved watching the elegant self-consciousness of women; like birds in a garden they fed daintily, took flight at his approach. He even came to enjoy the benign vigilance of his desire, that opportunism without opportunity. It was those moments of covert hunger that ached in him most, when he could stay still as a cat in a window, observing, wanting, forbidden, safe—gazing through the glass darkly.

Dom brown-bagged the fried egg sandwich from the twenty-four-hour deli back to his room to eat with the decent bottle of Barolo that waited to blacken his tongue. This morning he had woken up in a gray sweat and sleepwalked through his shower, dressing before the hangover arrived.

Just two subway stops in, he rushed out to find a McDonalds restroom and ruptured a hemorrhoid. Back on the street, he realized that it was too late to get back on the train and walked east to find a cab, which gobbled another ten minutes. As the taxi slugged its way across town, he bent down to tie his shoe. The lace came apart in his hands. He had meant to get new shoes too but thought that maybe these soft, rubber-soled, square-toed shoes, blunt and sincere, would export to his new, secular look. But he knew now they would not put his best foot forward. At the restaurant, he was forced to shuffle his feet through the revolving door. He kept his jacket buttoned to conceal the bloat of the fifteen pounds he had gained since the church closed down just after Christmas, like an underperforming chain store. His morning workouts had fallen away, and he was drinking heavily and eating badly.

What convinced him he was still alive were the all too real habits of his body: the movements of his bowels and the odor he lingered over during his morning toilet—all the evidence he needed to prove that his body indeed was longing for its final dissolve was provided in these daily mementos of his mortality. Diminishing returns, these little souvenirs, odorous of death. How the body uses food—ingesting, filtering the worthy nutrients, recycling the rest as waste—is how life itself uses the body, the soul thriving off its productions, convinced of its pleasures and then, in the end, eager to eliminate, bury its remains.

What a thing to leave behind.

Andrea leaned back from her desk and calculated how long it had been since she had gotten laid. She used to love having sex in the morning, before work, hoarding that little secret in her pocket all day. She considered the flat charge of fluorescent light on the crispness of her suit. She stood to inspect her dim reflection in the smoked glass window, the pointless profile her expensive outfit gave her body—her fit, undersexed, hard-won body—amid all the office noise: the chewy hum of terminals, the buzzy slip of fax machines, the clipped sashay of the photocopier. The red message light pulsed on her phone, five pink slips fanned out on her desk, the incoming e-mail gurgled on her laptop, the press of newsletters, solicitations, journals, invoices needing approval and proposals as ass-kissing as a tardy term paper—all of it coming at her while she sat blankly upon her office supply furniture. She was at home here, or, more to the point, essentially not at home here.

At first, she felt embarrassed by her rudeness with Dominic but soon grew resentful of the way she overcompensated during the rest of the meal, cooing sympathy and qualifying her statements with random prophylactics like "Don't you think?" or "Know what I mean?"—as if she couldn't drive the point through on her own and needed his consent.

He had stood up to her, and she felt as if she had been broken: not so much as a wild horse might be but as a triangle of balls on a pool table, sent clicking against each other in random associations. There were too many angles available for him to approach her. He had disarmed her by gently reminding her to behave herself.

She managed to get him to stay and finish breakfast, but they never exactly found a rhythm. In his conversation, she heard the tilt away from abstraction that she had picked up on in his writing. Commissioning a piece from a priest on the outs might not be the greatest career move, but she was attracted to his writing precisely because it sounded so different from the usual ego-infested landscapes her regular writers drew from their all-expenses-paid sensibilities. Those writers whose self-satisfied mediocrity enforced the high standards of excellence her magazine was known for; whose readers, so long as they made the right amount of money and had completed the right amount of education, counted on the magazine to present its worldview with not so much the challenge of discovery but the presumption of agreement.

But Father Dominic would be difficult to woo; he would be even harder to edit. There was a fair amount of rhetorical posturing just in their conversation. He spoke to her as if she were his public, as if he were up at the lectern. She spoke to him as if they were friends, beside each other on the pew, gently knocking knee on knee and whispering confidences. They each spoke as if they knew what was best for the other: he pure and moral; she frank and tough. The pauses in his speech irritated her: they were too deliberate, attentive, on call. She rushed in to fill all the empty spaces that were active silences for him.

He might just be the first man Andrea had ever talked to whose conversation was not in some way competitive. She had to slow herself down, give him a full beat in which to reply before she would be obliged to rush in and rephrase her question. He took his time—not because he was waiting for her to finish but because he gave himself room to consider and reply. How often she exaggerated just to keep someone's interest. She was more or less in control of most conversations, jerking chains, keeping people on their toes. She couldn't do that with Dominic; he paid too close attention.

In the end, this forced her to soften her voice and speak more slowly. She had to adjust to the fact that he actually listened to her, which laid the unfamiliar burden of sincerity on what she said.

After their second meeting, Dominic and Andrea agreed on two pieces he would develop for the magazine. It was also after their second meeting that Dominic knew he wanted to sleep with Andrea. It fell on him like a judgment.

Their various facts had emerged over the telephone: She was a single mom born in the same year as he. They had each majored in literature and philosophy in college; he had of course stayed at seminary and was ordained, while she had had risen to become an editor at a respected independent magazine. Recently divorced, she had a ten-year-old daughter; Dom told her he was midway through a six-month sabbatical and owed the Church an official decision about his future within a few months.

Soon they were e-mailing every day. She told him that he had an inadequate appreciation of the difficulties of her lifestyle; he had told her she was ill advised to replace the word *life* with *lifestyle*. He loved tangling with her. They found each other bright and clear within their disagreements, as if they needed to clamber up the damp rocks and through the shadowed bramble bush to get to a mountaintop meadow where they could regard each other under the hot, high sun.

Their third meeting was over drinks—a reconciliatory bottle of red—and they wound up talking for four hours on a single tab, as if they were in Europe. She seemed genuinely interested in what he had to say, but he also knew that was her job. She had a keen eye for the idea of the moment, which after living with all that eternal certitude suited him fine. It seemed the right way to live as well: commuting among endless interpretations of the self. He was trying the versions on, one at a time. It seemed reasonable, analytic even, hypothesizing, testing, disproving, abandoning, picking it up again. As a Catholic, he had been trained not to mistrust such an approach.

Their fourth meeting was at the clamorously loud Oyster Bar to celebrate the acceptance of his first article for the magazine. They had to sit close beside each other just to hear; cool oysters slid down his throat chased by champagne. Dom couldn't believe how well she could treat him. Every meal out could be significant. She paid for his overnights. There were gifts waiting at the hotel: chocolate, fruit, magazines. He was actually being courted.

Nevertheless, he stalled. Pointlessly. What was he waiting for?

He asked whether she thought people were essentially good.

For his own part, Dominic felt they were. Ultimately. They might need to be reminded how to behave, but they essentially would do the right thing. He believed this still despite the number of times he had been proven wrong.

Andrea told him that she shared in this magical thinking. But she wasn't sure. Was this willful naïveté? More than that: Dominic was so generous to other people and hard on himself; his inability to see the good in everyone he blamed on the failure of his own perception. For his benefit, she squelched her own cynicism about the matter. She would hide her conviction that the world was full of assholes, jerks, creeps and cunts. The remaining majority was simply more self-censoring, less willfully aggressive. And all of that was not such a bad thing: most people would never, could never, never even expected or wanted to be redeemed; that kept the world lively, pulsing with contention and advancement—what some called self-actualization.

By the fifth date, when they stopped pretending a work agenda, he was set on her. So what if she was the first woman he met since leaving the Church? Maybe God had sent her. All that waiting would have to count for something. He was free to make his first move yet didn't. What was he afraid of? Here was the moment he had been waiting for; he would take to it with a lifetime of anticipation but with the instincts of a natural. His skills would surprise him and delight her—as if wanting to do something gave one expertise in doing it. And yet his fantasies came right out of the movies. He imagined how he would put his cheek against hers. He would feel the softness of her skin against the grain of his chin. He would kiss the side of her mouth, peripheral openings. He would rub the small of her back, stimulating the flow of blood below. In his mind, they were enormous in scale: from their balcony seats they would watch themselves on the silver screen larger than life.

But what happened surprised him even more. They had shared a bottle of wine for lunch and stayed late at the bistro. She had told the office she would be out the rest of the day with an author. It was 4:15 in the afternoon by the time they stood, a little wobbly, outside the restaurant on the sidewalk. A late sun hit the mirrored windows of the building across the street and lit them up like movie stars. She gleamed like mica. He leaned forward to make his move as he had planned. His heart raced. She turned her head, but then leaned in to kiss his neck, right below the Adam's apple, where his shirt collar was freshly opened.

He felt it like a vision: lit and hooded, dark and lucid, the way a sudden and obscure light catches hard beneath cloud cover, an eclipse of the sun demanding revelation, an invention of god to transfigure the fear.

She came as if surprised at his bringing it on. Almost aghast; or did she mean a bit awed? Probably a little of both. She was aware that her moaning alarmed him; she voiced pleasure like a kind of hurt. Her cries were grated, serrated, ripped out of her.

Afterward, Dominic, prone to cosmic pressures, figured that this feeling he had (kind of like a blimp: buoyant, grand, unexpected and slow) must mean that he was falling in love; he tried to square the loft of the feeling with the physical deflation in the end, embodied but afloat. Why so much fuss over such little mess? He was desperate not to see sex as just another attempt to escape the accident of the body, the ambition of the soul.

She had scrambled some eggs at midnight. He was hungry and

ate quickly. But the eggs left him unsatisfied as they usually did. Why are eggs never cooked exactly, or as well, as you imagine them? Andrea uncorked the bottle of wine from dinner and poured the remains of it in a single glass to share. Dom was saddened by how quickly it was consumed; they drank competitively, matching sip to sip. He didn't understand the value of this moderation, as if satisfaction now required responsibility.

He woke up at 4:30 in the morning, the dreaded hour of prayer. He felt both sated and uneasy, like a gambler checking his wallet. He smacked his lips. He was really thirsty.

Andrea lay beside him in a strangely cramped crescent. She looked cold. He panicked, thinking for a moment that she must be dead, that he must have killed her. He covered her with the bedclothes and climbed out of bed.

She gave him a six-month contract, and he set about researching every day, all day, in the university library, rustling through the stacks like a mouse in the pipes. Dragging his haul to a study carrel he read, made notes and napped. All the apples and power bars he smuggled in got eaten.

In the evenings, he returned to the rectory. His key still worked; the archdiocese hadn't yet changed the locks or boarded it up, though the heat and water had been turned off. Everything else was as he had left it; he camped out wearing layers and layers to bed, making his way through the frigid halls with a lit candle and a blanket over his head. He imagined himself looking like a specter to anyone looking in on him through the windows. If only anyone were looking in on him through the windows. On Fridays he hiked over to the YMCA for a hot shower and shave to prepare for the weekends he now regularly spent with Andrea, when Ella went off to stay with her father.

Secular Sunday mornings made Dominic feel restless and disoriented, like a ranging dog in the streets—trying not to look lost, searching for the home that abused him. Andrea slept late on Sundays, catching up from her crazed workweek and taking advantage of her daughter's custody visits with her father.

One such Sunday, after raiding Andrea's cupboards and finding nothing but a thin box of ascetic crackers, Dominic decided to take himself out for a walk. He actually missed the regularity of celibacy a bit; it had been reliable as a subjective base, as good as a low-grade depression. Desire fulfilled, it turns out, would be no easier to manage than its denial. He had such meager context of pleasure within which to place his new love life: the sudden eruptions and the long intervals. He had the wary sense of having bitten off more than he could choose. Recriminations would be force-fed him. Reading the great poets of myth, he had always been impressed by the sheer energy of sex as truth, eros as prophecy. For mortals, though, sex merely had consequences.

Weekend after weekend, Andrea coaxed him to the sensual life as a process of rehabilitation: discovery, practice, initiation, control, mastery. She trained him in the intricacies of approach, led him to convert hesitation into restraint, eagerness into engagement. Even so, he felt a queasy resentment of her mentorship. What was wild for him was within her comfort zone. She had gotten there before him; she was so much more experienced than he. Sexually, he had to work backward, to get at the etiology of pleasure, the contingencies of impact. He suspected a silent criticism implicit within her guidance—a benevolent condescension that was downright Jesuit of her.

He left the apartment.

Walking down the street he was amazed at his impunity: he was merely a man walking down the street. On Palm Sunday no less. In yet another possible world. He no longer carried within himself that contagious goodness; he was no longer driven by the righteous ambitions of a thought virus. He gawked at girls.

Passing a woman at the crosswalk, he allowed himself to stare rudely at her cleavage and turned to watch the curve of her butt. And she turned her head and smiled back!

In the park, he disturbed a flock of pigeons, sending them off in deep-throated flight over the head of a girl thickly curled in the lap of her boyfriend. A vagrant dog sniffed at his shoes. An undershirt was folded carefully over a bench.

Religion was everywhere!

Cherry blossoms atomized in a sudden gust of wind; they seemed artificially lit as if they were indoors, on stage. The park blurred before his eyes. Always that urge toward abstraction. Was it based in the senses? Why did the brain insist on perceiving this way—as if purity was a quality outside the thing itself? To deliberately not see the something right before you, because one cannot trust its claim to completeness, to being all there.

There was a kind of hope from this, the positive despair of beginning again a new life in search of that which had gone missing. Epiphany was only ever to be glimpsed peripherally. Overexposed. He had been trained to expect the divine to honor the hard labor of faith in practice. It could be more like an accident. Unexpected. The enduring image of Christ is not the crucifixion but the empty tomb: never more present than when he was gone.

He sat on a bench and sniffed idly at his fingers. The scent of her: he can now add Andrea to his list of things that linger on his flesh: garlic, ammonia, rosemary.

A well-dressed group walked up the stairs of the handsome High Anglican church across the street. They seemed nice. He could be like them. He observed his custom of circling a church building completely before entering it, both wary and predatory but then followed them inside. He sat in a back pew and examined the protocols of the Anglican Mass. Variations on a theme. The choir was excellent, and the Liturgy had a civility that calmed him. The whole affair seemed satisfied; it did not appear to feel too bad about its past or future. At the offering, Dom was faced with a basket full of money, and for the first time in his life, he took out his wallet and put in a fiver. He realized how little he had ever paid for in cash. While his inner life had to a large degree been professionalized, he was such an amateur day to day. He took the host and sipped at the cup of wine—a sherry, no less—sweet, tart, acerbic. Its finish was brief, mindful of its limitations as a symbol.

As Dom tried to leave the church, the reverend blocked his passage out the door and held out his hand. Dom took it hastily, keeping an eye on his escape into the daylight.

"Hello, my brother," the reverend said with a friendliness that terrified Dom. He tried to let go of the hand, but the elder held a firm grip. He could feel the man tilt his head inquisitively, trying to make eye contact. And when Dom finally did raise his eyes it was with the look of a sprung ex-con, suspicious of this first moment of kindness in life on the outside.

"Are you OK?"

Dom opened his mouth to say, "Yes, Father. Thank you for your sermon today," but out came a brittle, little Tourette's yelp. The minister released, and Dom ran out the door.

The wind had died down; the cherry blossoms around the little square were nearly done. The wood was greening. Next Sunday would be Easter. Renewals seemed less and less convincing year after year. The efforts of spring become redundant. Its temperament was prepubescent, even insolent. Compassion for resurrections fatigues; miracles require belief; faith is the miracle itself.

• • •

Dominic was like some repatriated tiger who back in the wild from the zoo had learned to become more curious about than interested in his prey: he caught her, watched her still, opened her up, nosed around—fed. He was fastidious if remote, taking her guidance so seriously, an eager student in the pause before he overtakes his mentor. He seemed overly interested in her pleasure, had become a student of it. She tried to delay it, even pretended not to climax, just to see how far he would go.

If sex was a sacrament, what was she—the sacrifice? Andrea wondered what it was like for him to enter her. He had told her that over the years he had been with "many, many" prostitutes, but only ever budgeted for blow jobs, out of concerns both venal and venial. He had said "fellatio," actually. Hers was the first body he had ever penetrated. What was it like, though, for this man who had disavowed property to imagine possessing her? What was it to be dominated by a man whose only agency had been a spiritual grant? In the end, the thing that got to her was the will to appease his perpetual worried squint, his expectant cringe—the very thing that made her want to hurt him a little almost as if for his own good. The better he was, the less kindness she felt toward him. Did Dominic's God feel that sadistic impulse as well? Maybe good ol' Dom had a good reason to be worried. Just as every paranoiac has cause, so every person who cowers sees the coming blow.

He squeezed his eyes tight when they made love, like a little kid believing that when he opened them he would get want he wanted.

Lying beside her, on sheets that were so luxurious they felt vaguely buttered, he wished he would fall into a sleep from which he never woke. Surely he deserved none of this. Always a good scold, he had been disgusted by the "good life" that upwardly mobile people led with a ferocious vengeance against those who couldn't afford it, which were the same people who didn't deserve it. But he had to admit to liking this very much—this feverish spell that kept him between states, both engorged and light-headed. He nearly held his breath during sex, wondering just how long he was going to be able to get away with it. Reenchantment with the world: was that what he asked of Andrea? Would she be his witness, demand his deliverance?

The down comforter and the cashmere throw bothered him; he was too hot. All these pillows made his neck ache. His back was damp with sweat, but his feet were cold.

"What the fuck am I doing here?" he asked himself. It was too ridiculous, all this temporary tension and quick satisfaction. He was obsessed with their progress in bed, infuriated by his jealousy of her—that she was in a position to judge his performance. He wanted her to know him sometime in the future, when he would be fully formed and she equally met. And now that he had become technically proficient, she had suddenly become withholding. Now that he knew what to do, he couldn't get it done. Andrea became reluctant to climax. He asked her why.

"It doesn't have to happen every time," she said.

"I want it to."

"Shhh. You're embarrassing me," she said and punched his arm. "Anyway, I still enjoy every minute of it."

That wasn't good enough for him. He became a student of her orgasm: how long before she reached it, when it was likely to happen, how long it lasted. He studied the conditions of its elusiveness, chasing its retreat, probing every angle of access. He calibrated the transition between titillation and irritation. This became his new vocation, his spiritual exercise. He often forgot about his own pleasure in the process. If he couldn't complete the act, he would not be satisfied with merely finishing. He had discovered yet another way of feeling alienated from the surface of his life. Always hyperaware of the sense of Another watching and judging his every move, he had now become his life's own spy.

"Shit."

"What?" she asked him.

He hadn't realized he spoke it aloud.

"Nothing." He had to get used to the fact that now there was someone who actually heard him.

"Come on."

"Well, I was wondering."

"Wondering what?"

He had to make something up quickly. "This is probably crazy," he hesitated, "but is it possible that should we work out, would we ever have a baby?" He smiled generously. Could he possibly be this manipulative?

She got up on an elbow and looked at him.

"What?" she asked. "Silly, silly boy."

"I was just joking, you know."

"Listen, Father, I know we're breaking some new ground here"—she laughed—"and I know you're no stranger to miracles, but that's kind of what it would take at this point."

She kissed him on the cheek. "Anyway, aren't we getting a little ahead of ourselves here?"

"Oh, I know, I know," he said with a relief. He was going to have to watch his words; they were becoming impulsive. "I'm not even sure I want to start a family. And I need to get to know Ella."

"And she gets to know you."

She pulled up the comforter and laid her head on his chest.

A goose down feather floated free in the air in a more or less accurate pictograph of his anxiety: unstitched and carried off. He was getting ahead of himself. He watched as the white feather rocked gently in the air, and then blew it away out of sight. She closed her eyes and fell asleep.

Failed Prayer
You are the dream
We can never
Remember

Dominic had gotten word that the church was about to be fenced off, in preparation for its demolition. Andrea insisted on spending his last weekend at the rectory with him. They laid together in his little twin bed in his little bare room. The taboo of it all excited her at first; they giggled and whispered throughout the night as though they were being eavesdropped on. They huddled against the lonely, frozen bigness of the place, as if stuck in a storybook.

Andrea was impressed if not a little horrified by how little Dominic needed. There was so much he was expected to care for. He knew how to do things. Showing her around the place, examining the baptism well in the sacristy, inspecting the systems in the basement, he seemed to her like a native proud to show his city to a foreign tourist. His work as a priest often felt this way to him, imagining seeing his home through a stranger's eyes. With Andrea, he felt like he was hosting her first trip back to the old country, appealing to her sense of roots, the instinct of nostalgia, an ennobling sense of one's heritage which holds the restored state of your essential self within it. Only, as in any act of condescension, the joke's on you.

All this made Andrea feel protective of and resentful for him; he was so underappreciated. This church that he loved so much was being taken away from him. It would become like the institutional Catholic Church itself: oversized, underused, unmanned, demanding. And all of it going to hell.

In the morning he made bacon sandwiches on white bread whose crusts he cut off—all of it stale from the freezer. He threw away the frying pan without cleaning it. They ate in bed. He packed all his belongings in a backpack.

"You haven't even told me. What will you do when they finally shut this place down, after your leave of absence?" she asked, realizing that they had never planned longer than a weekend at a time.

"I really don't know. They have a parish ready to take me in."

"Where is it?"

"I actually went to visit, just before they shut us down. It was pretty incredible, in fact. A huge, modern church that people come to from a fifty-mile radius; lots of our New Haven people wound up there. Overall, they average a thousand plus on a typical Sunday. Incredible ministry, tons of programs. Makes me think Catholics still have a shot."

"Are you serious about it?"

"Well, I should be, but it's not for me." Dominic rolled his eyes and laughed, "The pastor is this really upbeat guy. Has lots of gimmicks. He does this bit every Sunday where he calls up anybody with a birthday that week and gives them a rose. And they line up, the men too! Couples celebrating anniversaries get bouquets. He's a real crowd pleaser; he hired a consultant to see how they could improve their—well, call it what you will, but it's basically customer satisfaction. Babysitting service—stuff like that. They even have a nutritionist on staff; I think they call her a wellness counselor. They replaced the choir with a rock band, power anthem stuff."

"Sounds revolting. So, what are you thinking?"

"That I won't be a priest forever. Haven't been one for some time, in fact. I have to come clean with them and tell them that. And I'll have to start it all up with the Vatican, a long bureaucratic process. All of which is OK—except that I love my ministry. I'll miss it."

Dominic hung his head and said, "Listen, the truth is I don't want to go. I don't want to leave you."

All of her extremities (nose, fingers, toes) went cold. "When do you have to tell them?" Andrea asked.

Dominic sighed. "Tomorrow."

She felt the part of her brain that sandbagged against the rise of rash acts lose out to her sinuses, which were flooding with feeling. "Well, don't leave, then. Stay with me. In fact, why don't you just move in with me right now?"

He looked at her.

"You know, for the time being. Until you figure things out."

The space between them went suddenly quiet.

"Thanks," he said.

"*Thanks?*" she repeated to herself, instantly regretting the offer; it was so ungenerous of him not to be more eager. It was too generous of her.

She considered how he would fit in with the expensive look of her apartment. After spending a fortune on a high-end decorator, moving in depressed her. She didn't resemble the place at all. What was wrong with the picture was that she was in it, with all her imperfections. Now she would have to corrupt it further in order to accommodate Dom, with all his ignorance of style and torment of spirit.

Later that day, Andrea called her car service to pick her up at the rectory earlier than scheduled. Dominic heard her do this but did not argue against it.

She usually felt better at the end of their weekends together.

After she and Dominic parted, she believed that she was a better person than her life up to that point would have suggested; that she could and would make it all better from now on. She felt warm with revision, solid with promise. What would happen when they moved in together: would she catch up to where he needed her to be?

Alone, Dominic considered his next steps. Could this actually lead to a normal life in a committed relationship? And what did he know of such things? Would Andrea always love the best of all possible Doms even while he inevitably failed to realize it? Could he still hope to be loved in all his incapacity?

Dominic closed all the lights and climbed the steep stairs to the bell tower for the last time. The effort winded him, and he felt as if whirled about in a time machine, ascending in order to spy on himself as a young boy, praying on his knees in the attic, whispering into the hollows of his hand. Climbing up to the close air of the bell tower as if to get closer to God, to outwit the pressure of logical objections, to engage the opposite of certainty. Climbing as if to escape the things that still kept him there: the parishioners, Mrs. Alfano, Signora, James—but mostly the undertow of Dolores's pull. He hadn't seen her in the few months since Father Carl's funeral. At Christmas, he received a card from her that said, "I've run away to have my baby in peace." She said she would be in touch when little Dominic was born. Everything would be fine.

Dominic held on to the bell rope in the tower—whose ring had quickened his blood, gathered his thoughts, clarified his purpose for long decades now—to stare at the city sky at night, orange with impending snow. He breathed the cold air deeply into the very body that had now betrayed its special fate. Dissolution; disillusion. He was no less lonely, just lonely like an ordinary man.

He opened his mouth one more time as if to cry out, to utter a sound of sheer helplessness but knew no comfort would come from it, that he might even be punished for it. *Lord, open my lips. And my mouth will proclaim your praise.* Instead of the wall of silence he expected, he might feel the hard slap of being silenced, that a hand from the heavens might clap down over him. *Whatever you say, say nothing.*

The next morning, the last morning, James had already arrived at the church and was deep into the Toccata and Fugue in D minor when Dominic walked in.

"Hey, sounds good," he called out.

"They won't make them like this anymore," James said. The 1926 Wurlitzer was a gift to the church from the local mill family before they lost the fortune that would leave whole sectors of the city bust. The organ fit snugly into the chancel as if the church had been built around it. All through the fall, James and Dominic had been working on a grant proposal to restore the great organ; they had commissioned a professional evaluation of the damage incurred over the years as well as its repairability. They were still waiting on an appraisal of its worth. There were nearly a thousand pipes that would have to be removed simply to reach and examine the bellows. The temperamental sound of the organ—its wheezing in the winter and reediness in the summer—betrayed the fact that there were probably holes in the original leather bellows. Releathering work would be easier on an organ of this vintage, as the manufacturer would have used animal glue which could be dissolved in hot water without any damage to the wood or the leather.

But now they were talking about an excavation. There was a church in Essex that was eager to have the organ, and the archdiocese was weighing its proposal against that of a museum that wanted to buy it. The old Harwood baby grand had already been moved to a small rec hall in East Haven.

James opened the cover to the keyboard; the smell of the organ hit Dominic like a sensation, sharp and sentimental, mothballs and cinnamon. On day one, the casework, action and open wood would be removed. He pointed to the custom wooden packing cases stacked against the wall that would be used to pack the keeps, the brass reed and the giant soundboard. Next, the entire console would have to be removed, to be followed by the Great and Choir pipework. The pipes and console parts would be packed in bubble wrap and moved by a crew of six specialists.

James had already interested a reporter from the *Almanac*, though he had warned that the whole metro desk had been decimated and he alone was covering much of the civic beat, so he didn't know if he could actually get to the story.

"We should commemorate this church with a plaque on the organ," Dominic said.

"Like what? "In honor of the derelict Our Lady of Fatima that once stood in the inner city slums of . . ."

"Something like that," Dom murmured.

"I guess all things come to an end."

Dominic was silent.

"You know the musician Glenn Gould?" James asked.

"I know his Goldberg Variations," Dom replied. "Why?"

"Which version: 1955 or 1981? Never mind. Anyway, Gould had this idea that maybe art should be "given the chance to phase itself out, to preside over its own obsolescence."

"Interesting . . ."

"I've been carrying that around for you for weeks now. Thought you might like it."

"Because you think maybe the same could be said for religion?" Dominic wondered aloud.

"Maybe. Or classical music. Or communism. You know, one big prevailing idea around which you build a life."

"Take control of our own dying. Decay like a thing of beauty: faith for faith's sake."

They went quiet.

"This can't be easy, your losing this church. But, listen. Just do good. Do what you're good at. What more do you want? You know, blow the cosmic scale of it. Take the thorn out of your side."

"Thank you, Brother James. You know, for an atheist, you're pretty benign."

They both laughed.

"So what will you do?" Dominic asked.

"I don't know. Do the recital; see what happens. Maybe follow this organ, rebuild it. I'm loving this chance to learn it."

"You were going to try to find your father and invite him to the recital. What happened?"

James snorted. "I asked my mother about that, and she just got ripped. She asked why on earth would I ever think of doing that. Didn't I know that he would only think of himself? He'd just resent it, say shit like, 'No one gave me any extra opportunity to better myself.' She said he would ultimately fuss where the money for lessons came from and why it wasn't being sent his way. My mother said, 'Just like the Scriptures say, James, call no one on earth Father.' "

Dominic nodded sympathetically. "That's what they've been calling me half my life."

"So, what about you?" James asked. "Heard you have a lady friend."

"Yeah. Andrea, you know, "la figlia di Signora."

"That's good. Really good." James laughed.

James laid his hands on the organ keyboard. "You know, when they take apart this baby, it's going to cover the entire church floor, even with the pipes laid across the pews."

"It'll sound nice in Essex, though."

"Yeah, that church has beautiful acoustics. Much better than a museum."

"Here, much as I love it, you began to sound as if you were playing under water."

"Weird. That's how Signora Rosa describes the way I play sometimes. She urges me to swim away from the music."

"Hmm. Does she always speak in such riddles?"

"Yes, actually."

"She'd make a good priest."

"How come you don't introduce me to your friends?" Dominic asked Andrea after their second month together.

Reasons tallied in her mind. They were cheap and mean.

She was afraid he would strike one of those moonie looks at her as he settled yogi-style beside her, rocking himself into place and planting another one of his huge, loud, insipid, way too frequent popcorn kisses on her lips.

She hated how Dom always pointed things out for her to appreciate—the late light on the trees, the carpet of pine needles, etcetera—as if he were God's impresario, here to focus our attention on His glories. As if none of this was apparent to her before he came along!

He would be likely to blurt out, when a friend complimented her new dress, that the word *sheath* actually comes form the Latin for *vagina*.

The way he lifted a cup of coffee or a glass of wine with both hands as if were an offering.

Her primary strategy for guaranteeing a successful social evening was to direct most of the conversation toward the personal interests and histories of her guests. Dominic was flummoxed by these friendly invitations; it was as if his past were an embargoed country.

She was afraid he would wear ragg wool socks beneath his Birkenstocks. And, at home, he would pick up those same socks, dump them in the laundry bin and then do the wash at the end of the week for all of them. Her ex used to leave his socks on the floor for her to pick up. And while she always expressed irritation, she was fond of those dirty socks. They were proof that the man needed her to take care of him. While she judged that dependence to be a kind of weakness (and wound up, in the end, resenting him for it), it did offer an illusion of security, a kind of bond, bondage even. Dom's self-reliance prevented him from needing her.

He had no clue how to run his life now. Where was the financial drive, his lust for things?

The way he said, "You're welcome" after being thanked—instead of just "OK," or "It's nothing," or "No problemo," or just say nothing like regular people?

The solicitous quality of his voice after sex.

It wasn't annoying enough that he actually thought there *was* a soul—but that that it was there to be saved, to be fulfilled, rather than just driven and tormented.

"What a bitch," she thought to herself. Of course she would say nothing of this to him; she had long ago reckoned with the sadistic power of honesty and tried to use it judiciously. But she was surprised it had happened so soon—the comfortable tug of resentment that comes with living with someone, the reassuring leverage of blaming every problem in her life on the behavior of someone else. What right had she to complain? He was a pilgrim at her body come at last to a promised land, filled with wonder as well as a respectfulness that was unnecessary if not misguided, she thought. He really was so sweet, with those big sincere eyes, even if he was the cause of her every unhappiness.

Why, at this point in her life, did she still think that a man would be the answer to her problems? She threw everything she could think of at it, to kill this relationship that nevertheless seemed to be nearly working. She was suspicious of their conviction that they were somehow right for each other. Their opinions were becoming more and more like-minded, and she hated that too; their worldview was growing pink and scratchy and cottony with its insulation. She even felt a bit glamorous with him. Lovers all act like movie stars in the beginning. She and Dominic were deep into the screenplay in which of course people are better off with other people. The movie was devolving into the Vaseline-lens montage in which their candlelit dinner conversations might as well mute beneath the cover of a swelling soundtrack; they might as well find themselves laughing underneath the spray of a water hose or trying on silly hats or playing folk instruments in eccentric boutiques—all of it so vague and gauzy that actual words would become unnecessary.

As if on cue, Dominic told her that he had not been to the beach since he was in high school, and so she took him there despite the fact that she hated it: the imagined crab bites in the soft arch of her foot; the terrible trick of the mirroring horizon; the urgent, strangulated call of the seagulls. As a child she heard them as the cry for help from the ghost of a dead girl. She had never been able to get rid of that. The poetic delusion of the waves crashing with their irregular heartbeat thud, like the slap of a back of the hand to take a child's breath away, that terrible silence before the seething and stingy and sinister withdrawal of the tide, which to her ear always sounded like some fatty food blistering in a frying pan.

But there he was beside her as if photographed with a soft

lens, benevolent and handsome. Despite everything, she couldn't bear to think, couldn't bear not to think, of lying beside him, drawing her thigh over his hip with the grip of a drowning thing coming up for air. She had never met anyone who better illustrated the phrase "He doesn't know his own strength." His physicality was evolving daily, as if he were at last embodying. He moved both gingerly and powerfully, with a middle-aged, ascetic, gym-innocent bloat at the hips, the fur that lined his skin and rubbed against her electric with static. Even his footfall made her tremble inside like crystal glasses in a cupboard.

With her, he began to do things to make a home he had never had the chance to do: light a fire and let it roar through an entire Sunday afternoon, wrap sweet potatoes in foil and roast them in the embers, simmer long soups and braises in the oven. In the rectory, he barely even remembered what he had eaten for dinner the night before. Now, he perused her hundreds of cookbooks and experimented in and out of the stands at the farmers' market. On a Saturday morning, he helped her crack nuts for a pie. So this is what the erotic life was: attachment, bondage, materialism, mortality.

Waiting for her in bed was like being buried alive with anticipation. His body, swollen and heavy and eager to dissolve, imagined itself pure gnostic spirit. He wanted to have too much of her, to kill himself with the stuff of her. He had always dismissed the mixed metaphor of sex and prayer, but now he saw, at the very least, some parallels: a partnership that was intensely private, potent, invisible to others, a complete immersion in the subjective self, defenseless, with some apprehension of the unobservable self. "This is what it feels like to be known by you."

He touched every inch of her, every toned limb. She worked out every day and was very proud of her single-digit body fat index. In his fantasies, he had always pictured himself with an amply figured woman with big hips and generous breasts. It was curious to find out that what you end up loving is not what you always thought you wanted.

He dove headfirst into her library, which throbbed with entitled anxiety; the luxurious, oversized photography books of the destitute in Brazil and the tortured of Kosovo. She collected the diaries and letters of dead writers. She loved their groping after the condition of writing, the positioning of oneself, the apologies that were disguised defenses, the chronicling of struggles (with drink, money, depression, marriage)—all of it without the pressure of summary or conclusion. She loved the performative aspect of these books, preliminary and daring as a rehearsal. He dipped in and out of the big and small lives of Pepys, Boswell, Virginia Woolf, Julian Green, Cheever, James Lees-Milne. These journals had a cunning sense of sport that appealed to her—the anticipation and manipulation of one's own critical legacy, as if it were a good idea for an animal being hunted to leave tracks. What would editors do with the ephemera of e-mailing novelists of the future? What would they do with the novelists themselves? Dom joked that Andrea too had a habit of loving things on the verge of extinction.

She also collected interior design books: big lavish perfect and furious. But none of these comforts were something to live up to. They were nothing but a strategy to cover up his mounting guilt of giving up the godhead. It ran in him like a low-grade fever, the collective mumbling of gossip. He experienced new and various sorts of delusions:

On a train trip to the country, he sat in the quiet car, keeping a vigilant eye on every passenger with a cell phone; he would hush the speaking violations and worry about what the conductor meant by suspicious behavior.

Every manhole was to be sidestepped gingerly; Dominic was

prepared for it to blow its cover and shoot its shrapnel into the air.

Every Con Edison plate might electrocute him.

Without God to protect him, the world was becoming animated with evil intention.

Even Andrea's beautiful apartment troubled him. Facing a little green park surrounded by a wrought iron fence, her building was a converted parish house that had once sat beside its church. Her bedroom featured a stained glass window. He couldn't get past the overdetermined nature of it all; that he would at long last get laid in a bed lit by light coming through a rose window—Episcopalian, granted, but still!

She had come to him that morning and lay across his middle at a perpendicular angle. He couldn't help but see the intersection of their bodies forming a crucifix; some things just get too engrained. As he stroked her lower back he felt his whole body press into the coolness of her morning skin. He couldn't believe his life.

All this sacrilege was a better fate, he guessed, than the alternative of his own dead church in its failing neighborhood: desolate and purposeless, growing faintly menacing. Ronnie had called him to report that the archdiocese had indeed installed a chain-link, barbed-wire fence around the property, as if to keep the church in instead of intruders out, as if it were we who needed to be protected from it.

"A group of us are wicked pissed," he told Dominic. "We're gonna hold midnight vigils there until they give us time to raise money to save the thing."

Dominic ignored his parting shot, "Would be nice, Father, to see you there."

Google-mapping the abandoned church gave Dominic an unsettling vantage of his beautiful building, which, while alive, coveted nothing more than affectionate acknowledgment from the heavens.

Yet the photograph on the computer screen was merely documentary; it had no configuring eye, no intentionality—the image demonstrated another annulment of the deity, another flattening expansion. Dominic imagined the building itself getting angry, being leaned on by body shops and striptease bars. The gate off its hinges. The parking lot reduced to rubble; asphalt erupted through the long winter, shooting gravel into the air like a faithful geyser. His garden, the remains of the little plot where the retired men of the parish harvested the last of the autumn tomatoes and the dusty marigolds, pruning the tender green shoots with their big fingers, had gone to junk.

It was these places of transition that touched him most—those places between use and uselessness, left behind, waiting. Manhattan had become hysterical in the way it wanted to finish itself. There were almost no spaces left for filth and graffiti; the polish of privilege expanded across the island, pushing up high into its sky. For the first time in his life, he could feel the city running out of space; there was less and less room for someone like him: at odds, without money, vaguely artistic, unambitious. He even missed his little, half-ugly city up the coast which in its majority always felt like outskirts—outskirts that collected themselves in the inner city, like an errant seed in the wind taking root. He missed the church lot where weeds sprouted from sidewalk cracks like hair from a mole and sneakers hung from the electric lines. Plastic bags collected in the fences, ripping in the wind. The empty chapel and its pews stripped of prayer books. He found similar copies of the chapel's wooden Madonna sculpture and Raphael copy on eBay. He imagined the dirty noise from the interstate and the abandoned fridge with the curling orange peel and used condom—all this new emptiness, frank and unreceptive.

• • •

An angel fallen is still an angel, and, in the best moments, that is how Andrea saw Dominic. At worst, she felt he was a bit of a fool and wished she could roll him around in the mud he had fallen to, help him realize he was irrevocably earthbound, bruised and dirty. But she could not reach him. Dom gave Andrea no access; it was always about him pleasing her. This was new for Andrea: someone else's pain wasn't legitimate until it could be felt by her, saved by her, shaped by her.

She couldn't help but feel a kind of contempt for him. What was his tragedy, really, except to realize that he was merely human? His faith had led him to extraordinary expectations, yet it was undone by ordinary problems and everyday feelings. All his life he had been protected in study and prayer; in him were preserved the remains of a childish, spiritual idealism, a paternalistic fantasy. Andrea was of the opinion that the answer to the problems of childhood was, simply, adulthood, the acknowledgment that existence is difficult and one must cultivate discipline, drive, cunning in order to survive.

So this is what it had come to: a love for/ at the end of history, with the last Catholic priest, conveyed from the platonic ideal, uncovered amid the stripping of the altars, released from the clutch of institutional faith, translated without dying into the vernacular, a life returned to itself, merely that which must learn to self-subsist, the chubby hunger artist, the last fucked priest, not quite defrocked but lying nonetheless naked here beside her.

She would not indulge his fantasy tragedy. He wanted tough love? Just watch: this fallen angel would become a mere embodied man in which the essence of Him met the stuff of him. Why should she stand for his existence at the vanishing point of the either/or. I and Thou.

That is what sex with him was like: when he came, it was a leap of faith. A leap from faith. His concept of love, his ability to know someone intimately, was engineered by his faith: asserting any knowledge of God was a corruption of the very idea. She would get to him still, her body to his. Coming down to life-size could still be a kind of transcendence. She could show him how—with all the weight of mortal flesh falling in love.

"The only one you can really love, I mean REALLY love, is your child." That is what she told her husband two months before he left her. And she meant it, even at the cost of saying it. Even as the girl grew out from the center of her mother's life, Andrea knew hers was the love that could withstand all of Ella's tests of it.

How Andrea missed her little bedmate: the way Ella's woolly head nestled under her chin; the way her wriggling body so slippery all day long fixed itself in sleep, cooling and setting. The sound of her skull chewing when her mother placed her head beside her daughter's at breakfast as if listening for an inner life. Until Dominic moved in, Ella was still innocent enough to keep the bathroom door open whenever she peed—or "made water," as Andrea still called it, just as her own mother did. The tinkle in the toilet was a sound as lovely to her ears as any fountain in a garden. Its funneling sound concentrated her attention, gave her a feeling of peace, a secure knowledge that her daughter's darling body was working just as it ought to.

Ella's well-being was the only thing that made Andrea feel safe. In fact, the only times she suspected in God were those irrational moments when she feared for her little girl's life. She would believe in anything that might save the girl from the doom that always seemed near. Andrea was always so scared for her. How could someone so lovely and delicate be spared? The girl's prescient beauty, when she looked her mother in the eye, suggested, without modesty, a cosmic intelligence, a precocious maturity—a forecast of the woman Andrea might never get to know, a woman no longer in need of a mother to predict her.

"An old soul; that's what your daughter has. She's an old soul." The comment was probably meant as a compliment by Ella's kindergarten teacher, but Andrea was enraged at the impropriety of it. She yanked the girl out of the New Aged bullshit school and installed her into a blueblood, mainline institution.

Nonetheless, the comment haunted Andrea, satisfying a deep craving for another level of regard for her daughter. It referred to a time extending before and after the little girl's life on earth as witnessed by her mother. She felt the eventuality of her own death as a tragic event not so much in her own but in her daughter's life. She couldn't bear to leave this little girl or cause any grief for this future woman.

The puppy was now a year old. She had wanted to surprise her family with it, but her husband turned that into a "thing" too. When she apologized for springing the dog on him, he tried to explain to her, "It's not only that you got it without telling me; it's that you got it without bothering to ask me first." Never mind. They needed the dog more than ever since he left, even if it was just a hybrid lap dog, banal in its white fluffiness, basically a Beanie Baby with a heartbeat. Andrea was slightly repulsed by the ever-ready affection of the dog. Dog love was undignified, too needy, too constant, too urgent, too indiscriminating. Andrea made the mistake of asking her daughter, "Don't you think it's weird how Puppy (the daughter didn't want any other name for it) can love just about anybody?"

"But that's exactly what I love about her."

"You spoil her." Dominic knew it was a mistake as soon as he said it. At first, Andrea thought he could only have meant the dog.

"She's really a sweet little dog, really," Andrea had tried to convince him.

"Of course she is. That dog has never known anything but a full stomach and lots of affection. Treat it less well; then you'll see its true nature."

But Dominic hadn't meant Puppy was spoiled. He meant Ella.

"So you're saying you should treat my daughter 'less well' in order to know her true nature?" she said, her voice getting tighter and louder. "Is that what you're saying?"

More than the judgment itself, Andrea resented his presumption in making it. She hated the arrogance of people without children who judge every indulgence as if it stood on its own, without understanding the great balance of negotiations, the give and take, the yielding and insisting, the tallying, the balance act that was parenting. As if there weren't that fine line between setting limits and cementing limitations.

"So, we should feed her cheaper food? Send her to school in protective rags? In fact, why send her to school at all? Why not have her clean the house and do the laundry herself? We could save lots that way."

Dominic was silent, struggling to feel unfairly treated and misunderstood even as he reckoned with his guilt in the matter. He might have been content to be put in his place if that place were not constantly shifting.

Ella was kind to Dominic, more or less on her best behavior; she had enough social pride to keep her in line when other people were around. She was always polite and charming; she had the confidence to know that people lit up around her. Ella even gave up her spot in Andrea's bed that she had slept in since the divorce without much of a struggle—but the effort itself was distancing her from Andrea. She wouldn't have that.

Dom had only been living with them for six weeks, but deep

down Andrea knew it couldn't work. She was going to dump him. His falling in love with her was a kind of grief. She knew she couldn't bear him up; she felt sad and tired. Who would love this man when she asked him to leave?

The next morning, Andrea was up before the dawn, showered and ready. Dominic woke to the sound of a knife slicing a carrot, as Andrea prepared a boxed lunch for the girl. He lay in bed listening to the sound—so wet and curt.

She was going to dump him. Dominic was convinced and somewhat hopeful. This too shall come to pass, must pass. He understood and expected it, wanted it. Leaving the church would mean the end of permanence in all future things, including Andrea.

What had he been thinking? What had she? He was even more surprised by her naïveté in setting up this living arrangement than his in accepting it. Surely she might have known this was impossible. He was lucky in a way; he would have not just a once but a twice in a lifetime opportunity to overthrow a world he had in good faith accepted. While his life of faith and falling in love felt like conversions, his disavowals felt more like convulsions, violent and toxic, like throwing up something indigestible.

She was too busy for him in any case. He was awed by how much Andrea accomplished every day, whereas he had too much time on his hands. He sat on her couch and tried to write, but every day he would end up letting the laptop screen dim into hibernation. His first piece had appeared in print, triggering hundreds of Web site comments both positive and negative. Then it was over just as quickly; it didn't change his life, and he had not been able to work since. His lack of progress was a constant source of trouble between them.

"Why are you so interested in my story, anyway?" he asked her. "You don't share these beliefs."

"I wouldn't be with you if I didn't believe you could write."

She had meant that as both compliment and warning. Time would draw its conclusions, they understood.

If his faith had become skeptical, her skepticism had become cynical. He felt her atheism came too easily; it was just a default position. She had not reckoned with God in any serious way, and it was that kind of arrogance that would finally do in the divine. People would just ignore God rather than reckon with the tragic absence. After all, it is harder to lose something you have than to want something you don't. Neither of them had an appropriate perspective on what ought to be sacred in their lives.

Dom told himself that he should just shut up and feel lucky in love: he didn't know how good he had it because he didn't know what he was doing. Instead, like an academic resenting university life, he started to write a novel in which a priest vacations at a friend's New York apartment, hiding from God. Dom felt buoyed by the projection of this useful, hopeful fictive self who tries to rationalize his religiosity while fending off the inertia of anomie and momentum of irony. But he soon gave even that up. Every afternoon at four he turned on the TV and zoned into its incandescence, his attention like the soft static that crackled between the screen and his fingers. On the talk shows he watched people with similar problems to those he had tried to help all his life. He pondered their dull, endless godlessness, the thud of their hitting bottom without the promise of bounce, the flatness of their speech. When had language given up the fight with the magical, the ineffable, failing dutifully before what it cannot or must not name? Or had language prevailed? Had we overcome and superceded the mystery?

He figured he watched more television in the months since he left the Church than he had in his whole life. He did purgative push-ups and sit-ups during the commercials. He bought pajamas—his first since he was a boy—and stayed in them until just before

Andrea came home. He asked her every day where she ate, how much lunch cost and who had paid. He was jealous of these other writers who dined out on her dime. Why did it seem that all her writers were men?

Andrea had once told him that she thought too much agreement in a marriage was the equivalent of cultlike groupthink. Couples risk the danger of cultivating a crippling insularity between them. "That's why I made it a principle to counterpoint my husband's opinions, to democratize the level of discourse. And he was so pathetic about it: 'Why can't you just be supportive of how I feel?' he whined, just like a little girl."

So Dominic obliged her arguing with her in imagined conversations throughout the day. Why did he need someone listening to his monologues all the time? He didn't have private thoughts so much as soliloquies. Why must they always have an imagined audience? He judged the narcissistic core of his faith; his prayers had followed the same trajectory that his depression now tracked.

He limited himself to one call to her office, between noon and three, calibrating his suspicions about the duration, the location and the content of her luxurious lunch dates. He carried on pitiful conversations with her overworked assistant:

"Oh, well, do you think you can interrupt her and tell her it's me on the line?"

"OK, she knows where to find me."

"Oh, you mean she's left for lunch already?"

"Oh, you mean she's not back yet?"

"OK, can you tell her I called?"

Her apartment was overheated; New York seemed not to want to admit the coming of spring. He opened the window every fifteen minutes for three minutes. This gave his day structure. He paced the rooms, scratching himself distractedly until his skin reddened while picturing her empathic posture at the restaurant table. Her forearms on the tablecloth wiped clean of breadcrumbs. Leaning forward; her expensive shoes crossed at her sexy ankles beneath the chair. Things only worsened when she did call back and condescended with her concern about his lack of progress on the manuscript, his moods, his grief.

The religious life at least held the promise of a life accumulating, thickening toward an earned conclusion, becoming dense with promise. There were rituals to fill out every day. Now, between his futile attempts at work, Dom was faced with an endless leisure replacing his devotion to sacrifice, work and self-improvement. He missed not having enough time with too much to do.

Not that he could ever be really idle—not with Andrea. He now understood what she meant by the "work" of a relationship. Her emotional state was not merely a feeling; it was an event. It was supposed to happen to him, but left him feeling a bit fuzzy, as if cognitively challenged. This was over his head to some degree, but that feeling itself was comfortable; he liked the fact that his primary relationship exerted a mysterious emotional force beyond his understanding.

Tapped out, he watched the *Jerry Springer Show* and imagined Dolores appearing on the show with her reticule of complaints: abuse, bulimia, incest, teen pregnancy, vagrancy, indeterminate paternity. They would make her cry onstage, make pornography out of her vulnerability. Dominic thought that maybe he was the last person alive who could see her innocence. He decided to call the clinic, only to discover that Dolores had not kept the appointments he had scheduled for her; they had never heard from her. He immediately phoned and left a message on the answering machine in her mother's apartment.

He was surprised when she called back and left a message several hours later: "Oh so Father Do-mi-nica-nica-nica," Dolores mocked. "Listen to me, the Singing Nun. Mr. DJ Clueless.

What up my home-fried skillet biscuit? Tell James I talk ghetto better than he do." She giggled. "I guess I'm in crowd having your number now. Anyway, thanks for the call. I got a little confused by it, actually. You know—were you like reaching out to me out of some professional duty? No shrink ever did that before. When they're done with you, that's it. So I figured the same for you. Were you calling me out of some kind of freak wonder—'Whatever happened to her' kind of thing?"

There was a pause. "Or were you . . . ? Are you some kind of friend to me? Well, whatever. It bugged me."

The message outran its time. A few hours later, Dolores left another. "I'm really sorry. I was too jokey on the phone. I'm always messing up with you, aren't I? Saying the wrong thing, doing the wrong thing. I'm just really sorry." Dom heard a thickening of her voice before she hung up. She was right; he was always doing the wrong thing with her as well. He resolved to make a day trip up to see her, take her to a nice lunch, talk to her, escort her to the clinic, maybe even help with the delivery. Her due date had to be coming up.

He wanted to be useful again; he wanted to do good. He wanted to help Dolores, to counsel her, to console her, to be her priest, her friend.

It was still dark when Andrea left the apartment. Dom heard her greet Connie, the nanny, and listened for the grateful click of the lock. He rolled over to her side of the bed, where the scent was sweet and warm under the covers already pulled up tight. Dom had always jumped out of bed, like a little child, even when facing his failed prayers. But not now. He stayed in bed every morning, sleeping through or waiting out his old hour of prayer. Lying in bed, he realized that prayer had some of the character of sleep—

but a sleep captured in mindfulness. If sleep is a necessary relief of consciousness, prayer is a focusing of it. Unlike sleep, prayer is experienced by the one praying but must be fulfilled by Another. Prayer's end, grace, cannot be grasped, only received. Likewise, desire for Dom now had an end—as well as an ending. Satisfaction was something that must literally be grasped and left Dominic more depleted than the endless spiritual longing of his priesthood. Sex demands satisfaction; prayer resists it at all costs.

If Andrea complained that loving Dominic was impossible, she also made it be known that loving her would be unimportant. Andrea would not change her life for him. In their third month living together, she acted as if he wasn't there. She had been out *again* the night before, and he was desperate when she returned after midnight: "You're too old to have this many friends!" he shouted at her. "Get an inner life already!"

In his abandoned novel, he imagined how the argument between them tonight might go.

SHE: *I think you've been duped, brainwashed to believe all kinds of nonsense: that self-mutilation is salvation, that the flesh and soul are not only distinct but at odds. That one should walk the earth humble and underappreciated.*

HE: *So what, your way is better? Your mind, your soul—they live hand to mouth. You hang on to ideas as if they were junk food. You buy, you binge. You get bored and disgusted; you trash. You can't tolerate any big idea that might distract you from your self-obsession, your own delusional drive toward self-realization. In your condescending attempt to defy the basic human need to mythologize, you enslave yourself to consumerism.*

SHE: *Right, and you're going to tell me that someone of your supreme intelligence actually believed all that crap? You bought wholesale the whole idea that we belong to a God and a Catholic*

Church, which has discovered truths as if unaware of having created them? Come on, pal. Admit it. You were just a lackey for the greatest mind control scheme in history.

HE (JEERING): *So you're saying that faith in God is nothing but superstition, an evolutionary anachronism; its only validation is our need for false comfort.*

SHE (COOLLY): *You said it.*

HE: *Even if deeply felt?*

SHE: *Yup.*

HE: *So you feel the same way about any deeply felt emotion? Even love?*

SHE: *Even love.*

But the conversation would never happen. Even in his daydream, Dom had given her the upper hand. What did happen was much more mundane and irreversible. After dinner, he and Ella had fought over who got to watch what on TV. In a grab for the remote control, he accidentally kicked the puppy off the couch. The girl started to cry, ran to her room and slammed the door. After a while, Dom assumed she had fallen asleep, but the girl had apparently been sulking all night. When her mother came home she stormed her, clutching the dog, pent up with rage.

"It's not fair!" Ella wailed, filled with tears. It was strange. Her outraged sense of injustice and the guilt it provoked made Dominic see her as a real person—as if for the first time.

"I hate him. I wish he would just leave!" she shouted, and with that Dominic saw his fate sealed. He had wronged her, and this was intolerable. Ella would always come first. Andrea followed the girl into her bedroom.

She was exactly the excuse each of them was looking for.

He downed a few vodkas and fell asleep during the second rerun of *Everyone Loves Raymond*. Andrea woke him up and sat down on the coffee table, folded her arms in her lap and leaned forward. The gesture had resolve and experience behind it; she had done this before.

"It's not working, Dom," she said.

"OK."

He sobered up. They discussed practical matters.

She had climbed into bed around 3:30 while he pretended to sleep. "Good-bye, Dominic," she said in a room temperature voice. She imagined he would not hear it.

He would move out in the morning, as she had asked him to. They would end just as they began, unlikely and precipitous. Another way of life would spit him out again. So much for love. He would look elsewhere. Consolation is defined by what it appeases; it is only ever as good as that. It felt right, actually; he didn't belong in her luxurious bed. He was too hairy and too big for it: the funk of him lying amid all that toile and lace.

Things would really begin again tomorrow. He would seek out Dolores; help her raise the baby. Unlikely. All he really wanted was a small room, a single bed, a white sheet, a gray blanket. He would write the Vatican and leave the Church too, officially. Everything familiar: he would leave it all behind. He wanted nothing but the simplicity of a cold-water flat, a seat at a table in the library, a productive solitude. He craved an equivalent naïveté to that which had graced his priesthood: a willing unknowing, a silly dream of perfection that was a more engaging way of living than skeptical reduction. Generous was the spirit that allowed for a transcendent goal, a craving for meaning, the possibility of God.

Connie knocked on the bedroom door. "Mister?" she called out. "Father? Teléfono."

• • •

The coroner rolled the sheet off her bit by bit, revealing what was left of the girl's head. Dominic came prepared to recognize Dolores, expecting to be repulsed, to wretch, to scream out with anger—but what he saw oddly touched him.

"Oh God," he heard himself say. Involuntary as a reflex, the words of Psalm 69 echoed in his head.

Save me, O God!
For the waters have come up to my neck.
I sink in deep mire, where there is no foothold.

The dead never look surprised.

She smelled vaguely like a riverbank negotiating its shape with the water. Her face was layered and ragged, as if made of papier-mâché; she had finally donned a mask answerable to her reality. He had seen too many corpses for one lifetime.

Then he remembered.

"What about the baby?" he asked.

"What baby?" the coroner asked, checking his report. "There is no evidence of a pregnancy."

"What? She must have been, I don't know, around seven or eight months by now."

"Sorry, Father. Suspended abdomen but nothing else to support that."

He checked his report again.

"In fact, the hymen is intact; the girl is a virgin."

Dominic leaned over to examine the belly.

What were those episodes of morning sickness, the tender swelling of her breasts, the thickening of her middle? Almost every sign of a pregnancy had been true except for the heart of the matter. Dominic even remembered Dolores smiling at the quickening of the baby in her womb. The coroner told him about the possibility of pseudocyesis, a hysterical pregnancy. Dom would later look the condition up: "an intense desire to be pregnant creates internal conflict which, in turn, charges up the endocrine system to inspire her body to simulate pregnancy."

Her wish for it to be so made it appear so. Her belief in, her fear of, her attention to the body, to interpreting its signals and investing them with significance—all of it seemed essentially Catholic to Dominic. The need to believe had directed her body to literally live the lie. Her physical life would support the mind's desires, her delusions. Prove them.

"If all other factors are equal, then, when there is free access of air a body decomposes twice as fast than if immersed in water and eight times faster than if buried in earth." That was Casper's Law. Dominic pitied the small, preserved, distended breasts. The wrinkled yellowed skin that looked as if you could pull it off until it crumbled in your fingers like an old piece of tape over the spine of a book. He imagined Father Carl's innocent head lying there. Dolores petting it. Father Carl's petrified skull.

No, he would never have anything of the divine in him, could never send a child to her death or bring him back to life, would never see the value of a life as merely symbolic. No life would not be worth saving. Dominic would have finished her life otherwise if he could, let her grow into her own beauty, her own libido, her own life force. He would have undone the heartlessness, the meaninglessness of her end. But he couldn't finish another's story; in fact, he wanted relief from the expectations of stories, delivering redemption or tragedy. Was he ready at last to give up the dream?

Are you tough enough to do God's will? He fell to his knees and held the sheet to his breast.

Prayer.

And in our sleep

Pain, which can not forget
Falls drop by drop
Upon the heart
Until in our own despair
Against our will comes wisdom
By the awful grace of God
—Aeschylus.

It was Dolores whom Dominic prayed for, his sudden angel. In his fleabag hotel off I-95, prayer rushed at him intimate and urgent. It wasn't the suicide itself so much as the pain of the young girl in the weeks before, deciding to take her life, that made him cry for the first time in years. He positioned himself for it on the floor, the acidic smells in the carpet stinging, sitting back on his heels, in child's pose.

She was a "suicide," the coroner's report read, fusing her life with the way it ended. The baby that might have saved her was never real, born only out of her desperate need for it to exist. An immaculate misconception, a plagiarized miracle. She was a martyr who gave her life precisely because it carried no meaning.

Dominic cried for her innocence. For Father Carl's innocence. For his mother's innocence. For the grief of innocence. Could he in fact call it something so archaic? Innocence may never be proved; despite what the courtrooms said, the burden of proof always lies with the blamed. Maybe he meant Dolores's naïveté, really, her belief that the soul does exist, but that it is only accessible through an act that transforms it in death—as if the end of a fire were its smoke. He was the naive one, convinced that she was up to her life, at the level of its circumstance. He was very wrong.

What her death insisted on was a kind of argument: irrefutable and tautological. Suicide might be an insult to God and an act of violence against one's family. But what were these arguments to the state of mind essential to committing the act?

Was it the kind of argument that perhaps was right but on the side of wrong—like arguing against the illusion of God? The argument compelled; it drew you to its side even as it failed to convince. He had to shake it off. All he had needed to persuade her to do was to take her pills, eat well, go to bed when others did and trust that she could do it again the next day. But he had never called her back; he had never pulled her back. None of it mattered now. The dead won't be argued with.

They had this in common: the world would do fine without either of them, the martyr and the ex-priest. He had always believed that it took faith and hope to believe in the future, but that it took good common sense and hard work to get through the day. He cried at the hopelessness of Dolores having neither skill. He cried for himself, for his belatedness, for the grief at the fact that he had misjudged Father Carl, abandoned Dolores, had arrived at her side too late, for how much he now knew he loved Dolores, for her apology which in the end was not a request for but a granting of forgiveness; for the love he now knew he was capable of giving, of losing—for a love so specific and big enough for one person to infer a more general and grander Love. God's Love.

He had been a little afraid of her; she tried to break through the boundaries of self-knowledge; she refused the inability to see ourselves for what we are-wholly, truly, simultaneously. What, in the end, did he have to teach her—that we can believe neither in perfection nor in redemption but a kind of transcendence of one self into another, over another, maybe even with another?

He imagined Dolores slipping into the water, the indifferent water, the current tugging at her body, stronger than her ability to swim it, letting herself be led by the river, urging her downstream while her head bobbed at the surface growing cold and senseless until it too was carried away.

> Floating down the river singing a song and the rocks listened and the forest listened.
>
> You are free to be here. Walk here. Or not.
> Let the earth forgive her.

There was chicken three ways: Scarpariello, thighs on the bone with sausage, onions and potatoes. Thin cutlets rolled with fontina and prosciutto. Chicken al limone with capers. Eggplant Rollatini, stuffed shells, Spaghetti Carbonara, escarole sautéed in garlic and olive oil. All of this steaming in chafing trays along the credenza. The coffee table was laden with desserts. A white sheet had been pulled over it. Mrs. Alfano had gone into overdrive as had the able ladies of the parish. They had gathered in her apartment, stripped it clean. They had even lifted the carpet and buffed the floors. Their husbands had painted the walls. All of them had avoided the place while it reeked with the stink of death but had come now to celebrate its passing.

Dominic scolded himself as he helped himself to another plate of pasta; he had spent too much of his life as this community's negative oracle, calling people out on their hypocrisies. He was as resentful as an unproduced playwright.

Dolores had, of course, been denied a proper funeral by the Church, a damned suicide. The regulars had registered a complaint, insisting on a Catholic burial for the girl in her family's plot. Some of them tried to sneak into the old church to hold vigil but were preempted by the hastily erected chain-link fence that circumscribed the perimeter of the building. Ronnie had paraded the daily Mass regulars and the AA workshoppers down to the church site for a sit-in.

Dominic went to try to talk them out of it and invite them back to the Alfano apartment for lunch and company. He approached the group warily. It was the first time he had seen them without wearing a collar. And even though he knew and accepted some of their darkest secrets, he found it hard to forgive them now for witnessing his own fall from grace.

They stood up from the sidewalk and formed an imperfect arc around him.

Ronnie gave him a slap on the back, shook his shoulders with his big hands and said, "You know, Father, we're all human."

Carmen Cruz gave him a kiss on both cheeks and a big hug. "It's all right, sweetie, we love you, honey. Welcome home."

Even Sister Agnes came to him and touched his elbow and said, "I hope you find your way. You deserve that much."

They loved him, they said, and Dominic knew that he loved them too, loved them for accepting his weakness, his foolishness—for caring in any case. In his obsession with the closing of the church as his failure, he had failed to acknowledge their own loss or allowed them time to grieve with him. This had happened to each of them. He wiped the tears from his eyes and tried to persuade them to leave the site. Seeing these old friends surround him, he realized that he had perverted the Golden Rule—by treating others exactly as he would have them treat him: largely tolerant, vaguely wary and, for the most part, left alone.

But he got it: he saw that every single one of them was beautiful, magnificent really, radiant even. Why had he been so modest, too embarrassed to acknowledge that? He saw it now, in an instant but just for an instant. He knew too that he could never, ever make any one of them see it. No one would ever convince anybody of that. It was hardest of all to see oneself in that light. He had failed to connect to any of them individually but had dreamed of connecting (with) them to a larger truth, the consolation of millions living in the same lonely dream.

"I'm staying right here, Father," Ronnie said. "I mean, is it still OK to call you Father? Anyways, what matters is we're ready to go down with this. We're gonna sit here right on the sidewalk till they come in and try to take us out."

Dominic looked at his big cold church behind the fence. Never had a building so consistently impressed on Dominic what it expected of him. And here it was, closed off and marked for demolition.

"All we want, Father, is a peaceful vigil," Carmen said. She had brought devotional candles and lined them up in a semicircle around the group. The words of the Funeral Mass came to Dominic, and he almost said them to the makeshift crowd as the squad car that had been circling the block set its lights and parked in front of the church.

"It's not dead yet, Father," Carmen continued. "Remember what Father Carl always said, 'to believe in something greater than yourself is to believe in something greater for yourself.' "

Dom had once repeated this line to Andrea, who snapped back, "Great. I know someone at Hallmark. I'll hook you up."

Johnny Patrillo, son of the pizzeria Patrillos, got out of the car. He was a young man, not even a year out of the academy.

"Johnny," Carmen called out, "what do you want here? Go home, baby."

"Hey, folks. Tell me what's going on here?"

"We're not moving," Ronnie said, full of purpose.

The young cop sighed and looked at Dominic, who had known him as an altar boy. "Come on. It's OK right now, but later it's supposed to rain, maybe even some snow."

He was met with silence. "Father?" he said.

"Come on," Dominic said. "Let's go. This is over."

No one moved.

"It's our church, Dolores's church," Ronnie said.

"Father," Officer Patrillo pleaded, "talk some sense into them?" He was obviously frustrated. "People, let's understand the situation here. Think about it for a minute, please. Don't make me do my duty," Officer Patrillo said.

A few stood up.

"Carmen, please walk with me back to the house?" Dominic asked as the woman got up stiffly from the ground. She was embarrassed and wouldn't look at Ronnie, who remained sitting there with his mouth open. She blessed herself and tied a kerchief around her head.

Only Ronnie sat. "Hell no, I won't go!" he shouted.

"OK, Ronnie. Let's go," Officer Patrillo said wearily and secured the hands Ronnie offered with plastic cuffs, led the man to the squad car and gently guided him into the backseat. Ronnie beamed at them out the window as the car drove off. Patrillo had requested a backup van, which drove the rest of them back to the widow Alfano's apartment as a fine drizzle started.

Now, facing the steaming chafing trays for the third time, Dom filled his plate again and wandered through the crowd in the small apartment. Many warmly embraced him and welcomed him back. He began to overheat with the bloat and could feel the sweat collecting at the back of his neck and dripping down his back. The wine was a homemade brew, dug up from the cellar of one of the widows attending. It had turned a bit but no one minded, and they were well into the second case.

The metal taste in his mouth convinced Dom he needed to get some air. Kissing the bent head of Mrs. Alfano once more, he caught a glimpse of Dolores's boots under the sofa, the beige suede with the woolen lip and the stain of snow at the scuffed toe.

He made his way quickly to the door, ran down the stairs and into the project's quadrangle. A cold sweat broke quickly all over him; his shirt applied cool and damp to his back. He sat on the bench and hung his head in his hands. Little daffodil spears peeked through the dirt pocked with rock salt.

He felt a slap against the back of his head. "Jesus Christ, what did you do, run here? You're soaking wet."

Dominic turned to see Marc wiping his hands on his pants leg. "I don't know; I suddenly didn't feel so well in there."

"Yeah, I guess we're all pretty shaken up," Marc said, and Dom softened up again. The man's sudden hints of compassion always confused him.

"Especially you, I guess, with, you know, how you felt about Dolores and all," Marc said.

Dominic stiffened. "What does that mean?"

"You know, I don't wanna say nothing, Father, but sometimes my sister, you know, when you hugged her? Sometimes maybe you held on too long."

Dom stood up, staggered a bit. "You are a true son of a bitch."

"Whoa, Father, come on now. I know this is tough on everyone, but—"

"Just shut the fuck up!" Dom shouted, surprised at the power in his voice. Was it possible that this was the first time he had shouted in decades? He tasted the meal repeating itself in his mouth.

"Please shut the fuck up," he repeated. It sounded a bit off, as if spoken with a foreign accent.

"Father, are you drunk?" Marc asked, as a grin spread across his face.

Dominic took a step toward the man and poked at his chest. "You are a shit."

Mark opened his palms to the priest. "Yo, Father. Back off."

Dominic turned to leave but halted. He grunted deep in his belly and hooked his right fist against Marc's lips. He felt the instant give of the flesh and was shocked at how crisp and fragile the man's face was, like a bug underfoot. He heard the kindling crack of a tooth dislodging. The sensation drew Dominic's lips back into a hiss. He grabbed Marc's head and brought it down against his raised knee. Hard. A fine mist sprayed from the man's nose; Dominic paused to look at the red dash it made against the last pile of gray snow.

When he looked up, Marc no longer looked surprised. He saw a rage rise in the man, in the swelling of his split lip.

Dom was shaking. His hand ached tight and cold, like a wrench around a stripped nut. He brought his left hand over to rub it.

Marc rushed him and punched him in the gut, slapped him across the cheek with the back of his hand.

"You think you're pretty special, don't you?" he heard the man gasp.

"Should I turn the other cheek?" Dominic thought as a tender warmth radiated across his face. The pain felt affectionate. He *did* care what happened to him after all. He was hurt. This was happening. Right now. To him. Marc's punches were thrown harder, better, more efficiently, with conviction with righteousness, even. Dominic felt the weight of them in the lightness of his knees, as he sank to all fours. Brought to his knees again. An involuntary confession. He felt Marc grab a fist of his hair, as if to raise him up.

"I'm going to be sick," Dom croaked and spewed all over the polished shoes of the other man.

"Jesus Christ," Marc spat.

Dom wretched again as he saw Marc hop on one foot and wipe his shoe on a corner of Dom's overcoat.

"Jesus fucking Christ," Marc said as he toed the back of Dom's leg to clean the other shoe.

He heard the man walk away, the sound of his heel breaking through the crust of ice. Dominic climbed up to all fours. The pain in his body had an immediate and focusing clarity. Repentance—not to feel bad but to feel better, to rise above his own self-loathing, over the isolating sense that he was always offending *someone*—or *something* that had the power to banish him. He had come home, the prodigal son—and was meant to pay for it.

Minutes later, an ambulance arrived—Marc must have called for it himself—and Dom was driven to the hospital in the vehicle which, after silencing its alarm, obeyed all the traffic lights.

SEVEN

James watched the auditorium slowly fill up from behind the curtain. Lots of nervous parents. His own mother sat toward the back, dressed for church. Behind her, in the last row of the house sat Vanessa, still unacknowledged by his mother. Signora Rosa sat beside Andrea and (Father) Dominic. He was badly bruised; his left eye was swollen.

But it was Signora Rosa James worried about. That very morning, at the end of their session, he had asked her, "Do you believe in me?"

She stared at him then. "Play something."

He sat down at the piano and played a little capriccio.

"Stop, stop!" she yelled at him. "Good enough is never good enough. I must have told you that. What do you think you are doing here, young man?" she asked him.

"Signora? It's me, James."

She clucked at him. "Of course it's you." She laughed and looked earnestly at him. She put her good hand on his cheek; an affectionate smile spread across her face, "Oh, James, you are just too handsome. Maybe we should just get married."

"Signora."

"People will talk, you know. But it's none of their business."

He paused. "OK."

"And I want to go home. You can live there with me. We can eat out of the garden. The strawberries are better than anywhere else in the world."

James was quiet; she sounded like a little girl; then her expression became stern again. "You worry too much about being different. You don't realize you're not here to express yourself; you're here to approach the music, ask its permission and then leave it alone. Let it use you."

"I understand that."

"No, you don't. I hoped for something more from you than some Magical Negro myth. Stop lifting yourself up from the ground already. Just stay up."

He forced a smile at her. "If I win, I'm going to take you out to a big, celebratory dinner."

"Oof. Don't count your chickens. There are two things an artist must beware: success and failure. But don't worry; you'll never know success, James. At least, you'll be spared that," she said.

James took a dry swallow. He was going to be kind to her. She had not had enough kindness in her life.

"Well, then, I'll still take you out. Someplace with fresh strawberries."

"Did you wash your feet tonight?"

"Yes, Signora, as instructed."

She nodded. "You won't make it, you know."

"That's OK. I'll end up on easy street, you know, just like you, practicing the lucrative art of piano teaching."

She looked worried. "But you will still marry me?"

"As soon as I'm worthy, Signora."

She looked as if she were trying to remember something. "What can I tell you now? Yes. Let me teach you what a good musician knows. You have to say, 'I love you' and mean it. It has to convince. Even if you have to say it over and over—1,111 times even. Don't be bored; never let her hear your boredom. Never."

Andrea settled herself beside her mother, adjusting her shawl. Signora Rosa sat straight up in her chair; her good hand covered her bad in her lap. Ella sat on the other side, and Andrea was moved by the affection she showed her grandmother, taking her good hand in hers and playing with her rings. She wasn't just tolerant of her wandering mind but protective of it. She followed its peculiar turns as if they were playing a game, sharing a secret code. She wouldn't tolerate any talk of her grandmother's infirmity.

When Andrea began researching assisted living homes, Ella had insisted that her grandmother move in with them. Andrea had resisted but finally gave in. She actually looked forward to giving her mother some comfort now when she wouldn't realize how much she needed it. Andrea relished the generational symmetry; besides she couldn't waste any more time waiting for her mother to turn into that magically good parent—as if the awareness of being badly parented were enough to suddenly correct it. Deserving love never secures it. Her past was so hungry all the time, setting its teeth deep into her future; it was her own private religion. Dom, on the other hand, craved the ideal future, dying into fate the way she was born into hers. She and Ella even took her mother to church every Sunday, though truly she wished the whole God thing would finally just go away so she could stop deflecting it so proactively. She was annoyed by that curving of her spine, the busy work of denial that credentialed the very thing it negated.

It had been only ten days since he had left the apartment, but nonetheless Andrea broke her own rules and called Dominic to see if he was going to James's recital.

"I won't be pretty," he warned her and told her about the fight he had been in with the drowned girl's brother. Still, she gasped when he walked in with his black eye and split lip. She waved him over and removed her coat from the seat she was saving for him, even though the auditorium was only a third filled. He looked sheepishly at Andrea. She kissed the warm top of his head. The smell of this man got to her every time—dull, salty, sweet, like a paperback after the beach, word become flesh. She breathed deeply to take him in.

Dominic looked at her through his swollen eye, satisfied at finally having the physical correlative to the pain he carried around with him always. Now she could see how much he hurt.

The night before he left, Andrea had asked Dom what he could still believe in. His answer, instantly and confidently spoken, surprised both of them: "Love," he had said.

"He wants to believe he loves me so badly," Andrea thought to herself. "He wants me to believe he loves me so much. One was almost tempted to believe him. Almost."

Dom took a cough drop out of his pocket, concealing it between his palms to minimize the noise unwrapping it. Andrea impatiently reached over and ripped the wrapper off and shoved it back in his hand. He let the lozenge stick to his fingers for a moment before popping it in his mouth.

The auditorium lights dimmed, and as James walked onto the stage, Andrea sighed with the portent of it all. All this pressure on our attention. All these hierarchies: the artist and his audience, the priest and his congregation. The utter narcissism of it all: performance and prayer. She had never been able to stay awake through the entire Goldberg Variations. She sat up straight and vowed to listen to each of them with devout attention this time.

Signora Rosa thumbed through her program looking for her Christmas list. What was that thing she wanted? A record, yes, but not of Bach. Beethoven played by Artur Schnabel, who said that this was "music composed better than it played." He was wrong about Beethoven but right about the principle applied to life.

She took a deep breath; the concert hall—with all these rigid bodies erect in their seats—was beginning to agitate her. She tried to concentrate on this Bach coming now from the stage—the way every note took you along the steps of its argument with the suspense that at any moment it might stop and drop you. Down you would plummet. And even as she chased the music she knew it would go on with or without her. Think you can catch it? As you get closer it draws away: the spirit that eludes you then when you grasp the hardest.

She watched James on the stage in his solitude. Oh, the loneliness of the piano life. And her daughter beside her: alone, alone, alone. And the priest. She looked at his hands folded so properly in his lap—nice hands, might have done well on the keyboard. But he had his own brand of loneliness too; he was wrapped in it. He was losing his shape within it. She became alarmed. The priest seemed to be disappearing, right there while she watched. The ground would rise and overtake him. Who would mark their grave? People in the back were already coughing. But just then she saw Andrea take one of Dominic's hands in hers, and she saw the priest accumulate and become solid right there before her eyes. He congealed in her daughter's grasp even as she felt the auditorium go heavy with pressure.

She was excited; her heart raced as she turned her attention again to Bach. This time, she might at last hear the whole piece at once, in a single moment. Perhaps thirty pianists onstage. Why stop there? Maybe hundreds, tens of thousands of pianists playing in rounds. Every single note of the Goldberg Variations struck simultaneously as one white sound. She could walk among them, float above them. The pianos submerged, the notes would liquefy. She needed to keep her head above the rising waterline. Then all of it would become clear at once, simultaneous rather than the usual experience by increment, variation after variation, measured out in time to accommodate our own incapacity.

She is terrified that it will stop, must stop—with that curious obsession of things to end beautifully. Will she end beautifully? And then drop her like that? What a silly thing to leave behind.

All these years of music: that at least was something—especially Bach, he who left nothing unsaid. Said everything. More than any composer, she loved to be on the arm of this dear, severe, generous Bach.

Dominic settled deeper into the chair and let the music bring him into focus. When Andrea took his hand, he flinched at first at the soreness in his knuckles, at the unexpected tenderness. He marveled at her hand; it was so small and elegant; a manicured finger lightly traced the vein above his thumb. He felt calm: obedient matter. Everything he was afraid of had already happened.

James had told him what to listen for: the Aria always stands alone, in the beginning and in the end, a haunting of the self. Each of the variations investigates the Aria—annotates, contradicts, rebels, accelerates, elaborates, retards, enhances, subverts—but is always contingent on the original Aria. Everything we can think of in order to change ourselves only brings us to the same place we started. We transubstantiate, take other forms, mean different things, perhaps, but we are the same in the end: simple, obedient matter.

Dominic listened to the pianist run through each of the variations like the soul trying on different selves. Bach, beginning with purity, filled in with ornamentation, brought on the accretions, the complications, believed in progress through reason, thought away the darkness. Nevertheless, each of the variations, the dances, the marches, the advances and retreats were all contingent on the essential original. The doing of a thing over and over until its power sneaks up on you and you realize it has changed you, made you what you wanted to be. To be deliberate is to trick fate, to be original even if deviating just perceptibly from the origin, to be judged by what you've done; to practice until it is perfect.

A return—another chance to get it right, another chance to wrest something more from it, to tease out every intuition before returning to simple assertion. The fate of this melody: to become experienced yet remain essentially unchanged.

You are only ever as good as you are. Practice ideal versions of the self; every variation against the ideal. Commit to an identity until it begins to restrict. Then commit to another. If you cannot live these selves simultaneously, live among them. The varieties do not fragment but overlap; the variations anticipate and make each other, lead into each other. They are contingent on each other. Respond. Love.

"It is God that is primary," Dom thought, "indivisible, irreducible. All the rest variations on a theme."

And when, at last, this music has learned to go so beautifully, one wants it to slow down. But so it goes on, inevitable, tortured, bruised, but at last itself. Ending where it started, a true odyssey.

The beginning often predicts the end—but for the beginning to be the end! That is what catches the breath here; that one is born in order to die—and everything in between good and bad, deliberate and accidental, saved and doomed, nothing but variation.

One yearns to hear it simply, to hear it originally, as if for the first time.

ACKNOWLEDGMENTS

I am indebted to the Yaddo Corporation for its congenial support. I am also indebted to the following authors and books: Robert Orsi, *Between Heaven and Earth*; Russell Sherman, *Piano Pieces*; and Peter Williams, *Bach: The Golberg Variations*. I am grateful to those who read early of this novel and gave valuable feedback, especially Andrew Krivak, Mark Larson, and Lee Siegel. My agent, Bill Clegg, and editor, Jack Macrae, were peerless readers and steadfast believers. And my biggest thanks and love go to my wife, Betsy Lerner, again and again.

ABOUT THE AUTHOR

JOHN DONATICH is the director of the Yale University Press. He is the author of a memoir, *Ambivalence, a Love Story*. His essays and occasional pieces have appeared in *Harper's* and the *Atlantic Monthly*. This is his first novel.